They heard a shout from one of the approaching men, and saw Gumpson again, this time standing next to a vertical rocky outcropping. The men gave an excited shout and began running at Gumpson, just as Kinney and his friends had done earlier.

Gumpson turned to face them. Kinney had no gun, but by God, he would bring this vexing villain down. Without thinking it through, and with more speed than he knew he possessed, he sprinted at Gumpson's back and launched himself through the air.

He seemed to move in slow motion, approaching Gumpson. As he made contact and his momentum carried them both down, his ear came close to Gumpson's twisted mouth. The world seemed eerily silent as they crashed to the ground and he thought he heard Gumpson say something.

"Help me," Gumpson said.

Everything went green. Kinney felt himself flying backward through the air, and he hit his head on the ground, hard. Then everything went black. When he awoke, South and Hayes stood over him, giving him looks of concern crossed with annoyance.

"Why didn't you just let me shoot him?" South asked.

"What happened?" Kinney said. "I had him. I was right on top of him."

"He did his trick," Hayes said. "He turned all green, and then he disappeared."

The shouts of the other men indicated that Gumpson had reappeared further away. Kinney was not up to the chase anymore.

"Something weird is going on here," he said, and his friends did not argue.

BAEN BOOKS by BRETT DAVIS

The Faery Convention
Hair of the Dog

Bone Wars
Two Tiny Claws

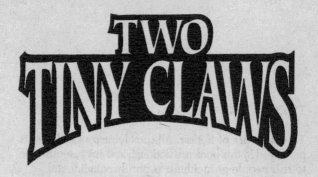

TWO TINY CLAWS

BRETT DAVIS

BAEN

TWO TINY CLAWS

A Baen Books Original

Baen Publishing Enterprises
P.O. Box 1403
Riverdale, NY 10471

ISBN: 0-671-57785-9

Cover art by Bob Eggleton

First printing, January 1999

Distributed by Simon & Schuster
1230 Avenue of the Americas
New York, NY 10020

Printed in the United States of America

Dedication:

To Mom and Dad, for everything, and to Darshan and Jeety Kang, who introduced me to Montana.

Acknowledgments:

As with *Bone Wars*, anyone reading this book hoping to learn history will be sorely disappointed. That said, there are some sources of actual fact I would like to thank, particularly John Horner and Don Lessem's *The Complete T. Rex* and Roland T. Bird's *Bones for Barnum Brown*.

ONE

"I think I'll be getting off here, old man," Luther Gumpson said.

He was in a bad mood, and he knew his words offended on many levels. The man who had given him a ride was probably about forty years old, just a few years ahead of Gumpson himself, so he could easily have avoided use of the word "old" had he chosen to be civil. He also knew that the wagon was close to its destination, and that night was falling, so the old man did not want to go to the bother of stopping the wagon, giving the horses something to chew on to keep them happy, and unpacking Gumpson's tent and supplies. Nevertheless, the man quickly agreed, which meant that he was glad to get rid of his scraggly, disagreeable rider.

"Jordan is not far," the man said, making a token effort at keeping Gumpson aboard.

The old man was mannerly, one had to hand him that. Probably trying to set a good example for his two little girls, who were a principal reason why Gumpson wanted off the wagon. They giggled. They cried. They tried to play with him. They wanted him to pet their dollies and comb their dollies' hair, which he did, grudgingly; if the boys back in Missouri could have seen that, there would be big laughs all around.

The old man was right. Jordan was not far, but from what Gumpson had heard there was not much to

1

recommend the place. It was supposed to be dull, even for Montana. A few log houses, a tiny store, no bar, not even scenery to amount to anything. This place looked good enough for the night, maybe even for a day or two. No one out here to ask questions. No one out here who might ever get a gander at a newspaper. Just the dark sandstone walls and towering rocks that rose straight up, leaving little sunlight to nurture the scrabbly patches of grass that eked out an existence below.

The old man stopped the cart and sent the girls to entertain the horses. His wife sat up front on the plank seat, as grim and immobile as a mummy. She was no doubt younger than her husband, but looked older, and was so motionless that for a good portion of the trip Gumpson had genuinely wondered if she had passed away and the husband just couldn't bear to part with her company.

"Much obliged," Gumpson said after the old man had tossed down his tent and pack.

"Think nothing of it," the old man said, coughing against the dust that his actions had raised.

"Getting dark," Gumpson said. "You better get going."

He handed the old man a wad of money that had just a little more in it than they agreed to. This was the result of intensive calculation. Gumpson did not want to underpay the man, which could make him mad. Neither did he want to pay exactly the agreed-upon sum, which might also make him mad. On the other hand, he did not want to pay him too much, which would make him suspicious. He wanted the old man to forget he even existed, and to do so as quickly as possible. The amount he had selected was engineered to do the trick, and it had the added advantage of fitting within his regrettably meager budget.

"Take care," the old man said, although his tone indicated he was not going to worry too much about Gumpson's fate. "Might be varmints out here."

"Nothing I can't handle," Gumpson said. "Just wildcats and wolves to worry about out here now."

The girls reclaimed their space in the wagon, and their dollies waved stuffed-arm goodbyes. *Too bad they didn't leave one of those yarn-haired dollies*, Gumpson thought. He could really use some kindling.

He had the tent up just before the sky went completely purple with sunset. It really was beautiful out here. The rock cliffs caught the light like ancient temples, and somewhere down in his heart Gumpson said a little prayer of thanks for the beauty, although not to any god who would demand work or allegiance from him. His tent looked a little forlorn, perched as it was against the gigantic splendor of Montana. It was a good, rugged Army tent, but looked as insubstantial as a child's twig fort. It would have to do, at least until he reached California, where he could get a place that was a little more comfortable.

Gumpson had heard about the lignite coal that blanketed the area, and before too long had a decent fire burning, one that combined coal with clumps of the patchy grass that grew up to his knees. It didn't smell too good, but he could live with that. In the morning he would walk over and examine the rocks that rose all around the tent, just for fun, but tonight he didn't want to fool around in there and risk breaking a leg. Once the fire was well under way he poked around in his pack and brought out a hard biscuit and two strips of hardtack, along with a small tin of whiskey to wash them down.

The attempted job in Hannibal had probably been overkill, in addition to being unsuccessful, but the police were still in an uproar when he left so it probably didn't matter. He didn't get any money out of the deal, but they didn't catch him either, and that was the main thing. His only regret was that his string of jobs had made it fairly clear that he was heading west, although surely nobody would expect him to go this far. He was a city boy, everybody who knew him knew that. He couldn't stand to be away, off by himself, they would say. He would show them. He sat in silence, chewing slowly. Or maybe they were right. The quietness of the night was beginning to feel oppressive, as was the incredible parade of stars above his head. He didn't have so much as a mouth harp to entertain himself, and for the first time in his life he felt lonely and small. The glorious array of nature that surrounded him seemed designed to make him feel insignificant.

"Hang in there, buddy," he said to himself. "You made it this far, you'll make it okay."

No sooner had the words left his mouth than he heard a rustling sound from the darkness, off to the right. He dropped the biscuit and whipped out his pistol, although he kept the whiskey firmly in hand.

"Who's there?" he asked, taking care to keep his voice level and free of fear. "I'm armed."

He heard the rustling again, but no response. It was probably just some varmint passing through. He was not sure if he should stay close to the fire or venture away. He seemed to remember hearing that wolves and their ilk did not like fire, and so perhaps he should stay close to it. On the other hand, by staying close to it he sacrificed his night vision and the ability to see whatever this beastie might be. Well, he had a gun, so surely it wouldn't matter that much. Gumpson rose to his feet and stepped away from the fire.

What happened next occurred so fast that his mind could barely process it. Some sort of thin green fire, for surely that was the only applicable word, appeared from the darkness and froze his right hand, forcing him to drop the six-shooter. The line of fire made no noise at all, but the sickening thump of his gun on the ground was sound enough. Gumpson let out a whoop of surprise and crouched low, trying to locate the pistol with his other hand. He found it just as another green line appeared, heading straight for him. With a speed that he hadn't used in weeks, he rolled over and avoided it. Just like old times. He righted himself and got off a shot in the direction of the fire, and was rewarded with the sound of a grunt of surprise from that end.

"Stop and you won't get hurt!" he shouted, but his assailant was not to be denied.

He saw a figure approaching through the darkness, a figure now revealed to be a man, a tall man with long hair. Gumpson jumped to his feet and fired another shot. The approaching man somehow managed to avoid it, but Gumpson wasn't quick enough to do the same when the green fire reappeared.

The fire caught him right in the midsection, knocking away his breath. He dropped his gun again, this time from the pain. It felt like a steel band had been tightened around his stomach, squashing everything inside of him. He raised his head to inquire of the man why this was being done, but no sound came from his mouth. The stranger approached, and Gumpson could see now he was a pale man with blonde hair the color of straw, like the hair on the departed dollies. He wore a nondescript shirt, trousers, and duster, but there was something odd about him.

The green fire reappeared, jumping from something the man held in his hand. This time it hit Gumpson's left knee, which froze like a branch in winter. Gumpson toppled over on his right side, hitting his head most painfully on a rock. That was the least of his problems.

He heard two sets of approaching feet. The pale man loomed over him, now joined by another man who looked almost exactly like him. This man was also tall, pale, with long blonde hair. Seen together, they looked like members of some sort of vindictive theatrical troupe. Gumpson longed to ask them questions, find out what was going on, maybe even join this strange long-haired gang, but words failed him. Soon consciousness did, too.

TWO

Barnum Brown studied himself in the lavatory mirror. His entire world had come unglued, become disrupted, almost ceased to exist, yet he looked exactly the same. Strange how that should happen. He would have thought the death of his wife would leave some physical mark, yet it did not, not so much as a scratch. His mind howled with loneliness, yet two inches away there was nothing at all on his face to mark her passing.

His jaw was still firm and tight, and when he clenched his teeth he could see the muscles twitch behind his cheeks. His nose was still aquiline. At thirty-three, he had the beginnings of bags under his eyes, but they hinted at hard-won knowledge and lent him an air of solemnity, not sorrow. His gaze ascended to his round, nearly hairless skull. The death of his hair had preceded the death of his wife by some time. He had to admit to himself that there were times that he mourned the pending extinction of the modest brown covering that used to adorn his head, but on the other hand he felt his head was so finely balanced that the fuller hair of his youth was not something to miss. He sometimes imagined that some far-future paleontologists might dig up his milky skull and declare it to be the perfect specimen, and perhaps it would never even occur to them that fur should be added atop such a well-shaped bone structure.

Time to abandon these thoughts of death, hard as it

was to do in a building full of bones. Brown wet his fingers lightly and patted his face, taking care to let no water run down his neck and under his stiff collar. It might feel good—New York was absolutely roasting under an early summer heatwave—but it would play havoc with the careful starching.

Brown flicked his fingers dry and stepped back into the hallway of the American Museum of Natural History. All the fabulous dead beasts in the museum's collection were out of sight on the other side of the suite of rather drab offices never seen by the tourists. The creatures of yore and lore stood proudly in the open air, while he, who had put many of them out there, walked through dim lighting and bland corridors that would not have looked out of place in an insurance building. Such was the price of progress, he reasoned.

He opened his office door and regretted it instantly once he saw the face of Miss Lord, his secretary.

"I'm sorry, sir," she said in a hurried, worried tone. "She insisted she had an appointment with you."

He had almost forgotten about the crank, but now she had made it all the way into his inner sanctum. He should have lingered longer in the bathroom, although he doubted it would have made any difference. This was not the sort of woman who would give up and go away quickly.

"It's all right, Miss Lord, I'll handle it," Brown said, which did not seem to lessen her distress.

The woman's back was to him when he entered his office. He had half expected to catch her snooping around in his desk drawers, but she sat quietly in one of the fine oak visitor's chairs, contenting herself with examining his favorite paperweight, a clear half-circle of glass formed around what looked like a stone drinking straw.

"That's a fossilized interior piece of horn from a dinosaur called Triceratops," Brown said as he entered.

The woman nodded as if that was the sort of greeting

any man would give upon entering a room. She gave
the horn core a last look and stood and turned to shake
his hand as he approached.

"They have been found in Montana, I hear," she said,
an answer that surprised Brown a little. He knew from
previous (and unfortunate) correspondence that this
woman was keenly interested in dinosaurs, but he did
not realize her knowledge had some depth as well as
breadth.

"Yes, that's true," he said, as he took his seat and faced
her across the sea of papers and knickknacks that occupied
much of his desk. His working surface might look
cluttered to untrained eyes, but he knew where everything
was.

"My name is Alice Paul," the woman said. "I indicated
to you by letter that I would be coming for this visit."

"Yes, you did," he replied blandly.

Mrs. Paul did not look particularly insane. She was
perhaps in her mid-forties, but appeared to be in excellent
health and would have looked a great deal younger if
her hair were less enthusiastic about displaying its many
silver strands.

"I understand you are thinking about going back to
Montana to look for further dinosaurs."

Brown nodded with exaggerated solemnity.

"Yes, ma'am, I think I will. That is my job."

"Did you read the magazine I sent you?"

Brown sighed. In two days' time he was going to lead
a sizable paleontological dig in the Hell Creek formation
of Montana. Preparing for that was difficult enough, given
the still-primitive condition of the area. He really did
not have time for this, too.

"You're a talented writer, and perhaps you will give
H.G. Wells a run for his money, but really I prefer to
read scientific articles," Brown said.

"So you think I made it up," Mrs. Paul said.

Her tone of voice was not at all angry. Brown laughed,

although he hadn't intended to. One had to be careful around lunatics. He had been led to believe they did not have senses of humor about themselves.

"You mean you didn't? Mrs. Paul, your article—what was the title?"

"Bone Wars."

"Yes, very catchy. Your story told about Othniel Charles Marsh and Edward Drinker Cope, and how they competed with creatures from outer space to dig up dinosaur bones in Montana some three decades ago. Does that sum it up adequately?"

"Well, it's a little artless, but yes," Mrs. Paul said. "Thirty-one years ago, to be exact. 1876."

He leveled his world-weary eyes at her, so she could see he was a serious man not given to this sort of fun and games.

"Mrs. Paul, Mr. Cope and Mr. Marsh were esteemed giants in my field of science, that of paleontology. Their stature has only grown after their deaths. Now, your article was accurate in its portrayal of the unfortunate bone-digging feud they carried on, but these were very proud men, Mrs. Paul. If they thought they had been the first to come across life that had originated off of our planet, I can assure you we would never have heard the end of it."

The woman nodded slowly, as if ready for this argument. She bent down low, to match his level gaze. It was going to be a long day.

"Consider this possibility, Mr. Brown. If Marsh had breathed a word of this, Cope would have branded him a lunatic in the papers the very next day. Marsh would have done the same thing if Cope had tried it. It's one thing to take credit for old bones you dig up. People will believe that, you can show them proof. They had no proof of these creatures, and neither Cope nor Marsh were going to say one blessed word about them for fear of what the other might do."

Well, she did have a point. Neither man was ever big enough to let his competitor forget a mistake.

"You talk as if you knew them, Mrs. Paul," Brown said, trying to figure out a way to cut this meeting short.

Mrs. Paul sat back in her chair. He had to admit she did not look the sort to spin wild fantasy stories and publish them in the rag press.

"You didn't read the article all the way through, did you, Mr. Brown?"

He gave a weak smile.

"I'm a very busy man, Mrs. Paul."

"Did you read any of it at all?"

"I did read some. I skipped around. It was . . . interesting."

"Do you remember a young man in the beginning by the name of Al Stillson?"

"I believe so, yes."

There was some sort of youth in the story by that name, he recalled.

"Had you read more carefully, you would have seen that Al Stillson was really Alice Stillson. My maiden name is Stillson."

"Oh."

It took him a long moment to realize what she was saying.

"So you were there? You were there with Cope and Marsh?"

Mrs. Paul smiled, a smile that quickly became weak and wistful and then fell away entirely.

"Yes. Everything in the story happened. I saw some of it and pieced some of it together afterward. I was there. It was the best time of my life, and the worst time."

"How so?"

"Again, you should have read it all. I fell in love with a man there. An Indian man, sort of. There was a lot of Indian action back in those days, Mr. Brown. My beloved was killed, and I miss him to this day."

Brown leaned back in his chair. She spoke her painful words plainly, yet they hit him as if each sound carried an electrical charge. Thirty-one years, and yet she mourned still. Did it never end? Would he be this way, too, three decades hence? The burden seemed unthinkable, but Brown kept his face impassive.

"I did love him. And I love my new husband, too."

He was not sure how that answer made him feel, and stayed silent for a moment.

"That's very nice, Mrs. Paul, but I really have things to do, a great many things," he finally said.

Mrs. Paul stood and leaned over his desk, placing her hands on stacks of paper, shifting things out of order.

"I don't think you should go," she said, her passionate side having completed a victory over her dispassionate side. "Mr. Brown, every single thing I wrote in that story is real. Those creatures will be back, they may already be back. And they want those bones."

Brown stood as well. He had a height advantage, he might as well use it.

"I work for the American Museum of Natural History. I can assure you, Mrs. Paul, that I want those bones too. And I will have them. Now please take your fairy stories and go home."

Her face turned crimson, but she waited to speak until her natural paleness returned. He sat back down, wishing that she was gone. Not go on the trip? It was impossible. He had to get away from his house, had to combat his newfound hatred of death by going far away to seek evidence of deaths long since occurred. He would go mad if he stayed in New York, which already bore an uncomfortably close resemblance to a concrete mausoleum.

"I am sure you are sometimes a nice man, Mr. Brown, but I did not come here for your sake."

Brown rolled his eyes, unwilling to humor her any longer. He could give her his empathy but not his time.

"Why, then, I ask, in God's name, why are you here taking up my time?"

"I'm afraid for my son. He is a scientist, too. He is going with you."

Well, this explained a good deal. He imagined that her son the scientist would be mortified to find his mother spouting about creatures from outer space. Perhaps the young Mr. Paul should take up with Dr. Freud in Vienna as a vocation.

"I do not believe there is anyone named Paul on my trip."

"He is not named Paul. His last name is Burgess."

Brown scanned the paperscape of his desk and located a list of the scientists and assistants who were signed up for the trip. An S.L. Burgess was indeed supposed to link up with them once they reached Montana.

"S.L. Burgess?" he said. "I admit I have not met him."

"Sitting Lizard Burgess," Mrs. Paul said, and tears came to her eyes.

That must have been the name of his father. Brown felt a faint twinge of guilt for not reading her story more closely. He had scanned it in haste, letting his eye linger on only the more outrageous parts, missing the human element altogether. So Sitting Lizard Burgess was the son of her dead Indian lover, going back to where his father had perished. No wonder his mother had gone so far out on her mental ledge.

"Mrs. Paul, if your son has made the decision to dig with us, I can do nothing to stop him. He must be of an age where he can do what he wants. I will assure you I will take no undue risks, but I can promise no more."

Her eyes dried remarkably fast. She reached in her bag and produced another copy of her wretched manuscript.

"Take this with you. You have to promise me," Mrs. Paul said, and her eyes would not let him argue. "Promise me. Take it and read it carefully this time. They could be out there again. I have already lost one man over those stupid bones, and I don't want to lose another."

She kept her gaze locked on him for what seemed like minutes, and then finally recovered her manners.

"I suppose you have many things to arrange. Thank you for meeting with me today."

"My pleasure."

"You're a charming man, Mr. Brown, but a bad liar. Please take my article with you. Read it."

"I will read it. All of it," Brown said, words that he hated to let past his lips.

She extended her hand for a curt handshake, and then she was gone. Brown ran his fingers across his head and sat down behind his desk, sighing. Perhaps some other person who had taken leave of their senses would soon come in and order him to commit the King James Bible to heart backwards, and he would have to promise to do that too since he was in such an agreeable mood.

He picked up the copy of the *Wild West Weekly* that she had left behind. "Amazing absolutely true activities in the Wild West!" it proclaimed. "On what was witnessed in the wilds of Montana, where famous men of science cavort with Wild Indians and Creatures from beyond God's Earth!" It was festooned with lurid line drawings of dinosaurs, poorly posed and overweight, clumping around on stumpy legs like reptilian elephants. They were even less accurate than the bovine Iguanadon that Gideon Mantell had conjured up in England, and that was more than eight decades ago, before anyone knew any better. The story "Bone Wars" took up nearly the entire paper, page after page of tiny print separated by tiny lines. He would go blind halfway through it, but he said he would read it, so he would read it. Maybe after that he could use it for a pillow.

THREE

Luther Gumpson blinked a few times. An orange blob floated before his eyes, but the blinks disciplined it, ordered it until it was revealed as a human face, the lean face of a brown-haired man.

"Hello," said the face. "How do you feel?"

Luther thought about that. He was used to taking inventories in the morning, but he was usually checking to make sure all his money was in place and his weapons were ready. Now his brain was working on something more elemental—making sure his body, his temple, was still intact. He felt a slight pressure behind his eyes, felt small sparks of pain arcing across the top of his head.

"Fine, in general, I believe," Gumpson heard himself say. His mouth had moved before his brain had advised it. "Who are you?"

The face stood frozen before his, and did not reply. The man seemed to be sizing him up. Probably looking for a fight, looking to kick him when he was down. Why exactly was he down? The last thing he remembered was sitting before the fire, eating his biscuit and hardtack, drinking his whiskey. Now he was here, wherever here was, and this strange man was staring at him, ready to mix it up. Gumpson made a fist and got ready to duke it out.

Or at least he tried to make a fist. His brain sent the signals but his fingers steadfastly refused to move.

14

"Don't be alarmed," the face said. "You can't move just yet. You're under observation."

The face was not kidding. He literally could not move at all. His eyelids seemed to work, and his mouth, but no muscle that could transport him anywhere seemed up to the task. Gumpson looked around. He was not near his campfire anymore. He was not even outside anymore, by the looks of it. All he could see was a silver room, which was brightly illuminated even though no candles or windows were evident. The light almost hurt his eyes.

After a moment, when his eyes cleared a little further, he could make out movement. Flaming torches were moving around in the background. Well, that was it. Luther, old boy, you obviously are dead. For a minute he thought maybe the old biscuit had done him in, but then remembered the intruders who had appeared from nowhere and blasted him with something. He was not aware of any Colts or Remingtons that could shoot green fire, but maybe that was just what a dead man saw when a bullet was fired at him. Whatever sort of gun it was, it had obviously done the trick. Here he was in a room lit by no visible light, surrounded by what looked like angels. This was not of this Earth; he had to be dead. The only thing he was not quite sure about was whether this place was Heaven or Hell. If it was Hell, he figured it was not so bad. If this was Heaven, it was definitely not up to expectations.

The orange-faced stranger noticed where Gumpson's eyes were pointed.

"I see your eyes have not quite adjusted. Blink three times, please."

Upon lengthier inspection, the torches were revealed to be people, all milling around like clerks in a bank. They were dressed like no bank clerks he had ever seen, and he had seen more than a few. They all wore what looked like metal suits. The suits obviously weren't really metal, because he didn't hear any clanking, but they were shiny like silver. The people in them all seemed to have bright blonde hair, just like the strangers he had seen the night before. In fact, the only people in the room who didn't have blonde hair were Gumpson himself and this orange-faced man who was looking at him.

"Where the hell am I?" Gumpson said, a choice of words he instantly regretted. "What is going on here? Who are these people?"

One of the blonde-haired men appeared at the side of the orange-faced man. His face suddenly appeared orange, too, as if he was basking in the light of a fire when he peered at his captive. Angels would have blonde hair, wouldn't they? Gumpson thought.

"Initial scan done," the new man said. "Intelligence below average. No major physical defects. Small mole on left arm could be pre-cancerous, but initial scan inconclusive. Blood stream indicates recent alcohol consumption, but no long-term liver damage detected. Subject has a slight headache, possibly as a result of last night's encounter, or from the alcohol, or both. Aside from that, he is in good shape."

"Fine. Is that all?" said the other man.

"There is one thing. Subject indicates very high hand-to-eye coordination, involving primarily the right eye and the right hand. Very high. Among the highest we've encountered among your type."

The orange-faced man nodded gravely. Fear shot through Gumpson's mind. He had been dwelling on the insult about his intelligence when he was heartened by the news that his liver was okay, but now this. What was wrong with his hand and his eye? He was a good shot, a quick draw, and hadn't noticed any problems. He could pick a bottle off a fence at two hundred yards without hardly having to aim. Had he lived some decades before, he could have been one of those Wild West gunslingers all the penny novelists wrote about. What was wrong with his hand and his eye?

"Will I live?" he asked the orange-faced man in a voice that betrayed a tremble.

The man's face drew close.

"That's really not up to us," he said and, to Gumpson's surprise, winked.

Gumpson remembered his earlier confusion.

"Am I alive now? Is this Heaven?"

The man smiled but did not respond. He did something with his left arm and suddenly Luther felt very sleepy.

FOUR

Barnum Brown walked along the edge of the rocky promontory, the one that from a distance resembled an old woman bending over, stooped from age. The men in the camp had already dubbed it "The Widow," and it did sort of resemble an elderly woman grieving for her lost husband. He winced every time he heard it. Most of the men did not know his own wife had passed away recently, and would have been abashed to learn of the inadvertent pain they caused him with the nickname, but he didn't want to make them feel bad so he kept silent. Marion. It was only six years until death did them part. She left a hole in his heart that was too big to contemplate; he could not even walk near its edge to look over. He would turn away and busy himself by digging in the dirt like a little boy.

The Widow. The men were clever. Maybe he would just have to work them so hard they would not have time for such things. He should really draw some strength from the nickname of this rock, though. The image of the old woman, her agony frozen into a towering pile of minerals, should give him comfort, let him know that others had felt his pain since time began. He thought about that but it really didn't help. Only work could make him feel better. He needed to quit looking at this woman as a woman and start looking at her as a pile of rocks, a pile of rocks that could hide a treasure trove of dinosaur bones. Now, if anyone knew something about pain, it was dinosaurs. They hurt so much they had ceased to exist, had fallen forgotten into the bowels of the earth. He intended to bring them back.

"Around this way, men," he said, and the first three assistants to arrive on the scene walked with him.

They were students from Kansas, so eager to learn they had gotten here first and had camped out for three days waiting for him to arrive. They must have been in dire need of entertainment, and he hoped they were at least good conversationalists or had a complete deck of cards, because there was nothing out here for a young man to do except work. The town of Jordan was little more than a few houses that happened to be close to one another, and around it stretched miles of emptiness. The rest of his party had gone to Miles City, a hundred miles away, hopefully bringing back enough supplies for at least a month. In the meantime, he had locations to scout.

"We found parts of some very significant dinosaurs here two years ago, near this very site," Brown told the students, and they nodded.

"Yes, sir," said the one named Raymond. "We have read about that. I believe Professor Osborn named it Tyrannosaurus rex."

Brown smiled. They had done their homework. The find was not widely known outside paleontological circles.

"That's right. King Tyrant Lizard. A pretty impressive name for a pretty impressive beast. What else do you know of this specimen, Mr. Harryhausen?"

"Not much, unfortunately," Raymond replied. "You didn't find the skull or the arms, so you're not sure exactly what it looked like."

"That's right. We just know it was big, probably the biggest predator in the Cretaceous Period. Maybe the biggest predator in any period, which is why Professor Osborn's name wasn't so far off the mark."

He chuckled at the thought of his friend Henry Fairfield

Osborn. They had once dug fossils together in the field, even had a bit of a rivalry, although nothing along the lines of the famous Cope-Marsh feud. As Osborn's middle had expanded, he had come to prefer the familiar comforts of civilization to the rigors of field work. Brown was beginning to see the attraction of the idea, but he still felt his blood pump a little faster as he looked at a column of rock and imagined the bones trapped inside.

"I think we will make this rock face the base of our operations," Brown told the students. "We'll start about here and work our way down. The ground's not too steep so we shouldn't have much trouble getting the carts around this to pull the stuff out."

The Widow dominated the extreme southern tip of an expanse of rock which had worn to the point that the dinosaur bones should be fairly easy to find. Most of the area had weathered down to the Cretaceous Period, the last great age of the dinosaurs, the end of the Mesozoic. The Cretaceous was the dinosaur swan song, the last defiant roar before the tiny, insignificant mammals took over. On his last trip here, some fossilized bones were sticking right out of the rock, like the ribs at some Cretaceous buffet. Getting them out was no easy trick, but at least they were not hard to find.

Edward Drinker Cope had once had some luck near here, where he found a very good skeleton of a Mono-clonius, a Cretaceous herbivore. Brown wondered why he had not done more digging in Montana than he had. Just for an instant he remembered the strange woman and her tale of space creatures, but he quickly brushed it away from his mind. Space creatures or no, Cope and Marsh wouldn't let anything scare them away from good bone ground. Or would they? He walked close to the rock, so close he could barely focus on it. No bones were evident, not yet. He heard the students whispering behind him.

"I heard he can smell the fossils," Harryhausen whispered to his friends.

Brown smiled slightly, although he didn't let them see. Osborn had started that rumor about him, in jest, of course, but he had to admit it pleased him and so he felt no inclination to dissuade its spread. He did have a demonstrated knack for finding bones, so perhaps it was not far from the truth.

"Let's walk around here," he said, straightening up. The whispering stopped. "I want to see if there are any shortcuts through the rocks so we don't have to run the carts the long way all the time."

He began striding around the western edge of the Widow, the students following behind like ducklings pursuing a mother duck. The rock wall edged southwest for a while and then moved back to the center, forming a natural windbreak, one that would make good shelter. As he approached, he saw that it was being used for just that purpose.

"Hands up!" a voice called to him. He froze and put his hands in the air, and the startled students followed suit.

A man edged around the rock face. Not a man, actually. A boy, one who needed a few years on him to even be as old as the students who stared at him with fear and disbelief. Everything they had heard about the old Wild West was true! The young man approached, working his jaw slowly, like a malevolent cow. His clothes hung on his lanky frame. His face was unlined and round, but his blonde hair was dirty and stuck out at all angles like straw. The young man looked like a living scarecrow, a scarecrow that packed a pistol.

"What are y'all doing here?" the scarecrow drawled.

Brown could see two other young men hunched in the windbreak, a half-empty bottle and a pack of cards between them. They watched the confrontation with mild interest, as if confident that any one of them could handle three interlopers.

"I said what are y'all doing here?"

"We're looking for fossils," Brown said, looking him straight in the eye. "Mineralized dinosaur bones, to be exact, dating from the Cretaceous Period. Herbivores, carnivores, omnivores, what have you."

The young man looked suitably baffled. He frowned and gave a tug on the waist of his ill-fitting trousers with his free hand, but Brown noticed that the gun barrel did not waver an inch.

"Well. Are they worth any money?"

"No," Brown said, which was not exactly true. "We are searching for them purely in the interest of science."

What little light was visible in the young man's eyes dimmed immediately.

"Oh."

"May I ask what you are doing here?" Brown ventured. "There does not seem to be much in the way of entertainment."

The young man's companions interrupted what looked like a poker game to laugh. He turned and spat a thick brown stream of tobacco juiced and then joined them in a chuckle.

"There will be plenty of entertainment real soon," he said. "Yes, sir. Didn't you hear nothing about Luther Gumpson?"

Brown shook his head.

"I—I heard something," said one of the students, a young man named Simon. "He robbed some banks back east."

The scarecrow moved the gun to point at Simon when he began speaking, as if he was ready to shoot upon hearing anything objectionable.

"That's right," the scarecrow said, nodding.

Brown noticed that the gun barrel stayed dead level no matter what its owner did with the rest of his body. If he nodded his head, it stayed stock-still. If he moved the gun, it traveled in a plane exactly horizontal to the ground. This kid knew what he was doing when it came to the shooting iron.

"Anyhow, Luther Gumpson took off and headed west, and word is he's out this way. A farmer said he gave him a ride to these parts, dropped him off not half an hour away. There's a big reward. Shooters from all over are coming to collect. I intend to be the one to do it."

"Well, good luck to you. If you don't mind, we need to be heading along," Brown said.

The scarecrow eyed him curiously.

"Say, you seem to be dressed a little fancy for someone digging in the dirt," he said, running his gaze along Brown's neatly pressed shirt and creased slacks. "You sure you're not a sheriff, out with your deputies looking for me?"

It took Brown just a second to follow him.

"Looking for *you*? I thought if I were a sheriff, I should be looking for this Gumpson fellow."

The boy snorted, but Brown could not tell if it was from disgust at Gumpson's name or if he merely needed to clear some undesirable substance from his nose.

"Gumpson's good, but I'm better. You may have heard of me," the scarecrow said. "I'm William H. Kinney."

Brown paused for a moment, looking upward to the right and the left in a parody of thought.

"Don't recollect. Should I have?"

The kid seemed frustrated. He shrugged his shoulders and spat another thick stream of tobacco juice, although again Brown noticed the gun was as steady as a tree limb.

"Didn't you hear tell of the Fort McCagle massacre? The shootout at Plains City, Kansas? None of them?"

Brown heard a murmuring behind him. He turned his head, slowly, to see the students whispering again, in some agitation.

"Deputies!" Brown said. "Have you heard of this man?"

"Yes, sir," Harryhausen piped up uncertainly. "They call him the Plains Kid. He's sort of notorious. The papers write him up now and then."

"Not enough," the Plains Kid said, a scowl on his baby

face. "They also call me William the Conqueror sometimes, and I like that one better. I don't know where they got that name, but I like it."

"William the Conqueror," Brown said. "He was the Duke of Normandy. He took over England at the Battle of Hastings in the year 1066."

The kid seemed impressed.

"Well, that's something fine. But even Billy the Kid gets wrote up more than I do, and he's been dead a long time. He only shot twenty-one men."

"You have beat him at that, I assume," Brown said.

"Yes, sir, I have. Fifty men by my last count, and I ain't so good with numbers. Ain't that right, boys?"

The young men behind him, now bored with the conversation, grunted their agreement, never once taking their eyes off their cards.

"So you think you want to try to run me in, lawman?"

"I was joking," Brown said. "I am no sheriff and these two men are certainly no deputies. My name is Barnum Brown. You may search us until you grow tired and you will find no weapons or badges of any sort. We are as I said, scientists. I am dressed in the manner I am because we are not digging today, and at any rate I hold the fossils we find in great respect, and don't mind dressing up for them a little."

"Let him alone, Kid," one of the Plains Kid's companions said. "No sheriff talks all fancy like that. Shoot us something to eat if you want to shoot something. He don't look to have enough meat on his bones to suit me."

"Shut up," Kid said. "Barnum, huh? You any kin to that feller that runs the circus?"

He had heard this question before.

"No. There is a connection, however. Mr. P.T. Barnum was passing through my hometown in Kansas when my mother was carrying me. When I was born, his name stuck in her mind and so she gave it to me."

The Plains Kid had clearly been counting on a more

interesting story than that. Like his companions, he
appeared to be growing bored with the confrontation.
He seemed the sort who would find it difficult to carry
on a conversation unless it eventually resulted in shooting,
or a fistfight at the very least.

"So you was never with the circus? Never saw the lions
and tigers and all?"

"I hate to disappoint you, but most of the creatures I
have any dealings with are long dead."

The Plains Kid nodded.

"All right, mister, you can go. But keep your eyes out
for that Gumpson, and tell the folks around these parts
that William the Conqueror is in town. And if you hear
any shooting, don't bother to duck. I only hit what I'm
aimin' at."

In the space of time it took Brown to blink his eyes,
the scarecrow had put his gun away and stood smiling
at them through stained teeth.

"Well, fine," Brown said. "That's very comforting. Nice
to meet you, Mr. Conqueror. We will attempt to stay
out of your way as best we can."

"Your choice," William the Conqueror said.

Brown and his students headed back the way they had
come. They could wait another day to find a shortcut,
but he certainly hoped the scruffy youths were not going
to make the rocks their hideout for the duration of their
stay. Being around hotheads with guns would not make
for a relaxed work crew.

"Some people don't seem to have it through their
heads that the Wild West is over," Brown said once he
figured they were out of earshot. "Those boys should
be riding with Wild Bill Hickok's show, not be out here
fooling around. They're only about twenty years too
late."

"Why did he tell you his name if he's a wanted criminal?"
one of the students asked, nervously.

"It does no good to be wanted if no one knows you're

here," Brown said. "Even the notorious have to do a little advertising now and then."

"I *have* read a little about him," Harryhausen said, and his companions nodded nervously. "He did shoot a good number of people."

"Well, let's steer clear of him, then. Maybe I should alert the authorities, if I can figure out who the authorities are."

"First this Luther Gumpson and now the Plains Kid," Harryhausen said. "You said this would be a quiet, boring dig."

Brown laughed out loud and clapped Harryhausen on the shoulder.

"I did, at that. I may have miscalculated. Boys, this summer could be more lively than we expected. Be ready for anything."

FIVE

Brown paced by the wall while the crew looked on expectantly. It was the first day of the dig, and he wanted to give them an idea of what he expected, although most of them knew already. S.L. Burgess rubbed dust from his eyes, adjusted the brim of his hat and waited while Brown spoke about the need for careful digging and the value to science of what they would find. Careful digging. Burgess almost laughed. This was the only careful digging he had ever heard about that involved the use of dynamite.

They were dealing in bulk, Brown said. They were going to cut great hunks of rock out of the sandstone, hunks of rock that contained hunks of mineralized bone. Rather than try to dig out all the scattered bones of the great animals of yore, they would identify their location as best they could and blast out the rocks that surrounded them. They would take the portions of hillside, load them in the wagons and drag them more than one hundred miles away to the nearest train station, where they would be given tickets back east.

"We will excavate what bones we can, but some will have to make the journey encased in the rock that has contained them for so long," Brown told the group. "It will be hard work, but I invite you all to the museum to see the fruits of your labors. Just give us a few years to get it together."

This last was meant to be a joke, and the crew laughed on cue. Except for the students Brown had agreed to take on, all the men in the crew seemed to know their way around a pickaxe, and seemed eager to begin cutting into the rock. The students affected a pose that suggested they, too, were ready. Burgess supposed he looked like all the rest of them. His skin had a built-in tan, but if you didn't know it was natural, he could pass for one of the crew members who had spent years in the sun, and he had certainly done that, too. His hair was black, but a black that was only a shade removed from brown. His eyes were brown, but a light brown. He did not look like a half-breed Indian. Right now, as far as he could tell, he just looked like a paleontologist.

Brown was still talking when Burgess heard a noise behind him, down on the rutted path that passed for a road. It was the unmistakable clop of horses approaching, a slow clop that suggested they were pulling a heavy cart. He looked back, expecting to see the bone cart Brown had been telling them about. What he saw instead were the upturned faces of three baffled men, staring out from under wide-brimmed hats with mouths agape. The sight of so many men standing around got them excited. They began yelling up at Brown, forcing him to stop his monologue and turn around.

"Hey!" one of the men shouted. They were all thin as sticks, as if they had passed the time with a weight-losing contest. If that were true, this man had won. "Hey! Is the posse already ready to go? We just got here. Can you hold on a little bit?"

"What?" Brown shouted.

"The *posse*! Is it ready? Are you heading out?"

Brown stared at him in stupefaction for a moment, and then broke into a chuckle.

"You misunderstand, sir," he said. "We aren't a posse. We aren't after that Luther Gumpson. He's all yours."

Now it was Burgess's turn to be stupefied. He had

ridden in last night with most of the crew, bringing supplies, and was not aware of anything going on that might involve posses.

"You should be aware," Brown shouted, "that the Plains Kid, also known as William the Conqueror, is also around these parts, looking for Gumpson. He has blood in his eye, so beware."

The skinny men exchanged glances and then squinted back up at Brown.

"Who's here?"

"The Plains Kid. A notorious outlaw."

"He ain't too notorious," the man said. "I ain't never heard of him."

Brown shrugged.

"Just a warning. You looking to camp around here?"

"Reckon we were."

"I'd prefer it if you moved on down a little. We're going to be doing a little dynamiting around here. Might be messy."

"Dynamiting!" The men exchanged glances again, glances of wonder. This seemed to impress them. "Can we watch?"

Brown shrugged.

"Not up close, it might be dangerous, but otherwise suit yourself," he yelled through cupped hands.

The men nodded excitedly and then moved slowly away waving as if saying goodbye to old friends. Brown resumed speaking, but was again quickly interrupted by the sound of arriving horses. Burgess turned to look, and saw that this time it was the actual bone cart. Brown waved to the driver and then clapped his gloved hands together, which made a thump that was muffled but still surprisingly loud. Sound seemed to carry farther out here on the edge of the country. It was as if it had so much room at its disposal that it might as well take some of it. Sound was more tentative and apologetic back east; here it was as loud and bright and bold as the sky.

Since Brown was done with his presentation, it was time for work to start. Burgess selected his section of wall and poked it with an uncertain finger. It was sandstone, but there was nothing sandy about it, at least not this part. It was dark blue, almost black, and there was nothing on the surface to indicate the treasures within. Burgess had not dug in this part of the country before, although he had certainly heard about it. He had heard there were places here where the bones stuck right out of the rock, but this didn't seem to be one of them. Just as well. Finding a fossil that way would take away all the fun.

He was so intent on examining the rock wall that he didn't notice the approaching footsteps until Barnum Brown was almost right in his face. Burgess stood up straight, startled.

"I'm sorry," Brown said. "I thought you heard me."

Burgess shook his head and smiled. Brown smiled back, a smile that bunched up his cheeks like a squirrel's and gave some shape to his thin face.

"I've met everyone in the crew except you," Brown said. "You must be S.L. Burgess."

Burgess nodded. Brown extended a gloved hand and Burgess shook it with another gloved hand. Two patches of human skin separated by cow skin. Brown's grip was firm through the worn leather.

"It's a pleasure to meet you, Mr. Brown," Burgess said, trying to make his voice sound respectful but not obsequious, just one scientist speaking to a colleague of a higher stature. "I've heard great things about you."

Brown shrugged off the compliment and looked away. "Well . . ."

He couldn't think of anything else to say, and Burgess saw that he was genuinely embarrassed. He would not have expected embarrassment to come easy to a halfway famous scientist like Brown, but here was the knight-errant of the American Museum of Natural History, averting his eyes, smiling like a schoolchild getting a compliment from a teacher.

"So," Brown said after a moment. "S.L., how did you get interested in paleontology?"

This was a strange question, and now it was Burgess's turn to have trouble thinking of something to say.

"The usual method, I guess. Started digging things up in the yard and then didn't know when to quit."

Brown laughed.

"I know all about that."

"How did *you* get involved in paleontology?"

"The same way, generally. My family has some land in Kansas. We used to farm but we'd also dig up coal and sell it. I got used to digging things up. Then in college I narrowed that a little bit and got interested in digging up dinosaurs."

"I guess you have to be really interested in this to come out here," Burgess said, indicating the barren landscape beyond the rocks with a sweep of his hand. He noticed a gaggle of people in the distance, beyond the bone cart, looking at them. To be such a deserted area, this place was getting crowded.

"I think you're right," Brown said. He seemed distracted.

Burgess started chipping aimlessly at the rock, assuming that Brown was done chatting and was ready to move on. He didn't. Burgess looked back at him. Brown was just standing there, chewing on his lower lip, looking at the rock as if expecting Burgess to unearth a dinosaur bone any second.

"I'm glad I finally ran into you," Brown said. "I—well, there's no easy way to say this. I talked to your mother. She came to see me in New York before I left."

Burgess stopped chipping. Well, he shouldn't have been surprised it had come to this. He told her not to tell anyone her story, but she had not only published it, she had gone to talk to his boss. He was thirty-one years old—just a year or two younger than Brown himself, judging by his looks—and she worried over him like he was a kid.

"Well," Burgess said. "That must have been interesting. What did she say?"

"I suspect you know."

"I believe I do."

"She expounded on some incidents she had published in an article in the *Wild West Weekly*. I have read part of the article and may read it again. It's very interesting."

"I have read it myself. Yes, I would say interesting is probably the word for it."

Burgess struggled to keep his face as expressionless as possible. He would speak to Mr. Brown about his mother as if speaking of some distant acquaintance only dimly remembered.

"So—you don't believe it's true. You're out here to dig bones, not to hunt for creatures from space."

Burgess looked at Brown sharply.

"I am out here because I want to dig up dinosaurs, sir, and nothing else."

His mother had done it this time. All his years of work gone up in smoke in the eyes of perhaps the most distinguished bone hunter of all. Still, Brown should know his work. He should not be asked these questions.

"I have gone on paleontological expeditions with Charles Sternberg and his sons," Burgess said. "He was mentioned in my mother's article and he knows who I am. He never said anything about anything from outer space, much less people from there."

"Did you talk to him before the article came out, or after?"

Burgess struggled to keep the rising anger from his voice. He was a serious scientist, not some college kid. He should not be asked these questions.

"Before. The article is recent and I have not been on a dig with him for several years. But he knows who I am and he never said a word."

"Your mother must have spoken to you of this when you were growing up."

Burgess gave Brown a level look.

"It came up. But she didn't dwell on it."

"You can see why I would want to come talk to you about it," Brown said, a note of apology and embarrassment in his voice. He obviously did not want to anger one of his crew on the very first day of a major dig. On a paleontological dig, people were like members of a small community.

"I do," Burgess said. He resumed chipping absently at the rock as he spoke, his words coming in time with the pick's cadence.

"I would have done the same if our roles were reversed. But I can assure you, Mr. Brown, I am not out here looking for any creatures from outer space. If I find any, I will tell you, but I am here as a scientist and nothing else."

Brown nodded quickly, too quickly, obviously relieved.

"I have wasted your time long enough, Mr. Burgess," he said. "I think I'll be moving along and see how the others are doing. It looks like our college students are going to need a bit of handholding this summer."

Burgess laughed, probably more loudly than he should have, to show that he and Brown were back on a professional basis, with no secrets between them. He nodded at Brown and then looked down where his pick was hitting the rock. A tiny spur jutted from the rock, a coffee-colored stab too smooth to be rock. He could not tell what it was, but it stuck out against the dark rocks like a fly in water.

"Mr. Brown," he said, and Brown turned back around.

Brown saw what he was looking at and advanced on it without a word. He was a bloodhound on the scent, a shark heading for a school of fish. Brown knelt before the bit of bone and ran his right index finger gently across it. It stuck out one and a half inches, nearly two, and that was enough. Brown turned his face up to Burgess's and split it with a grin.

"Good grief, Mr. Burgess. You have found something already. Imagine what you could have done if I hadn't been distracting you."

Despite himself, Burgess felt heat in his face, and thanked God for his dark skin which made it hard for Brown to see him blush.

SIX

All of the Swedes were physically large when they chose to inhabit flesh bodies, but Art Kan was bigger than most. He did nothing to moderate the effects of his size when striding about the ship. He took no pains to duck under doors or to avoid bumping into walls at the places where the narrow corridors converged. As a result his physical body was constantly bruised and scraped, giving it a primitive, rough-hewn look that Kan used to full advantage to motivate those under his command.

"I am not a scientist," he had said upon beginning the latest trip to the small planet. "We sent a scientist before and it did not work. Our job is to get there, get what we need, then get out, and we will do that with a minimum of difficulty."

The six Swede soldiers who were going on the trip had hissed in agreement, and Earth Reclamation Unit 17 had done so, too, although he was not sure it was required of him. Now he closed his eyes and listened; he could pick up a dull thudding sound, heading his way. He was the only one in this part of the ship, so that meant Art Kan was coming to see him. He opened his eyes and almost unconsciously checked his appearance in the reflection from the monitor. He was more stooped than he would have liked, but he was not sure how Kan would view him. Kan had largely ignored him thus far, but he

35

knew he had been brought along for a purpose and now
it seemed he would be put to use.

The thudding grew louder and came to be revealed
as stomping. The stomping came right up to the door
to the research room, and then the mountainous figure
of Art Kan appeared. He gave his forehead a good whack
on the metal frame at the top of the door, which then
moved to accommodate him. Kan stomped his way into
the room, not ducking one inch. Kan could have had
the doorways and other entrances of the ship adjusted
to fit his unusually large size before the mission began,
but he had obviously not done so and genuinely did not
seem to mind having to repeatedly knock his head into
the metal to get it to move. Earth Reclamation Unit 17
noticed the gash the frame left on Kan's forehead. It
was not the only one there—Kan's forehead looked like
someone had used it to practice surgery—but it was the
reddest one, for the time being. The red contrasted nicely
with his golden hair which, unlike the hair of the crew,
was cut short and stuck straight up from his enormous
head.

Kan did not waste time on any fripperies or niceties.
He did not ask Earth Reclamation Unit 17 what he was
doing.

"Our prior understanding of this area led us to believe
it was sparsely populated," Kan said. "It does not seem
to be sparsely populated now. A good number of residents
of this planet have appeared here in recent days. Some
sort of event seems to be transpiring, and the number
of people here will make continuing our work difficult.
I am under orders to attract as little notice as possible."

He paused for breath, sucking in air in great gulps.
Kan's physical body was not only bigger than that of most
Swedes, it required more of everything: food, water, air
and space under doors.

"You have been prepared to go out and mix with the
people," Kan said, not in the form of a question, and

Earth Reclamation Unit 17 nodded. "I do not suppose you can use the name Earth Reclamation Unit 17 and expect to mix."

"It is true," Unit 17 said. Most Swedes gave off subtle vibrations that relaxed him, made him feel peaceful and at ease. Kan most certainly did the opposite. His body, right now, was giving off only sweat. "I have decided to use the name Eric. It is a condensation of my longer English name. I will be able to remember it."

Kan eyed Eric suspiciously.

"Are you certain that you have been properly prepared for this?"

Eric nodded.

"I believe my training has been adequate."

"Current president of the United States?" Kan asked quickly.

"Theodore Roosevelt," Eric answered.

Kan seemed satisfied. The rocky planes of his face contorted into something resembling a human smile.

"Good. Mr. Eric, go out there and find out what's going on, and whether these people are going to be around while we're trying to get our bones."

Kan stomped away without another word. Eric had been doing research on the soil characteristics around the current dig site. The work would make it easier to find the bones they knew were under the surface, but now that would have to wait. Eric touched his monitor and it disappeared into a cabinet in the wall, which closed until only a faint seam was visible.

Eric walked through the doorway and down the hall to the equipment room. The door frame did not need to perform any acrobatics to let him through; he was a good foot shorter than any of the Swedes on board. He walked into the room, which at first glance didn't seem to contain any equipment at all. It was four walls, a floor and a ceiling, and now Eric.

"My clothing," he said, and a nearly invisible panel

opened, producing a rough set of trousers, baggy
underwear, a nicely pressed shirt and a straw hat with a
floppy brim. Eric ran his fingers over the trousers. The
fabric felt so abrasive he wasn't sure he could stand to
wear them, but then he couldn't very well go out in his
current outfit. He was wearing one of the simpler ship
ensembles, a silver uniform that was very light yet not
only resisted dirt and wrinkles but was impervious to
any sort of penetration and had a built-in heater. Kan
and the others wore more complicated gear. The Swedes
did not particularly enjoy being in physical form, so their
silver suits were designed to make the experience as
enjoyable as possible. The spartan suit exteriors hid a
series of tiny motors that constantly massaged their skin,
so many of the Swedes' moves were accompanied by a
faint whine. Kan kept his motors whirring almost all the
time, and the way he knocked himself around gave his
suit plenty to do.

Eric had worn these clothes before, or at least the model
he was based on had worn them. His fingers traced their
crude outline but he had to admit they still meant nothing
to him. He could remember how to put them on without
difficulty, and knew that they had no built-in heaters or
other advanced technology. He knew how to walk wearing
the trousers, even though they tended to bind at the
crotch. He knew how to wear them without the memory
of having learned and that bothered him.

Eric shrugged. Art Kan did not want to hear a report
about the memories that should have been in his head.
He would want a report on what was happening outside,
and there was only one way to find that out. Eric dropped
his silver suit, pulled on the old clothes and checked his
look in the reflection that suddenly appeared along one
wall. He tugged at the brim of the hat and smiled. He
looked just like everyone else outside. He turned his face
this way and that, watching the soft room light play along
his chin. No, correct that. He looked better.

Eric was tall, thin, and looked just slightly too grizzled to be the forty-year-old his body told him he should be. His brown hair was short and stubbly, matching the stubble on his chin that he had started to grow two days ago. His clothes were rough but hung on his body, accentuating his lankiness and keeping the rough fabric off his tender skin.

"Okay, hoss," Eric said, practicing the lingo to his reflection. "Let's go get the lay of the land."

He walked to the escape hatch. The ship was buried under loose dirt about half a mile from the location of the latest planned excavation. It was not the best location. Kan would have liked to have put the ship underwater, but the nearest river was quite a ways off. The land immediately surrounding the desired bones was either threadbare or rock-strewn, neither of which would accommodate a Swede cargo ship. The landing site that was eventually agreed upon was located just behind a sizable patch of trees, which was good. The site was also apparently in a flash flood path, which left lots of loose dirt, which was also good. It had taken less than one Earth hour to get the ship safely hidden.

Eric stepped into the transport tube and checked the scanner. Temperature, 58 degrees. Wind, 8 miles per hour out of the southeast. Humidity, 20 percent. None of that was what he wanted to know. Bipedal life forms present, none. That was what he needed.

"Up," Eric said.

Transport tube was a fancy name for what was actually a small boring device that could carry him to the surface. It stopped automatically once he got to the top, issuing a beep to let him know he had arrived, but he still had to push open the exterior door. He stepped out onto the crusty surface of Montana and took his first breath on Earth.

It was beautiful. He stood blinking in the sunlight, listening as the transport tube wormed its way back down to the ship. When it was done he was left alone with the sights and sounds of the Earth. Mountains loomed in the distance, their tops as hazy and faint as clouds. The sky sprawled everywhere around him, its blue blanket thrown over the blackness that he knew lay beyond. The creatures called birds whipped by like feathered meteors, chirping once they reached their destinations on tree limbs or the summits of rocks.

After several deep inhalations, he had to admit that the sensation of breathing the air of Earth was not quite what he had expected. He thought the air would carry with it some evidence of all the living creatures that moved within it and the nonliving things that rested under it or floated above it; he thought it would smell like it looked. He was used to the sensory deprivation of life among the Swedes, who spent most of their time inside their metal and rubber world. Their air was unnoticeable; it took pains not to be disagreeable, it slid through the nostrils imperceptibly. They rarely needed to breathe it themselves, so they did not care. This air was not the riot of scent he had dreamed about all those nights, but neither was the polite gas of the Swedes. It was clear but sharp, and seemed to cut its way down his nose. The first breath very nearly made him sneeze. A slow smile spread across his face. So this world would have surprises.

He took a step and marveled at the crunch of gravel under the smooth sole of his boot. It shifted as he walked, but it didn't throw him off balance. It was very different from walking on pads or smooth metal. It seemed to give a little, and with every step it left some sign that he had passed. He made his way through the copse of trees, rubbing his fingertips along the bark. If he forgot to duck now and then, he lost his hat and had to stumble around after it. The birds, now invisible in the branches overhead, seemed to laugh at him, and he laughed back.

He started noticing the people almost as soon as he cleared the trees. A few wagons were clustered a mile or so away, thin smoke rising from the fire that was heating the morning coffee. Many residents of this planet felt it necessary to drink this hot fluid every day, even on the hottest days, or their heads would begin to hurt. He knew that from his studies, which had been so complete that he had consumed some coffee himself. Its taste was not pleasant. It was mildly addictive, but much of its addictive properties seemed to stem from the behavior that went along with the actual consumption: the holding of the drinking utensil, called a *mug*, in both hands; the blowing on the hot surface to cool the drink. Truly, Eric thought, sometimes it did not take much to keep these people occupied.

Once he neared the first wagon, he could see further around the great rill of rocks and noticed other wagons spread out along the dusty road. The ground rose to dizzying heights on one side and then sunk to a flat plain on the other. The wagons were hunkered in the lowlands, as if pulled there by gravity. Thin ropes of smoke came from them all and ascended into heaven like vines.

Eric walked down the middle of the road that ran alongside the wall of rock. A group of more than half a dozen men were gathered about halfway up. He squinted to see what they were doing, but couldn't quite tell. He shut his right eye and activated the camera that had been installed in his left eye and zoomed in, close enough so he could see that they were chipping away at the rock wall with small picks. He opened his right eye and turned the camera off. Picks. They were chipping at the rocks with picks, at a rate that would take them forever if they were trying to exhume anything from the rock. He wondered how they ever got anything done at this rate.

A brief flurry of fear overtook him. What if they were scientists? Alf Swenson had run afoul of Earth scientists on his mission here, and returned with very little; surely such an event could not happen again. He shook his head. No, these had to be gold diggers, and probably intoxicated ones. There was no gold in these rocks, and they would give up soon enough. Only one thing bothered him. One of the men had been wearing what looked like a hairy, luxurious coat to ward off the chill. That didn't really look like his idea of something a gold digger should be wearing, but then again he couldn't be sure it wasn't appropriate. He felt the weight of his ignorance.

"What do you reckon they're doing up there?" a voice asked him, and he turned to face a rather dirty individual.

It was a man, about thirty years old, whose knotty arms spoke of a life of hard work. He had impressive stubble on his rounded chin and dark teeth that betrayed years of neglect, but those attributes paled beside the look of genuine pleasantness on his face. He was one of those sorts of people who liked to just chew the fat, as the phrase went. Eric had studied this tendency.

"They're digging for something. Gold, I guess," Eric said.

"Gold!" The man looked very interested. "I didn't know there was any gold around here."

"There isn't. Our mineral scan didn't turn up any," Eric said, before remembering he shouldn't say that. "I mean, I heard there isn't any around here."

"Digging," the man said, appearing not to have heard. "I hope they got guns or they won't keep the gold long if they find any."

They stood in silence for a moment, squinting in the sun.

"So that's what that racket is. They woke me up, and I was sleeping good. Had a bit of a long night."

Now that he mentioned it, Eric could hear the chink chink of the picks striking the rock. That shouldn't have been enough to wake anyone up, but perhaps the man was a light sleeper.

"Have a bit of a hangover," the man said. "I lost five dollars at cards and stayed up all night doing it, so I end up without sleep or money, either one."

Eric nodded politely. It sounded vaguely familiar, this activity, but he couldn't place why. He wrinkled his nose slightly. The Earth air was certainly carrying a scent from this man. Now that the air was performing as he had expected, he found himself wishing it wouldn't.

"So what are you hearing about him?" the man asked after a long silence, broken only by the faint ringing of the picks.

"Him?"

"Oh, you're one of those, are you?" the man said, giving him a friendly nudge with an elbow. "One of these big secret men, like you just come here for the *weather*. The usual summer visit to Hell Creek, just *taking the air*."

Eric gave him a faint smile. Why was the man talking about the air? Was he enjoying breathing it, too? It seemed he would be used to it by now.

Confused, Eric offered a vague smile and said, "Uh, yes."

The man nodded and gave Eric a conspiratorial wink.

"Me, I don't think he's here yet. I think that was just a rumor."

Eric activated his camera long enough to get a clear image of the man, then shut it off again. All of that took the time of two blinks. If he left the camera on very long, it gave him fierce headaches. He could record audio tracks with no problem, so he let his microphone run.

"Why do you think that?"

The man laughed, a jarring bark that made Eric wince.

"Cause he ain't shot nobody yet, mister!"

This response inspired the man to great hilarity. He wrinkled up his face until his eyes popped behind his lids, and then doubled over, hugging his sides. Eric thought he was having some kind of attack at first, and started to go to his aid, but then he recognized the bark.

"Whooo," the man said finally, his odiferous breath sounding around the ragged stubs of his teeth.

He looked up and caught the perplexed look on Eric's

face. For the first time, Eric caught a glimpse of meanness in the man's eyes.

"Say, mister, you really don't know what I'm talking about, do you?"

Eric shook his head. The man straightened up slowly, never taking his eyes off Eric.

"You never heard of Luther Gumpson," the man said, taking a step forward. Eric reflexively took a step back. "Mister, did you come from another planet?"

Eric's training surfaced. He recognized this as an exaggeration. The meaning did not exactly match the words.

"Of course not," Eric said, straining to put a smile on his face.

"But you never heard of Luther Gumpson, the only reason anyone is out in this godforsaken country. Except for them gold diggers."

"I guess I haven't."

The man shook his head, as if Eric had just declared himself to be able to fly or breathe fire.

"Mister, I find that a little hard to believe."

"It's true."

Eric put a bland expression on his face. He wanted to appear as stupid as possible, a task that he liked to think was difficult for him. The man studied him a minute longer.

"Then why are you out here?" he asked.

Oh, just here with an archeological team from outer space. Botched the job thirty-one years ago and had to come back, you know. Eric almost smiled. His training wouldn't allow him to say anything like that.

"I'm looking for fossil bones."

"*Fossil?*" the man said, squinting his eyes in confusion. "Is that a French word? Is that some kind of animal?"

"No. Well, yes and no. Fossils are the bones of extinct— of long-dead animals. They turn to stone over time. I'm looking for them."

The man nodded his shaggy head.

"Oh, I getcha. Like what they call the bones of the dinysaurs."

"Yes."

"Well, with all these people rooting around here, maybe some will turn up. Listen, mister, I need to get on back and get me some hair of the dog. A little whiskey is good on a day like this."

A memory dug at his mind. The Swede doctors said he didn't have those memories, the memories of when his parent lived here, but sometimes he felt he did. The grizzled man's words had sent the vaguest flash through his mind. What he had said was familiar, somehow, and not just from his training. Hair of the dog? Should that mean something to him?

"Looks like you could use a snort yourself, mister. Care to join me?"

The man gestured toward one of the more disheveled-looking caravans that hunkered beside the narrow road.

"No, thank you," Eric said. "I need to do some walking around. Scouting."

"Okay." The man gave him a half wave. "Nice talking with you. Good luck with them dinysaurs."

"Say, you don't happen to have a picture of this Gumpson, do you?"

The man paused and thought, and then sent a grimy hand searching through hidden pockets in his tatty shirt. It returned bearing a greasy, crumpled piece of paper. He unfolded it with great care, as if it contained gold.

"Here's the ugly bastard now," the man said when a line drawing was revealed.

Eric tried to keep his face as bland as it was before. He had heard of this Gumpson after all. In fact, he knew where he was right this very second.

"Hold that paper steady just a second," Eric said.

"You ain't run acrost him, have you?" the man asked.

Eric lifted his gaze from the paper.

"Never seen him before in my life."

SEVEN

"So how was it?" Kan asked, his forehead showing a fresh gouge from the top of the door.

"Fine. I think there's something you should see."

Eric stood near the wall and activated his camera, which sent its signals through his modified retina. A picture suddenly appeared on a wall monitor, a line drawing of a man's face scowling under the word WANTED and above the word REWARD.

"That's the man we are studying," Kan said. "The one in the red room."

"Exactly," Eric said. "It appears that he is not the low-impact subject we had imagined. All of those people camped out here have come to try to catch him. He is some sort of criminal, I believe."

"Excellent," Kan said, and Eric recognized the sarcasm, which was rarely used by the Swedes.

Eric took care not to say anything. He knew this mission was a heavy responsibility for Kan. The Swede who called himself Alf Swenson had completely botched his trip, returning with few bones, which was bad enough, and with having revealed himself to the native population, which was even worse. Kan did not intend to make any of the same mistakes, but it appeared he had already made a big one. Luther Gumpson should have been left alone when he was found wandering around the first dig site.

46

"So this man is being actively sought by his fellows," Kan said.

The Swedes, in their natural state, did not need to speak at all to communicate, but instead imparted information through the exchange of thought energy. That would not work for the flesh bodies they employed on Earth, and so for the purposes of this trip the crew had struggled into their fake bodies and learned English. If there were not sufficient words to describe them or their advanced technologies, they used whatever descriptions seemed to fit, such as by calling themselves Swedes when they obviously weren't. Sometimes the English they employed was not exactly up-to-date, and sometimes Eric—whose parent had learned English the old-fashioned way—found it slightly difficult to understand.

"They are chasing him, yes," Eric said, and Kan nodded.

"Then we should release him and let them catch him."

"That would probably be a good idea."

"Or perhaps we should kill him and let them find him. That should take care of it. What else did you come across?"

Eric showed the scenes of the scruffy man offering him the depressant alcohol, and the scenes of the well-dressed man standing beside the hill as other men chipped at the rock with their picks. Kan became visibly agitated as he stared at the screen.

"This is new?" he said. "You just got this outside?"

"Yes. About an hour ago."

The scenes finished and the screen faded back into the wall, as if it had never been there.

"Do you know what those men are doing?" Kan asked Eric.

He appeared agitated but not angry. His eyebrows bunched like hills against the flat front of his forehead. Although Kan did not sound angry, Eric felt his back muscles tighten as he leaned ever so slightly away.

"The man I spoke to seemed to think they are digging

for gold. I know our scans did not find any but the men
probably do not know that."

Kan scowled even more, which Eric would have thought
impossible. His face looked like a clenched fist, only less
attractive.

"You did not experience Alf Swenson's report of his
mission," Kan said as a flat statement, and it was true.
"I did. He encountered some of the rudimentary scientists
of this planet. They excavated bones, just as we are doing.
Their methods were very primitive. Earth Reclamation
Unit 17, they used picks."

Eric nodded, although he had stopped following Kan
for just a moment. He had started to think of himself as
Eric, and it surprised him to be surprised upon hearing
his real name.

"Those look like scientists out there, and they are
probably after the same bones we are. It appears that
they are digging at what was to be our next site. This is
intolerable."

Eric did not know what to say. Just at that moment,
one of the Swede crewmembers dashed into the room,
his appearance accomplished without the hollow clunk
that usually accompanied Kan's forehead-banging
entrances.

"Sir, we seem to have a problem. One of the indigenous
forms is examining the soil above the transport tube."

Kan touched a nearly invisible button on the wall and
the monitor reappeared, showing a view outside the war
freighter.

"Oh, no," Eric said.

"You do not seem to have covered your tracks with
aplomb," Kan said.

The knotty-armed, stubble-faced man who had spoken
to him that morning was now standing above the ship,
looking at the very place where the transport tube let
Eric out on the surface. Eric experienced an unfamiliar
feeling in his stomach. He could see his bootprints, stark

and clear on the ground, seeming to come out of nowhere, as if whoever made them had dropped down from the sky—or come up from below. He had forgotten to rub them away.

"This man Luther Gumpson is not the only one being pursued," Kan said. "What does this fellow want with you?"

"I don't know," Eric said.

"He seems to have followed you. Did you know he was following you?"

"No."

"Were you paying attention the way you should have been paying attention?"

"Obviously not."

Eric wanted to tell Kan how the walk outside made him feel, how it was new and strangely familiar all at once; but that was not the sort of thing one discussed with Art Kan.

"I knew it was a mistake to bring you," Kan said, matter-of-factly, completely without rancor.

Luther Gumpson may not be the only one left here for dead, Eric thought. The thought made him agree with Kan. He wished he had not come.

"Shall we use the shield, sir?" said the Swede, named Hern, who wore a standard-issue tall flesh body topped with long blonde hair.

Kan brooded in silence for a moment.

"No, I don't think so. Were you not telling me how this human in the red chamber appears to have exceptional coordination?"

"Our examination of him seems to indicate that, yes," Hern said.

"It was hand and eye, I believe."

"Yes. Right hand to right eye."

"Earth Reclamation Unit 17, given that he is a criminal and is being pursued by these other people, what would that indicate to you?"

Eric thought, and hard. He had failed Kan once already. "To be honest, I don't know."

"I have an idea. Hern, please release the man from the red chamber and give him back everything we found him with. I want to test a theory."

Ten minutes later a shadow fell across the ground where the knotty-armed man was standing. He had wandered away from the transport tube and through the trees to the flat land on the other side. He didn't hear the transport tube bring someone else to the surface. He did hear the heavy footsteps coming through the small patch of woods, and he turned to see who was headed his way in such a hurry.

"My God!" Luther Gumpson said when he cleared the trees and saw the man. "Mister! You've got to help me!"

"This will be interesting," said Kan, who was watching the monitor along with Eric.

"I get a bad feeling about this," Eric said.

"Get away from here, mister! You won't believe it!"

Gumpson grabbed the grubby man by the arm. The man rubbed his stubbled chin and frowned up at Gumpson's face while the terrified criminal tried to drag him away.

"You look familiar," he said, as the force of Gumpson's pull made him stagger two steps.

"Come on!" Gumpson shouted. "You don't know what's going on!"

"What did you say to him when you let him go?" Kan asked Hern.

"I said you planned to eat him but I felt sorry for him so I wanted to let him go," Hern said, barely able to contain his smile.

Kan's eruption of laughter hurt Eric's ears.

"I recognize you," the scruffy man said, planting his heels to keep from getting dragged. "Damn it, I know who you are!"

Gumpson, a wild look in his eyes, let go of the man's arm. He didn't appear to have heard his words.

"Suit yourself," he said. Free of the man's weight, he broke into a trot.

"He's getting away," Hern said, his smile gone.

"Don't be so sure," Kan said.

"Hold on," the man said. "You're Luther Gumpson."

Gumpson stopped, twenty paces away.

"You're Luther Gumpson and there's a price on your head."

Gumpson's fingers twitched.

"You're a dead man," the scruffy man said.

"Watch this," Kan said.

The scruffy man's hand went for his gun. Gumpson's arm seemed to twitch. There was a loud sound. The scruffy man seemed to implode, clutching at a hole in his chest. He fell to his knees and then sprawled flat on his face in the dust.

"Damn fool," Gumpson said, returning his pistol to its holster.

Eric gaped at the monitor. He wasn't the only one surprised.

"That was amazing!" Hern said. "I barely saw him move."

"Save this transmission," Kan said, looking extremely pleased. "I want to analyze just how fast this human is. Definitely get him back in the red chamber."

"Yes, sir," Hern said. He headed out of the room.

"And get him back quickly, before he gets where the other humans are."

"What about the dead man?" Eric said.

The scruffy man had not seemed like a bad sort. He had been pleasant enough, if a bit suspicious. Eric almost felt like he missed the man already.

"Leave him out there. Let the others find him, and then they'll be scared of this Luther Gumpson."

"It seems like this will just confirm to them that he's

here," Eric chimed in, trying to keep his voice from wavering. He was bothered by what he had seen, but it seemed to put Kan in a good mood. "Won't that make things worse?"

Kan looked at the man's motionless body on the monitor.

"Perhaps. But maybe not. We can release this Luther Gumpson as many times as we like, wherever we like. We can use him to direct the crowd where we want them to go. I think one good use would be to scare those scientists away from our next dig site."

EIGHT

The two Swedes stood close together, leaning on the wall, as near as they could come to getting completely out of monitor range. Art Kan was not noted for running a particularly tight ship, and was probably not checking the monitors at all, but they thought it best to not take their chances. They didn't look at each other much, just enough to appear they were having a normal, relaxing conversation.

"Did you see that?" the one named Bjorn said.

"Yes," said the other, who was named Lasse. "Killed him like nothing. Like he was a *frink*."

They had secretly connected one of the hall monitors to the outside monitor, which was easy enough to do, and had watched in mounting horror as the one human was released so he could kill the other human. It was not a clear-cut thing; the man was obviously trying to get away, and the dead man had indeed provoked him, but neither Bjorn nor Lasse doubted for a second that the outcome had been the desire of Art Kan. They were not entirely clear as to the situation the man had been released into, as their training for this planet was sketchy, but one thing they knew for sure: No human could escape from the red chamber without help.

"He is worse than we thought, I believe," Bjorn said.

Like all Swedes, they were tall and blonde when clad in their physical earth bodies, but there were some

53

differences. They were thinner than most, and their eyes bore a worried look that most Swedes didn't display. Their cheeks bore tiny lines that came from the grim set of their faces. None of these attributes were unheard of among the Swedes, who had occupied a dizzying array of physical bodies in their history, but it was unusual to see the traits gathered together in one place.

"What do you think he would do to us if he catches us?" Lasse asked.

They were also keeping their voices low, for fear someone might stumble upon them. It was hard to keep track of who was where.

"Did you not see what he did to those humans? He forced one to kill the other one, for no purpose at all. He would not treat us half so well."

Bjorn leaned his golden hair back against the wall and let out a long exhalation of air.

"I am becoming very afraid," Bjorn said. "I miss home. This is miserable, and it's just beginning."

"That is not the worst part," Lasse said.

"I know. Every single day, they dig up the bones of Mother Naga and they dishonor her."

They leaned in silence, listening as Kan's footsteps rumbled through another part of the ship. The footsteps of the devil.

"We need to restore our minds," Lasse said. "It has been too long."

"Do we dare? If we are caught, we fail. We will be out there with that human."

"Mother Naga will protect us."

The tremble in Lasse's voice revealed that this sentence was a triumph of attitude over belief, but Bjorn nodded.

They faced each other and extended their palms until their fingers were touching. They leaned their heads forward until their foreheads were united at the crest. They opened their mouths and released the sacred words, musical whistling words that could not be translated into English.

Their voices were below a whisper and just above a thought, but Lasse inhaled as if becoming energized, ready to run, ready to fight. He started to pull back his forehead, but Bjorn put a hand behind his neck and held his head in place.

"Blink," Bjorn said, and Lasse did.

"Why?"

"I am trying to see the *Nes* inside you," he said, ending the familiar word with the familiar whistle. "I am tired of wearing these monkey skins."

Lasse pulled his head back, and this time Bjorn let it go.

"So what did you see?"

"Only monkey eyes."

"No trace of *Nes*?"

"No."

Lasse smiled.

"Good. If you can see *Nes*, that would mean Art Kan could see it, too. And that would mean you and I would be joining the dead man outside."

"Three dead monkey men," Bjorn said solemnly, and then burst into laughter.

"Shush!" Lasse said.

Bjorn covered his mouth, his cheeks trembling with the effort to be quiet. The saying of the sacred words had a big effect on him, and Lasse began to be worried that he might get too boisterous, and all would be lost. Still, it was hard to keep from joining the laughter.

"Calm down," Lasse said. His eyes, the eyes Bjorn had stared into, were sharp and serious.

Bjorn slowly grew silent. He drew in a long breath and stood straight, his face impassive, in the traditional way of the Swedes when wearing human bodies.

"There," Lasse said. "We'd better get back to work."

He motioned for Bjorn to precede him, which he did.

Bjorn took a couple of steps, and then bent over as if
having trouble processing his dinner. He slung his arms
down as if carrying heavy rocks. He took a couple of
shuffling steps and looked back at Lasse, blinking his
eyes rapidly.

Lasse had never actually seen a monkey of any sort in
the wild, but Bjorn's impersonation looked about as much
like one as any of the library footage they had. Lasse
began to laugh, so much so that he had to lean on the
wall for support. Only the booming sound of Art Kan's
footsteps getting closer made him stop.

NINE

A six-inch bit of bone was now protruding from the rock face. A portion of the rock as tall as a man's head had been chipped away, revealing the jutting bone and the hint of others within, barely hidden in the rock, like fat fish in shallow water.

"What do you think?" Barnum Brown asked S.L. Burgess.

It was not that hot a morning, but the effort of sitting in one place in the sun and chiseling at the rock had overheated Burgess terribly. Sweat had formed minute rivers along the creases in his face. Brown was not helping much. Burgess felt that he was being tested whenever Brown spoke to him. Brown seemed nice enough, and had not mentioned his mother since their first conversation, but he felt like the famed paleontologist was just probing him for weakness, just waiting for him to crack and admit that he was seeing monsters in the sky. Today he was dreadfully hot and almost felt like giving Brown what he was after. Almost, but not quite. He had waited a long time to get here, and it was no small thing to be on an expedition with the great Barnum Brown.

Plus, Brown had put a lot of faith in him. He was now directing the dig on one section of the rock wall, while Brown headed another team that had moved a few hundred yards away, further down the rock face, away from the Widow. They had chipped up the rock and had

57

so far uncovered nothing but more rock. Because Burgess had found the first bone, Brown turned the dig on this part over to him. Burgess suspected that Brown would eventually get the credit for whatever they uncovered, but in the meantime it was an honor to have the responsibility. He would make no mistakes, at least no intentional ones.

"This rock is harder than we thought," Burgess said. "But this looks like a good specimen."

"Of what?" Brown asked. The bones could barely be seen; it could be a giant fossilized chicken for all anyone could tell at this point.

"I mean, it looks like it may be a good skeleton," Burgess said, mentally kicking himself. He traced a finger along a ridge of lumps that started low to the ground and slowly climbed the rock face. "This appears to be the spine, and the bone that I first found is probably one of the feet."

If the lumps in the rock were indeed the dinosaur's vertebrae, it would be his lucky day. If the spine was there, it meant that probably the rest of the animal was too, or at least the bigger bones, unless the dinosaur had fallen into a ravine or otherwise had its small parts washed away. If it hadn't, then at least some of the bones should be near the spine, and that would make for a very good dig.

"How long do you think it will be before we can dynamite?" Brown asked.

"Two days," Burgess said. "At this rate."

If the lumps were indeed the creature's spine, then they would not have to blow out much of the cliffside to get most of the bones. If they weren't, and the dynamite was set too soon, they ran the risk of obliterating the very bones they had come all this way to find.

"We're not having much luck down on our end, so I'm thinking about bringing everyone back here to work this site," Brown said. "How long then?"

"One day. This rock is harder than we thought."

Brown rubbed a finger along his upper lip. Burgess noticed the shirt he was wearing. Brown dressed for the field like he was dressing for the opera. Earlier this morning, he had even sported a fur coat and lacked only a tie to be ready for the finest restaurant in New York. That had been earlier in the morning, however. Burgess noticed that Brown was human after all. Fur coat long gone, he was now sweating profusely, sweat that appeared to be ruining a perfectly good dress shirt. It would be as brown as the bones he was digging by the end of the week.

"You know, I don't think I'll do it," Brown said. "One day won't make that much difference, and we'll all just be getting in each other's way here. Maybe we'll have some luck, too, and then we'll have all kinds of dynamiting to do."

Burgess nodded. The men on his team stood by, hands resting on picks, waiting for the conversation to pass so work could resume. They looked hot, too, and in no hurry to get back to it. The student Harryhausen was one of them. Brown had the other two students down on his end. His men probably wanted to take a break, but then his conversation with Brown was already a break, so he turned his attention back to the rock and they grudgingly followed suit. Burgess did not feel he had time to spare. The dinosaur was not going to claw its way out of the rock and lick itself clean; they were going to have to get it out.

For an instant, just before his pick struck rock again, he had a feeling that he had been there before, in that same situation. His pick hit the rock, but without any real muscle power behind it. That was an odd feeling. What was it called? Déjà vu. Everything about this moment felt the same: the presence of the men around him, the rock towering above, the blue sky spreading like an ocean beyond that.

Of course, he *had* been here before, in Montana, but
that was at the moment of conception and he was really
not paying attention. Maybe the feeling stemmed from
all the other times he had hunched in front of a rock
face with a pick. This was far from the only time he had
pursued a fossil into its hard bed. He had excavated them
ever since he was a kid in Connecticut. He could even
remember the first one he found. It was the print of an
ancient fern, embedded in a flat piece of shale. He had
taken it in his chubby hands to show his mother, who
had promptly identified it as a buggy track and threw it
out in the yard. He recovered it from the bush it had
fallen behind and showed it to a friend, who told him
what it really was.

More fossils had come after that. Trilobytes, which
could not be mistaken for buggy wheels, and teeth. His
mother had failed every estimate of their true nature,
and after a time he showed her his finds simply for
amusement, to see how wrong she would be. It was not
until several years passed that he learned she knew a
lot more about fossils than she let on.

His mother wanted him to be a doctor or a lawyer,
but live bodies alternately bored or disgusted him and
learning the law required entirely too much reading.
Fossils, on the other hand, never disappointed. He was
constantly amazed to see what could come out of the
ground, and the more he learned the more interested
he became.

He had not told Brown the truth during their first
conversation. Her tale, so luridly splashed in the *Wild
West Weekly*, had done more than just come up now
and then. It was the backdrop of his youth. The story.
Always the story. Burgess's mind was full of memories
of his head resting in his mother's lap as she described
Edward Drinker Cope and Othniel Charles Marsh and
the wilds of Montana and his own father. She even told
of seeing an actual dinosaur thundering across the plain,

its massive head dipping with each booming step. His mother's face was indistinct in his memories from childhood; all he could readily place was her lap and her soft voice as she told of things wild enough to dazzle any child.

"Digging the bones will do something to your head," she said, but her own tales just made the fires of paleontological desire grow hotter.

And then, when he had gotten old enough to realize what she was saying, he didn't want to hear the tale anymore. He got into several fights defending his mother's honor against friends who contested her sanity. Her story never changed, never changed a bit, and that alone gave him hope that she was not mad. The story always had Cope and Marsh, his father, the coward who killed him, the dinosaur, the creatures from outer space who looked more or less like people, except, of course, for the one who was really a lizard. He was fast and good with his fists and usually silenced his friends' taunts, but secretly he feared they were right.

Through all that, the love of fossils never left him. The fossil was the thing itself, an undeniable message from ancient times. Others—including his mother—could spin their theories, but he just liked to hold the rocks in his hand and dream.

"This takes *forever*," Raymond Harryhausen said.

He flexed his fingers, and Burgess could tell he had blisters under the rough cotton. Burgess laughed, without meaning to, and Harryhausen frowned at him for enjoying his misery.

"I'm sorry," Burgess said. "But if you think about it, fossilization almost *does* take forever."

Harryhausen gave what looked like a cross between a sneer and a laugh, opening his mouth just wide enough to show his gums. It was just insincere enough to be offensive. Then the dull pop of a pistol rang out, spreading up and over the landscape like an invisible cloud. The men on both teams stopped to gawk, as did the ragtag clans gathered around the wagons. Everyone had one thought: Luther Gumpson. The wagonfolk who were gathered in hopes the outlaw would show grabbed whatever shooting irons they had and began walking toward a distant copse of trees, forming a martial parade.

"I'll go check it out," Barnum Brown shouted. "I don't want things getting too excitable around here."

He wandered down the side of the hill and joined the group. As far as Burgess could tell, Brown was the only one without a gun. Burgess rubbed the sweat off his face and frowned at the departing mass of armed men. His mother's tales had been full of shootings and general violence, but he thought that part of the Old West was finished. Maybe not. He had to admit that those parts of the stories had always excited him the most, even more than the fossils his mother had described. Barnum Brown would not want him along, he was sure, but then again Brown hadn't heard all those stories. Brown's father hadn't been shot to death out here. If anybody should keep track of what was going on with this outlaw, it was S.L. Burgess.

"Keep working, men," he said. "I'm going with Dr. Brown. I'll be back."

The sweaty men grunted and continued their picking, secure in the knowledge that it would take more than a lone pistol shot to halt this dig. Before he stepped away, Burgess leaned down and whispered in Harryhausen's dirt-flecked ear.

"Take a little break and wrap something around your fingers," he said. "There are some spare bandannas in the bone cart."

He followed Brown's trail down the hill. Brown didn't seem to care, but Burgess wished he had a gun.

TEN

When Brown arrived at the shooting site, he saw what appeared to be some sort of five-legged half-man half-box, which had one arm that was flailing around, keeping people away from the body. As he got closer, he recognized the strange beast as a photographer. The photographer's rump, legs and madly waving arm were the only parts of his body visible from underneath the black confines of the camera, which covered a sizable portion of his anatomy with a cloth. Suddenly a head appeared.

"Don't touch him!" the photographer shouted.

He waved around a thin black rectangle about the size of a notebook, the dark slide that kept light from hitting the glass plate until he was ready. While the crowd watched, he removed a black leather lens cap and counted silently for what seemed like half a minute, holding the lens cap as if it were a weapon. Brown saw that he was younger than his gruff voice would suggest. His cheeks were still rounded, his jaw and neck only faintly bothered by the growth of whiskers. He had brown hair with numerous streaks of blonde, and wore a white shirt with a brown vest. Altogether, he looked like a gigantic chipmunk.

The crowd watching him was big for this part of the world. Brown estimated that there were nearly a hundred people gathered around, mostly men, mostly a bit dirty and a tad gamey, and entirely armed. They shuffled around, occasionally bumping one another in the heads with their rifles, and viewed the presumed handiwork of Luther Gumpson, master criminal and dead-eye shot.

The crumpled body of a man sprawled in the middle of a spot of ground so clear of grass or rocks it appeared to have been set aside by God for the very purpose of displaying bodies. He lay on his stomach, the left arm folded under him, the other out to the side. A trickle of blood proceeded from under the dead man's chest, but this was the only evidence that the man was in fact dead and not just sleeping. A sizable silver pistol was only inches from the fingers of the man's right hand. Brown was not familiar with firearms and did not recognize it, but some of these men could probably identify the factory and the year it was made and the type of metal used.

The photographer jammed the dark slide back under the cloth camera cover and replaced the lens cap. The crowd began to move forward, but he waved them off, shouting again.

"Just one more!"

He took the film holder off the back of the camera and stashed it into a black box at his feet. He reached down and extracted another film holder and maneuvered it under the cloth before holding out the dark slide again.

"Hurry up!" cried a man in the crowd. "He don't mean nothing to you but he was a friend of mine!"

"Here goes!" the photographer shouted back. He removed the lens cap and everyone waited for another thirty seconds. The dead man posed most obediently.

Brown eyed the man who had made the outburst. He was skinny to the point of emaciation, and clutched a flask for consolation. Brown was rather sure it did not contain water. A taller man, his face fleshier—not in a healthy way—stood beside the little scarecrow and rested a hand on his shoulder.

"Okay," the photographer said, and replaced the lens cap for a final time.

He grasped the black box to his chest and started walking to a small black wagon parked twenty yards away, in the meager shade provided by the trees. The horse had been unhitched from the wagon and was now tied to one of the slim trees, which it contemplated idly. Brown watched as the crowd moved in on the body now. The emaciated friend knelt over the body, but only put a hand on his shoulder and didn't try to turn him over.

Brown turned his attention back to the photographer, who had disappeared entirely into his other box, that of the wagon. The man poked his chipmunk head out the wagon's window, satisfied himself that no one was displaying any interest in his camera, and then pulled his head back inside. Brown wandered over and stood outside the wagon. He heard what sounded like the sloshing of water inside, and rapped on the wagon's wooden side. The sloshing continued.

"Yes?" said the gruff voice.

"You're a photographer, I gather," Brown asked, knowing the question was stupid but not sure of how else to proceed.

There was a laugh from inside.

"And you must be an intellectual. Yes, I am. What gave it away—the camera or the darkroom?"

Now that he heard the voice at a more moderate sound level, Brown detected strong evidence of a southern accent, although it apparently wasn't accompanied by southern manners. Brown gritted his teeth but moved ahead.

"I don't suppose you could come out."

"No sir. I'm developing my negatives. It will be a few minutes. I advise you to go look at the body with the rest of the mob and I'll be along shortly."

"I don't want to look at the body."

"Then keep an eye on my camera."

The camera was not doing anything interesting. The group of people now had the body rolled over and were arranging the dead man's arms straight at his sides. A few of the men were standing off to the side, whipping their pistols in and out of their holsters, demonstrating how *they* would have been faster had they the good fortune to have come upon Mr. Luther Gumpson.

Finally the photographer reappeared, a jug in one hand, a strong whiff of chemicals following behind him. He sloshed some water in a wooden bucket that was mounted in the front of his wagon. The wagon was small and boxy and appeared completely given over to the needs of photography; Brown could see no evidence of creature comforts at all. He looked to where the man's horse stood and saw a sizable bedroll on its back. This man's glass plates traveled in more comfort that he did.

"You seem well equipped here for your work," Brown said.

"Thank you," the man said, taking it as a compliment.

He put water into another bucket that rested on the wagon's footboard and then vanished back inside. When he reappeared, he was carrying two glass plates that bore images on them. Brown took the liberty of approaching the trays when the man put the plates in the water. When he neared, he saw that the whole front of the wagon had been revamped as a bucket holder; the man barely had a place to put his feet should he ever choose to ride in the wagon.

The chipmunk was not angry at Brown's intrusion. He seemed happy to have someone express interest in his work, and even tilted the sides of the buckets so Brown could look at the pictures. The glass seemed to disappear in the buckets, making the images they held seem to hover like ghosts.

"These are called collodion plates," the photographer said. "They're glass plates coated with alcohol, ether, cellulose nitrate and some other stuff that's too complicated to go into. This makes them sensitive to light. I can then put them in the camera and get my picture."

The image on each plate was indeed that of the dead man. One of the images was a little darker than the other, but on both, what should have been dark was light and what should have been light was dark.

"So these are negatives," Brown said.

He had friends who were interested in photography but he had never given it much thought himself. He had posed for a portrait or two, but had not paid much attention to how it was done. He had also seen pictures of fossils and considered photography a useful process for recording how bones looked, but that was about the extent of his interest.

"Yes. I'll take them back to New York and print them out."

"May I ask why you took a picture of this dead man?"

The chipmunk gave him a severe look and disappeared into the wagon. For a moment Brown thought he was going to stay in there, but he returned, wiping his hands on a cloth towel.

"You ever hear of William H. Jackson?"

Brown thought for a moment, but he wasn't sure.

"He was a photographer, right?"

The man seemed pleased.

"Yes. He ventured out west around forty years ago, and photographed what he saw. He saw a lot. He took some fantastic pictures of Yellowstone, and his work helped convince Congress to make it a national park, and you know what an ornery bunch they are."

"I have heard things to that effect."

"And have you also heard of Mathew Brady?" the man asked, leaning through the dark cloth in the wagon's front door to toss in the towel. It apparently didn't land where he intended, for a metallic crash came from inside the wagon and the man disappeared through the door again.

"Sorry," he said when he returned. "This damn thing is too small, but it's all I can afford. Where was I?"

"Mathew Brady. The portraitist and Civil War photographer. Of course I have heard of him."

"Well, anyway. You know he shot lots of pictures of dead bodies and all, to show the horrors of war. I am trying to do the same thing out here. I want to show the horrors of the Wild West."

Brown couldn't help but chuckle.

"Aren't you a bit late? The Wild West is gone, except for Wild Bill Hickok's show, and I hear that's not doing so well."

The man frowned and squinted off at some point in the distance.

"Well, it's not what I had in mind originally, I'll be honest. I'm kind of making up my mind about what I'm doing as I go along. I was trying to shoot some pictures like Mr. Jackson did, to sort of replicate his work. I even use some of the same processes he did. Everybody shoots dry plates now and don't fool with these chemicals, but I wanted to be as accurate as I can. Only it's hard to replicate. Where he used to see just trees and streams and things there are now towns. It was hard work to get anything good, or at least I guess it was hard work—I wasn't seeming to get anything good. I was on my way up north, thought I might even try Canada since it's not so cold right now, and heard about this bank robber here and everybody looking for him. Thought I might get in on one of the last of the Old West shoot-'em-ups. And I guess I did."

"So you think somebody will buy those pictures?"

The man shrugged, still seemingly fascinated by the nothingness on the horizon.

"Sure hope so. I even brought along some tin because it's cheap, and thought I might sell some of those old-fashioned portraits. I haven't had any luck so far."

Brown heard the clump of approaching feet, and turned to see the wizened little man who had shouted at the photographer earlier. He was approaching at a fast clip, one hand holding his hat in place.

"Hey, mister," he gasped when he arrived at the wagon. "You got any more plates?"

"Well, yes," the photographer said, trying to look noncommittal.

"We got Dexter back here all laid out nice. You took some pitchers of him when he was dead and messed up, and we was wondering if you would take some pitchers of him now that he's dead and looking kind of nice."

He stood panting while the photographer stared at him.

"Well, I suppose," the photographer said. "I could do a nice tintype for you."

"A *tintype*?" the man snorted in disgust. "A *tintype*? Mister, I got one of them Brownies and I'd rather shoot him with that only I ain't too good with it. Got shaky hands."

"Oh," the photographer said.

"We was thinking maybe one of those paper prints. He wasn't too good a while ago for you to shoot glass plates. Now he looks nicer than he did then and we want some plate shots, printed up nice."

"*Some* plate shots?"

The man appeared to know when he had overstepped his bounds.

"Well, at least one."

The photographer looked at Brown but Brown didn't so much as twitch a muscle, refusing to be drawn into this.

"I'm sorry," the photographer said after a moment. "I don't have any paper. I'm just doing negatives out here."

The man squinched up his face, which was already pinched enough.

"Well. How about giving us the negative then, and we'll get it printed up later somewheres."

The photographer shook his head.

"Those plates are expensive. I could give you a tintype for ten cents, but I can't sell the plates for anything less than a dollar."

"A *dollar?*" the man said, his voice shrill.

"A dollar. Can't really do it for less."

The man spun on his heels and began running back to the crowd, just when his breath had been getting back to normal. When he reached the crowd, Brown saw him gesticulating wildly. Other lean heads turned to look at the photographer's wagon.

"I think maybe you should have cut him a better deal on one of your plates," Brown said. "He and some of his armed friends are coming back to talk with you."

"Oh," the photographer said, craning his neck around the edge of the wagon to get a look. "I already cut him a deal, just then. They really do not understand the economics of this thing."

"They understand that their friend was worth more to you as a mess than for a nice funeral shot."

"Don't encourage them. They'll want it for a nickel."

Their conversation was drowned out by the approach of ten men, who made less time than had the single man by himself. Still, they were all slightly out of breath when they reached the cart. They did not seem to be getting much exercise, and Brown thought it a fair bet that Luther Gumpson would pick off a few more of them if given the opportunity.

"Mr. Photographer!" one of the men shouted. "We want to talk to you!"

The photographer rolled his eyes but stayed where he was, on the front of his cart. At least the men would have to look up to him, but otherwise he didn't seem to have much of an advantage.

"Why won't you sell us a picture of our friend?" the thin man asked.

"All of you?" the photographer asked. "That's a lot of plates."

The men looked at each other. Some nodded their heads and some shook theirs, but eventually the original visitor said, "No, sir, just one."

"One dollar," the photographer said, and Brown had to admit the man was cool under pressure. By the look of the crowd, he might be cool underground before too long.

The men began buzzing amongst themselves and at last the skinny man said, "We can give you fifty cents. Fifty cents. You took some for yourself, now you should take at least one for us."

There was much nodding of heads at that, but the photographer shook his slowly.

"Gentlemen, I've done the math, and I can't just go giving my plates away, which is what you're asking me to do."

The men looked at him as if he had insulted each of their mothers in turn.

"So you won't do it," the skinny man said, offering a last chance.

"I won't. Not for fifty cents."

As if they had plotted this out beforehand, three of the men quickly moved to the side of the wagon and got their hands under it while the others stood by, arms crossed.

"On my count," said the skinny man, who was not one of the pushers. "One."

The men rocked the wagon, and Brown could hear the sloshing of liquids and the clinking of glass inside. The action nearly threw the photographer off his perch.

"Wait!" he shouted, his eyes bulging, his puffy cheeks trembling.

"I think you better make a deal," Brown said.

"Two," the skinny man said, and the men rocked the wagon again, tipping it off one wheel by several inches. This time crashing noises joined the symphony of sloshing.

Brown considered trying to intervene somehow, but he wasn't sure he was up to fighting off ten men, and he also wasn't altogether sure that the photographer didn't deserve some grief. The men had a point; he was willing to use glass plates for his pictures of the dead man, but not for theirs.

"Thr—" the skinny man started to say, and the muscles on the three wagon tippers began to flex, but suddenly a dark figure appeared from around the side of the wagon and pulled the men away, all at once. They were so concentrated on leaning forward to lift the wagon that they toppled over backwards easily, like empty beer bottles.

"Stop it!" the figure said, and Brown realized with a jolt it was none other than S.L. Burgess. His face was drawn and angry and his hands were balled into fists, ready to begin bludgeoning the mob. The mob, for their part, appeared so astonished at this latest twist that they were completely unprepared to fight. While the three wagon lifters dusted themselves off and stood up, the other seven just gaped at the dusky man who had seemingly come out of nowhere.

"Who are you?" the skinny man asked.

"He don't look like Luther Gumpson," another man said.

"I'm not," Burgess said. "I work for a scientific expedition led by this gentleman over here. We will pay for your glass plate picture of your friend. That way you will get your picture and the photographer will get his dollar and everybody will be happy."

The men in the crowd looked at the photographer, who looked at Brown, who gaped at Burgess in amazement.

Noticing that some kind of reaction was expected of him, Brown nodded his head.

"Why didn't he say so himself?" the skinny man muttered. "Could have saved us a lot of trouble."

Brown chose to pretend he didn't hear the remark; he didn't want to admit that it just hadn't occurred to him. It was not the way he would choose to spend the museum's money, but it was a good way to solve the crisis. S.L. Burgess was a young man with a good head on his shoulders.

"I hope I wasn't out of line," Burgess said while the men were shaking hands with the photographer. All ten insisted on shaking his hand, as if the deal would not be good if only one or two were in on it.

"I don't think so," Brown said.

"You can take the cost of the photograph out of my salary if you want," Burgess said.

"I believe we have enough to go around."

He looked into Burgess's eyes, but the young half-breed seemed unwilling to meet his gaze for long. Whether this was from fear of having abandoned the dig, or anger for having to step in to help the photographer, Brown could not tell. Sometimes he felt he was better at divining bones than people.

"What did prompt you to step in?" Brown asked.

The photographer and the crowd seemed to have finished making their peace. Half of the ten were already headed back to where the dead body lay, awaiting its glass-plate immortality. The photographer had vanished inside his wagon to check on the damage.

"I dislike seeing people being bullied," Burgess said. "Even if they deserve it."

Brown supposed there was a story connected with that, but the sun was now well into its trek across the sky, and there was work to be done. He walked up to the wagon just as the photographer reappeared.

"No problems," the photographer said. "An empty jug broke, but the plates are fine."

He flashed Brown a relieved grin, perhaps forgetting that Brown was fully prepared to stand by while the gang destroyed his wagon. Perhaps the thought of a dollar headed his way was enough to cloud his memory in a hurry. Looking at the man's wagon, he had an idea, and was suddenly very glad that Burgess had stepped in when he did.

"What is your name, by the way?" Brown asked.

"Turnstall. Pete Turnstall. And yours?"

"Barnum Brown."

"Oh."

His face bore a puzzled look.

"I have nothing to do with the circus," Brown said.

"Well, I didn't think so."

"Listen, I wonder if you might be interested in earning more than just one dollar."

Pete Turnstall seemed very interested indeed.

"What do you have in mind, sir?"

"I am a paleontologist." Seeing the vacant look in Turnstall's eyes, Brown continued. "I dig up the fossilized bones of long-dead animals, along with my associate, Mr. Burgess, here."

Burgess gave a slight wave, and Turnstall gave him an even bigger smile, one that Brown thought was a good bit more deserved than the one he had been graced with.

"We are working on a rock formation just a bit over the ridge there, and I think it's going to turn out something good. It would probably be a good idea to get photographs of whatever we find, and I will be willing to pay you for them, and for your time."

"Well."

Turnstall rubbed his chin.

"If you're available. I know you are heading to Canada."

"Well, it's still early summer yet, so it won't be cold up there for a while. Tell you what, Mr. Brown, I'll do it. You tell me when and where. The only thing I ask is that if there is any more shooting action, you let me photograph it."

"That's fine. But if you get into another tussle like the one today, I'm afraid you'll have to handle it yourself. I would rather not have to pay a dollar every time someone gets shot. That could get expensive."

Tunstall laughed, and extended a hand—which smelled quite strongly of chemicals—for a shake to seal the deal.

ELEVEN

The world was sideways and slightly pink, and it hurt like hell. The tiniest movement caused ripples of pain to shoot across the universe, bounce off the far side and come back again with renewed force. Digger Phelps moaned and wondered, for what seemed like the millionth time, why good whiskey could cause such bad mornings. He wanted to look at his watch. It was already daylight outside, but maybe he had a little more time before work began. He could skip breakfast—not a problem this particular morning—and still make it on time.

He was not comfortable at all, apart from the crashing pain in his head. He was getting too old for this sort of thing. He should be in a four-poster bed somewhere, reading a big newspaper, sipping from a little hair of the dog, maybe nibbling on some toast to quell the raging horrors in his stomach. Instead he was sleeping in a drafty tent, on two blankets tossed upon the bare ground. Not soft bare ground, either, but hard, unyielding Wyoming bare ground that seemed to want to suck all the warmth out of his body. It was warm outside, but you wouldn't know it from being inside the tent. The tent had its own little weather system, and its sole aim and intent was to keep Digger Phelps hungover and miserable. Just when he thought it couldn't get any worse, the tent flap parted and old man Sternberg came in. Sternberg wasn't really that old—he was a year or two younger than Phelps himself—but it was a useful way to tell him apart from his three sons, who were also working this dig site.

"Not looking too good there, Digger," Charles Sternberg said.

He knelt next to his prone employee, and nudged him with a knee, an action that triggered the pains again. Phelps groped for some kind of witty reply, but could only groan.

"I'll be there in a minute," Phelps said. "Really. Just a minute."

Sternberg shook his head. He did not seem to realize how much of an effort those words had been.

"Too late, Digger. We've been at it for two hours now, while you've slept the sleep of the dead."

Phelps blinked up at him. Old man Sternberg had always had a hatchet face that looked sort of mournful, like he was always sad about something. Time and age had done little to soften it, and Phelps was getting the full-mournful treatment, the sort of look Sternberg might bestow on a dead dog or a wounded bird.

"I'll make it up," Phelps said, trying to keep his voice from sounding pitiful. "I'll work two hours past dinner."

Sternberg shook his head.

"If I do that for you, how will it look to the other men? They aren't asking for work hours like that. They get up when they need to get up and they go to bed when they need to go to bed. They don't stay up drinking all night and then sleep all morning."

Well, they should, Phelps thought, but he didn't say it.

"Even little Levi is out here working, and he's been at it as long as the others," Sternberg said of his youngest son, who was so little and scrawny he looked like he could barely dig up a blade of grass.

"Then dock me a day's pay," Phelps said. "I'll be up and around tomorrow. No drinking tonight."

Sternberg shook his head again. Now he was giving Phelps the look he might give to a dead person, and that couldn't be a good sign.

"Digger, I know you can work hard when you want to. I know we've been through a lot together, but I can't in good conscience pay you and watch you destroy yourself."

"What are you saying, Charley?"

"Much as I hate to, I'm going to have to let you go. But you're in luck. A traveler just wandered up, and he's wanting to get to Montana. I told him you have your own wagon and horse and you can take him. I'm letting you go, Digger, but I got you another job and I can't imagine you can ask any more of me than that."

He couldn't, really, but he could try.

"I don't want to drive to Montana, Charley," Phelps said. "You know what Montana is like."

"It's just another state."

"You know that's not true, Charley. You know what could be in Montana."

Sternberg puffed up his cheeks and gave a long exhale. He did not like to talk about Montana.

"That was a long time ago, Digger, when we were young. It doesn't seem quite real."

"But you know it was. There was a man from some other planet, and a lizard man and ships that could fly in the sky."

"Flying in the sky is not so much. The Wright brothers did it four years ago."

"Four years ago," Phelps repeated. He was getting used to the pain that jangled in his head when he talked. "I'm talking *thirty* years ago, and they weren't some flimsy thing like the Wright brothers flew."

Sternberg could not argue this point. The things that they had seen could submerse themselves in water and fly straight up into the sky, not to mention blast each other with some kind of red beam. He would like to see the Wright brothers try that.

"Well," Sternberg said. "I said long ago that I'm not going to talk about all that, and I'm not going to. Will you drive this man to Montana, Digger?"

"What does he want there?"

"I don't know. I doubt you will run into men from space or lizard men or flying ships. Just take his money and drive him there, and for God's sake stop drinking the whiskey. You're killing yourself."

"I could talk about it, you know, Charley," Phelps said. "I could tell people about everything we saw. I know you don't want me to, but I could. I could tell about you and me and Dr. Cope and Dr. Marsh and little Al Stillson and everybody. People might be willing to pay me to hear about it, particularly newspaper people."

Sternberg gave him that sad look once more.

"You just tell them, Digger. Let them get a good look at you in the state you're in and you just tell them anything you want."

He gave Phelps a pat on the shoulder, which Digger appreciated even though it sent new blasts of pain coursing through him. Charles Sternberg was a nice guy, everyone said so. He could fire you and still make you like him.

"So what shall I tell this gentleman?" Sternberg asked, as he rose to his feet to go. Standing up forced him to lean over to keep from hitting his head on the tent roof. "He's waiting outside, and he seems eager to get there."

Phelps closed his eyes, which made his head hurt, and then opened them again, which also made his head hurt. He took a breath and leaned up on his elbows, which made his head feel like it was going to fall off. He imagined the ride to Montana: two or three days' worth of bouncing around on what passed for roads. Just the thought of it made his head hurt even more, if that were possible. Perhaps he could offer the man a discount if he would knock Phelps unconscious, load him in the back of the wagon and drive himself to Montana.

"Tell him I'll be there in ten minutes."

Half an hour later he stumbled from the tent, his few belongings wrapped in a tattered duffel bag. It listed to one end where the big whiskey jug weighed it down.

There was still a good bit of hootch in the jar, and he could conceivably have consumed more last night had he wanted to, but he suspected old man Sternberg would fail to see this as a sign of self-control so he left it unmentioned. The workers were already occupied at the dig site a quarter mile away, so the only people to greet him were old man Sternberg, his youngest son Levi and the stranger, who turned out to be a compact man dressed head to toe in black. His face was as squat as his body; he looked a little like a bulldog dressed for a funeral.

"Digger, this is Mr. Winthrow Parnassus," old man Sternberg said. "He is a very patient man."

Patient or not, it would be quicker to wait for a man to properly prepare himself to arise from bed than to walk to Montana, but Phelps kept his mouth shut on this point, too. He was going to go out of here as a class act, or at least as much as his hangover would permit.

"Pleased to meet you," Winthrow Parnassus said, extending a stubby hand, although he looked more than a little worried about Phelps' condition. "I'm ready to go whenever you are."

Phelps sucked in a good lungful of air and tried to appear as steady as a judge, although he fell a bit short.

"I'm ready."

Old man Sternberg gave him a dubious look.

"Have a cup of coffee before you go, Digger," he said. "It will help."

That it would. Phelps started to walk to where the tin coffee pot dangled above the still-smoking remains of the previous night's fire, when Levi Sternberg took his hand. It was a little boy's grab at first, but one that quickly turned into a grownup-style handshake.

"I'm sorry you're going, Digger," Levi said. "I rode back in from the dig to say goodbye."

Phelps felt tears welling up. He was grateful for young Levi bothering to see him off, and he was also grateful because the moisture helped relieve his dehydrated eyes.

"Don't you forget what I taught you," Phelps said.

He knew this amounted to little more than knowledge of new and varied card games—an activity not altogether approved by the old man—but he had also tried to instill lessons about not giving up in the face of enormous odds, about treating yourself well; all the things he himself had failed to do.

"I won't," Levi said. He gave Digger a quick hug and then stepped away. "You take care of yourself now, Digger."

"Oh, I will," Phelps replied. "You know I always do."

Everybody laughed awkwardly at this, including Levi and Winthrow Parnassus, who appeared ever more eager to leave. By the time Phelps had finished his coffee, the man had already stowed Phelps' duffel bag and his own luggage in the wagon and was sitting on the passenger side of the board, tapping his fingers on one knee. Phelps gave the Sternbergs a last wave, and it was clear they were ready to get back to the field. So long, Digger. His passenger began to irritate him even before he had time to properly feel sorry for himself.

"Hurry, please," Parnassus said. "We need to make up a lot of lost time."

"And I need to make up for lost money," Phelps said.

That shut Parnassus up for a while, which gave Phelps time to concentrate on staying on the road and not becoming sick to his stomach, two objectives that took all of his energy. Parnassus further obliged by falling asleep, which was fine with Phelps because he did not snore and he had the amazing ability to sit up straight while unconscious, which was no mean feat given the way the cart was rocking.

After another hour the morning clouds burned off and Phelps' head cleared and became relatively pain free, a process greatly aided by the surreptitious mouthfuls of whiskey that Phelps took from a small flask that he always wore near his heart. Things were going fine until Parnassus gave a snort and awakened, looking around in surprise until he remembered where he was.

"Oh," he said. "It's you."

"Well, it's certainly nice to see you awake again, Mr. Sunshine," Phelps said. The sky might be clearing up, but his mood was darkening again.

"I didn't mean anything by it," Parnassus said.

Phelps grunted, and that remained their sole conversation for a while.

"Why are you wanting to go to Montana, if you don't mind my asking?" Phelps said when they hit a relatively smooth patch of road and his head began to feel better than it had all day. "Doesn't strike me as being that much more agreeable than Wyoming."

"I wouldn't say that it is, but there is a more fertile field there right now," Parnassus said.

"You are a farmer, then?"

"A farmer of men, sir."

Parnassus had a habit of tilting his head back after delivering an inscrutable comment, as if it was clear enough on its face and no more needed to be said.

"So you have a crop of men ready?"

"I have a crop ready to be planted. A field of men is ready. I have heard that men have gathered from far and wide, trying to catch an outlaw named Luther Gumpson, who has a bounty on his head. When men are willing to travel so far and endure so much, there is a need. They believe it is a need for money, and if they can just have some they will be happy. But I sense the deeper need within, and I want to show them that what they want is in the Bible, not in money."

"I'm sure they will be excited to hear that," Phelps said. "It will save them a lot of trouble."

Parnassus gave him a frown.

"It might do you a world of good too, mister. I saw you crawl out of that tent. You looked more like a beast than a man, and I must say you smell more like one, too."

"Don't make me stop this cart right here," Phelps said, but Parnassus just tilted his head back and gave a faint smile, and Phelps decided he was not up for a fight.

As long as Parnassus was not talking, he was tolerable, and they passed the next hour in blessed silence. The road was flat and relatively gentle, the horse named Othniel pulled smoothly but with some aplomb, and Phelps decided he would survive after all.

"Pull down there, if you would," Parnassus said, breaking the spell. "It looks like there's a stream. I wouldn't mind some water."

Phelps looked where he pointed, and sure enough a ribbon of green cut through the brown landscape, framing a small but swiftly moving stream. He pulled the wagon to the side of the road and walked down to the bank with Parnassus. Phelps knelt down and got a good throatful, but Parnassus walked downstream a little ways, where the water pooled deeper as it went around a slight bend.

"Easier down here," Parnassus said, extracting a tin cup from a valise.

Phelps stood next to him.

"Oh, look at that," Parnassus said, pointing at something on the bottom of the stream.

Phelps knelt down to get a good look, and Parnassus deftly booted him into the water. The cold kicked him like a horse. His brain, so recently quieted, seemed to thump against the walls of his skull. The stream was about four feet deep, and Phelps hit bottom and then angrily kicked his way back to the top, swallowing an inadvertent mouthful of water on the way up.

"Slosh around some while you're in there!" Parnassus shouted, retreating to the relative safety of the wagon. "I've been smelling you all day and I'm sick of it!"

TWELVE

Dusk was fast approaching when the gunfighter stepped out from behind a rock and faced a group of three bored-looking young men who were playing cards.

"You looking for me?" he asked in a monotone voice.

The men threw their cards to the ground and grabbed their guns. They were too late. The gunfighter had all the time in the world to shoot them. After all, they were sitting down, they had cards in their hands instead of guns and, to boot, their motor skills were impaired by the injudicious use of cheap alcohol. He should have filled them so full of holes that the wind would whistle through their chests, but he didn't. Instead, he was suddenly enveloped in a weird green fog, and then he vanished altogether.

"What in the Sam Hill was that?" said William Kinney who, by all rights, should really be dead now.

William the Conqueror was not afraid of death, but he would have liked a little advance notice. He had been working on getting two pair, not a bad hand at all, when suddenly Gumpson had appeared like a coyote and vanished like a ghost. The man had made him swallow a good-sized mouthful of tobacco juice, which was now burning its way through his stomach, and for that alone the man should die. Kinney squinted into the distance, pointing his pistol at nothing, trying to keep his legs from shaking.

"Was that—was that who I think it was?" said one of his companions, a dark-haired young man named Peck South.

"That hair, that nose," said the other, a man named Trevor Hayes. "It was him. Luther Gumpson. Or maybe it was his ghost. Where the hell did he go?"

This whole trip had been a fruitless outing for the three men. They had arrived, images in their heads of quickly bagging Gumpson and moving on to claim the reward. Each, of course, pictured themselves to be the one to do the honors while the other two looked on in admiration, and each had his fantasy about how life would be afterward. Kinney pictured his photograph in the papers, his outlaw legend only enhanced by the killing of Luther Gumpson. He might even pose for a picture before riding back out to the wilderness, and in it his wild hair would be slicked down to match his new suit, bought with the reward money. South, who lifted large rocks over his head for fun, pictured a young woman hanging on each of his well-muscled arms. Hayes, who was generally nondescript except for his clefted chin, pictured himself counting the reward money.

The reality had turned out quite differently. Kinney's hair still looked like an unharvested hay field, South had nothing but mosquitoes clinging to his arms, and Hayes was rapidly losing money at cards. To make things worse, it seemed that half the residents of the west had shown up hunting Gumpson.

What had been an empty rocky area near the tiny burg of Jordan had become a makeshift wagon town. Two enterprising visitors had set up supply tents, selling everything from soap (a slow-moving item) to whiskey (which did a much brisker business). The wagons bunched together on either side of the road, like cows near a pond. Everyone kept pretty quiet during the day, their watchful eyes on the lookout for any sign of the outlaw, their fingers trembling on their triggers. One man saw something move that he took to be Gumpson and in his haste to be the first to draw managed to shoot off a big toe. A later investigation by the bored owners of a nearby wagon determined that the man had in fact seen a rabbit, and not a particularly large one.

"Imagine if he had seen that Gumpson feller," the man joked with surrounding wagoneers. "He'd a blown his leg off."

At night, the place came alive. It wasn't as hot then, for one thing, and the men could drink more without getting headaches from the sun. Everyone realized that this was also the probable optimum time for Gumpson to be on the move, but after sitting around all day, not even able to drink as much as they would like, they did not care. Also, there were more of them out wandering around, walking from wagon to wagon, and most particularly to the wagons that sold liquor, so they figured somebody was bound to bump into Gumpson, get shot for his trouble, and then the rest of them could catch the sneaky bastard.

William the Conqueror knew that he was also a wanted man, which made his appearance here slightly risky, but he had to admit to himself that he really wasn't wanted that much. He got quite a lot of mileage out of the Fort McCagle massacre, where three train robbers had killed four Army guards. In reality, he wasn't even there and hadn't heard about it until months later. He had knocked over a general store in Kansas City shortly before that, a robbery where he had not been at his best. He was more frightened than the man behind the counter and had very nearly wet his own pants, but in the end he had made it out with fifty bucks and without causing any injuries, without so much as breaking a bottle. Someone later reported spotting him at Fort McCagle, which put a price on his head, but the drawing of him that was circulated looked nothing like him, and he didn't bother to correct the record and report that he was actually playing pinochle with his grandmother in St. Louis at the time.

As for the Plains City shootout, his other great feat, well, it had become rather exaggerated with time. He had been sipping a whiskey in the Plains City bar, trying to get a taste for the stuff that he knew outlaws favored, when he had gotten into an altercation with another tough in the bar. They took it outside and proceeded to blaze away with their guns, completely demolishing the bar's sign and killing a horse that had the misfortune to be standing in range, but otherwise didn't even manage to knock off each other's hats. In such a case, Kinney knew that he who makes the legend first can also make it last, so he spread the rumor that he had drilled his opponent with six shots, had reloaded and pumped six more slugs into his dead body. He had the good fortune of repeating this to a newspaper reporter from New York, a reporter who had not bothered about checking any facts, and so the deed had become enshrined in print. In actuality, he and his opponent crossed paths now and then and were generally friendly.

So, really, coming to the environs of Jordan, Montana, to hunt Luther Gumpson was not particularly risky for William Kinney, unless Gumpson were to leave Kinney's dead body like he had left that of the first man to encounter him. Kinney had thought it might be fairly easy to run across Gumpson in what he expected to be an uninhabited area, but he had not expected Gumpson to behave the way he just did, popping up to say hello and then literally disappearing.

"Where the hell did he go?" Kinney asked in frustration.

"There he is!" South shouted, pointing to the open patch of land that spread beyond the rocks. "He's playing with us!"

Sure enough, Luther Gumpson stood out in the field, just passing the time like there weren't dozens of men all around just ready to cut him down. South broke into a sprint, and Kinney and Hayes followed suit. Kinney liked to wear two guns, one on each hip, but it wasn't comfortable to sit with two while playing cards—the one on his left dug into his hip—so he had left that holster empty and in the excitement forgot to fill it as he began running for Gumpson. The two gunfighters did not exactly set a blistering pace, as it was hard to run in their boots.

As they neared, Kinney saw Gumpson's hand hovering, almost playfully, over his pistol. Kinney grabbed his own out of its holster and tried to get a running bead on Gumpson, a task made difficult by his heaving lungs. Gumpson just laughed. Quicker than Kinney would have thought possible, he produced his pistol and fired a shot. Kinney felt a burning pain in his right hand and realized he was no longer holding his pistol. He skidded to a stop and looked at his hand. There was a big red mark where the bullet had grazed it, but the skin wasn't broken. His gun, meanwhile, had been knocked twenty feet behind him. Kinney shook his head. He was a good shot, but he wasn't good enough to shoot a pistol out of a running man's hand from more than fifty feet away. Perhaps he had seriously misjudged Gumpson. The man probably shot the wings off flies for fun.

He realized that he was standing without his gun, presenting a terrific target. He took a few steps and then threw himself on the ground, grunting from the exertion as he grabbed his pistol and whirled to aim it at Gumpson. When he did so, the hammer broke clean off and fell several feet away. William the Conqueror, the true successor to Billy the Kid, found himself disarmed. It was just as well, he saw. Gumpson, in the meantime, had disappeared again. South and Hayes were now standing where Gumpson should have been. Kinney got to his feet, dusted himself off as best he could, and walked to where they were standing.

"Now what?" he said.

"He took off again," Hayes said, panting from the run.

"Yeah," South said. He was in much better physical condition than his companions, and was barely breathing hard. "We were almost on him and then that weird green cloud came all up around him again and then he was gone."

"Damn!" Kinney said.

Their antics had not gone unnoticed. Several curious wagoneers began walking toward them, no doubt wondering why all the running and the shooting. Kinney would rather have had the pursuit of Gumpson all to himself, but he knew that was impossible; gunshots did not go unnoticed out here, especially with one man already dead. They heard a shout from one of the approaching men, and saw Gumpson again, this time standing next to a vertical rocky outcropping that rose from the flat ground like a nail from a board. The men gave an excited shout and began running at Gumpson, just as Kinney and his friends had done earlier.

Gumpson turned to face them, and Kinney saw an opportunity. He had no gun, but by God, he would bring this vexing villain down. Without thinking it through, and with more speed than he knew he possessed, he sprinted at Gumpson's back and launched himself through the air. He was dimly aware of Gumpson firing off a couple of shots at his approaching attackers, and of Gumpson turning at the sound of his clomping bootsteps. He seemed to move through the air in slow motion, approaching Gumpson's back. As his fingers made contact with Gumpson's shoulders, and his momentum carried them both down, his ear came close to Gumpson's twisted mouth. The world seemed eerily silent as they crashed to the ground. The shouts of the men all around them seemed so distant they might as well come from Mars. The gunshots he heard were as soft as falling raindrops. Amidst the silence, he thought he heard Gumpson say something.

"Help me," Gumpson said.

Everything went green. Kinney felt himself flying backward through the air, and he hit his head on the ground, hard. Then everything went black. When he awoke, South and Hayes stood over him, giving him looks of concern crossed with annoyance.

"Why didn't you just let me shoot him?" South asked.

"What happened?" Kinney said. "I had him. You saw, I was right on top of him."

"He did his trick," Hayes said. "He turned all green, and then he disappeared."

The shouts of the other men indicated that Gumpson had reappeared further away, like an oasis that could never be reached. Kinney was not up to the chase anymore.

"Something weird is going on out here," he said, and his friends did not argue.

THIRTEEN

"How is he doing?"

Art Kan's voice was unnecessarily loud.

"He is fine."

Kan and four members of the crew hovered over the crewman named Par, whose shimmering green form was stretched out on a white table. A Swede in energy form would ordinarily be a shiny green, but Par was dull. To the Swedes who had paid attention to their research about the planet Earth, he looked something like a bunch of seaweed, one that was six feet long and two feet wide.

"I don't think we should do that again," said Fredrik, the ship's physician. "It was greatly stressful on him. It will take many days for him to recover."

Kan's massive face was impassive.

"I do not think we will have to do it again. Is that right, Hern?"

"Yes, sir," said Hern, who stood across the table from Kan.

Except for the unfortunate Par, all the Swedes were in their flesh bodies. They were under orders to stay that way, except in cases of emergency, to avoid any problems with the locals and to keep their flesh forms acclimated to the Earth environment. That policy was fine with Bjorn, who was one of those attending Par. He had been present when Par had been chosen to accompany the Earth person Luther Gumpson to the surface. He could easily have been the one chosen, and the game would be up; he could no more turn into a green energy ball than he could sing opera. So far, Art Kan didn't know that. It was the only thing keeping him alive.

"How are things coming along, Hern?"

"Fine," replied Hern. "Fortunately for us, the nervous systems of the residents of this planet are fairly crude, so we have a lot of leeway. We can install systems to intercept and change the messages that flow from the brain to the nervous systems, and interpose our own messages."

"Please!" Kan said. "The words you use. I told you this is not a scientific expedition. You mean we can make them do whatever we want."

Hern brushed his hair back from his face.

"Well, yes. We were conservative on our first test with the man named Luther Gumpson, since we employed what was essentially a language generator, with a minuscule amount of motor coordination added to it."

"So you could control what he said, and what he did," said Bjorn.

He did not talk much on the ship, but he shared Kan's dislike of needlessly complicated talk, and he saw that Kan gave him a conspiratorial smile.

"Yes," Hern said. "We were able to manipulate his voice—make him say what we wanted. We also took over his response for manipulating his shooting iron, as I believe they call it. His hand-to-eye coordination for that is really spectacular, quite extraordinary."

"And now—" Kan said.

"And now we are planning to go all the way. We are installing systems that will allow us to control Luther Gumpson's body completely."

Bjorn felt himself shudder, although he took care to look as calm and unconcerned as the others around the table.

"When will he be ready?" Bjorn asked.

"A few days," Hern said, casting a sideways glance at Kan to try to monitor his displeasure.

"About the same time frame it will take Par to recover the full capability of his energy form," Fredrik said.

Kan frowned, but he did not seem particularly upset.

"That's just as well," he said. "I believe we have accomplished our objective. Earth Reclamation Unit 17, has our attempt to redirect the attention of the human beings been successful?"

"It would seem that it has," Unit 17 said. "Most of the people who are here looking for Gumpson have now moved a couple of miles north. There are some rock formations there and a good number of trees, and they seem to be convinced that he is hiding there."

Kan nodded gravely and looked down at his motionless charge.

"With good reason. Par did a good job."

Bjorn bit his tongue, but was secretly appalled at Kan, as he found that he so often was. Kan had forced his man Par to take his energy body to the very edge of its performance. Kan himself had warned against going onto the surface of the Earth in energy form at the start of the trip. Yet here he was, praising the very person he had forced to do the forbidden.

It had worked to divert the attention of the humans, even Bjorn had to admit that, but the effort had nearly killed Par, one of Kan's own crew. Kan was rough on his followers; imagine how he would treat impostors on his ship. Bjorn felt like shuddering again.

"Let's leave Par now," Kan said. "Fredrik, do what you can to make him comfortable. Daytime is ending. Bjorn, what remains to be done here tonight?"

"Three skeletons," Bjorn said, trying to keep his voice level. "One is a plant eater, two are carnivores. The carnivores are part of what we are looking for, the plant eater is apparently not. We are taking all three to be sure, because they may have had some sort of interaction that we need to study."

"Do we have enough capacity?" Kan asked. "I don't want to drag around a bunch of bones just for fun."

"We have capacity," Bjorn said.

"Fine. We have work to do, and no better time to do it. We must make use of Par's sacrifice."

He walked out of the room, bumping his head on the top of the door as he passed, leaving a trace of blood.

"Please take some care with your body," Hern said, but Kan ignored him.

FOURTEEN

Brown couldn't sleep. He wasn't sure why, for it had been a long day. Maybe it was the sound of the men snoring, which resembled the noise of the internal combustion engines in horseless carriages. Maybe it was the wind, which would interrupt its soft blowing now and then to grab hold of a hilltop and let loose a lonesome whistle. Maybe it was the way the temperature dropped at night, forcing the men to retreat under their blankets, with only their infernal snoring to scare away the cold. One's body scarcely had time to get used to being hot all day, when it had to get used to being cold all night.

Then again, maybe it was the stars. He was always amazed to see them out here, all present and accounted for. The white curdle of the Milky Way sprawled above him, or maybe below. If he rolled on his back and craned his neck right he felt as if he were clinging to the bottom of the Earth, gazing at the snowy peaks of an impossibly huge mountain range far beneath him. He felt his toes tense in his boots and his fingers tighten on the blanket, angling for better grip to keep him in place. Barnum Brown rolled back over and crawled from his tent.

Things were going pretty well so far. Burgess had gotten them on to a find that looked more and more like a Tyrannosaurus rex every day. Getting just that one good fossil out would make the whole trip worthwhile, but he had reason to hope for even better things. The weather

certainly had been cooperating, he couldn't complain
about that, although now and then a rain shower would
be welcomed, both for the heat relief and because it
might soften the ground and wash away some of the dust
they had kicked up in their digging.

Even the things that weren't going so well were at least
interesting. He did have considerably more company than
he would have liked on this dig, but for the most part
the wagonloads of scraggly men who had appeared
seemed content to chase their dreams of an old Wild
West lifestyle. The only bones they were interested in
were the ones that held up the head of Luther Gumpson,
and as far as Brown was concerned they were welcome
to them. He chuckled to himself, thinking of how he
could relate these stories in a letter home to Marion,
but then he remembered that she was no longer there.
The scientific part of his mind offered the thought that
she was quite likely near bones herself, but the more
protective part of his psyche clamped down on that
thought and held it still until it died.

Marion always loved seeing the stars, and didn't get
to see half so many in New York City—the Milky Way
refused to commute into the urban hustle and bustle,
and hid itself just outside of the view of the lights. God,
she would love these stars. He felt a quick bolt of emotion
rise up in his throat, and he closed his eyes and thought
about nothing at all until it passed. Brown worked with
creatures that were millions of years old, and by that
comparison his own wife had lived for the merest blink
of an eye. But it was worth it. A butterfly might live and
flap its wings for only a summer, but to it the summer is
everything. All we know is this life.

The beasts whose bones slumbered beneath him knew
nothing of his presence or his interest in their location.
Wherever they were, if indeed they were anywhere, they
didn't give a tail's toss for his musings. Were they to shake
loose the dust of millions of years, they would shrug him

aside—or perhaps consume him for a snack—and wander down to the inland sea that once covered this place, and carry on as they once did. Maybe he would not miss his wife so much if he had a brain the size of a walnut. Maybe it would be a blessing.

There were good reasons for him to return to the Hell Creek formation. He had already made one significant find here—the first-ever bones of the largest predator ever found. Newspaper reporters seemed especially taken with the reports of the beast that were distributed by Henry Fairfield Osborn, his boss at the Museum of Natural History. Henry had an active imagination, and was not one just to lay out descriptions of the creature in a methodical, scientific way. He had described Tyrannosaurus rex as a ferocious eating machine—anyone who had ever seen the creature's skull could not disagree—and the reporters had followed suit.

One reporter wrote that it "dined upon elephants, with ancient crocodiles for dessert," and that was for one of the more respectable papers. Still, Brown couldn't say that such a description was necessarily wrong, except for the part about the elephants. If elephants had existed when T. rex did, he would have eaten them, too. The incomplete skull he had found here two years before was nearly four feet long, and the creature stood twenty feet tall. Stretched out, from nose to tail, it was twice that. Its teeth were six-inch daggers. Its huge rear legs could propel it across the ground like a locomotive, its muscular forearms could grab and hold any prey unfortunate enough to be in front of it.

He had actually discovered the beast twice. He had found the first one seven years ago in Wyoming, only he didn't realize what it was and called it something completely different, a name that had slipped from his memory for the moment. Dynamosarus something. It was a significant find at the time, but five years later he found Tyrannosaurus rex, a beast that had taken the name of king and kept it. Henry Fairfield Osborn had later deduced that both skeletons were of the same sort of creature, so Tyrannosaurus had made its first kill of the modern age, and Dynamosaurus was no more.

This part of Montana was good for discovering the bones of creatures from the Cretaceous Period, when Tyrannosaurs had lived. That was the last great age of the dinosaurs, and they had congregated around the inland sea like elephants lining up at a water hole. The great paleontologist Edward Drinker Cope had discovered a Cretaceous herbivore here, Monoclonius, a rhinoceros-like beast. According to S.L. Burgess's mother, he had done so with the help of people from another planet. Brown smiled at the thought, and the smile felt good after his earlier spell of melancholy.

This was indeed a good place to find dinosaurs, but it wasn't the only reason he was here. Osborn and his coworkers wanted him to come because they wanted to get his mind off Marion. Her parents agreed to watch Julia for the summer, and Brown agreed to go, not least because Osborn tipped off the *New York Times* and some other papers, and the reporters started bugging him for news about the great dragons of yore. The trip had worked, until tonight. He had dug during the day until his bones ached and then slept so soundly it was as if he himself had become a fossil. Until tonight. Tonight, Marion had come back to him, and the feeling was both good and awful.

He was still not sleepy, but he was getting cold. They had camped on the leeward side of the rocks, close to the dig site and suitably far from the three young gunslingers Brown had encountered. Those were creatures that should be as extinct as the dinosaurs. The camp was on a patch of ground that sloped gently down to the main road where the wagons full of Gumpson-pursuing men were parked. He could hear snores crossing the night air from them, too, in addition to the

racket coming from his own camp. It was very late,
probably two or three in the morning, and everyone was
asleep. Even those gunmen who had vowed to stay awake
all night looking for Gumpson had succumbed to whiskey
and were now snoring away, probably with their six-
shooters still in their hands.

Maybe he should warm up by taking a walk. If he moved
slowly he lessened the chances of breaking a leg, and
also lessened the chances of waking up the sleeping
wagoneers and getting shot for his trouble. He didn't
look anything like the Luther Gumpson of the wanted
posters, but in the dark a half-cocked shooter wouldn't
be too picky.

He decided to avoid the issue altogether by picking
his way to the right of the wagon road, heading toward
the rock called the Widow. Maybe she would bring a
widower comfort tonight. He knew the path to be rock-
strewn but relatively flat, and devoid of visitors. It must
have been later than he had originally thought, because
the edge of the horizon was just beginning to glow faintly,
which didn't help him see where to place his feet but
did help him avoid walking into any vertical rock
formations. Brown continued walking for several minutes,
trying to walk in as straight a line as he possibly could.
He thought that the ground here sloped gradually down
until it was also level with the road, but he must have
been mistaken, or he was walking in the wrong direction.
Ahead of him, to the right of where he thought the Widow
should be, was the edge of a cliff, which apparently
overlooked a drop he had not really noticed before. The
cliff edge was outlined in faint blue against the horizon,
but the drop itself was lost in darkness, and he couldn't
tell how far it extended. It could be a few feet or it could
be a hundred feet, and either way it was dangerous and
he didn't want to test it.

Brown was just on the verge of turning around and
heading back, perhaps to start building a fire for the

morning coffee, when he saw what looked like a faint green glow emanating from down in the drop. It must have been a fire from one of the wagons parked off by itself, but it shouldn't have been green. Even the lignite coal that fueled most of the fires out here didn't burn that color. He edged up closer to the cliff, being careful to take small steps and to make sure that his toes were pushing against terra firma before he put his weight down. When he came to what felt like the edge of the drop, he saw that there were actually several green lights, and they didn't look like fires at all. They looked like electrical lights, but that couldn't be; Montana wasn't wired for electricity. The green lights seemed to shimmer around the edges. Brown squinted and could just make out some moving forms. These were people down there, and they were doing something strange.

He heard a sound behind him, the unmistakable crunch of a pebble under a boot. Brown crouched and whirled, ducking what he thought would be a gunshot to the gut.

"I'm not Luther Gumpson!" he shouted, but heard only a grunt in response.

He could hear the shifting of several feet. Brown felt fingers close on his right arm. He tried to loosen those fingers with his left hand, but they held like steel. Brown then delivered the most solid backhand punch he could muster, but he might as well have sparred with a concrete block.

One of his attackers held something up, and suddenly Brown saw—up close this time—the same eerie green light he had seen below. The right half of his body was bathed in it, and that half suddenly lost the ability to move. Brown started to topple over sideways, and his attackers moved to catch him. There were two of them, he could now see, thanks to the light. They didn't look like the scruffy sorts from the wagons. These were tall men with shiny blonde hair, and they weren't scruffy at all.

As Brown went down, his left hand found what it was seeking in his pocket—his pocketknife. He had been toying with it absently as he walked, flicking it first open and then closed. As luck would have it, it was open, and just when he needed it. The thinner of the two tall blondes grabbed him to stop his fall, and Brown repaid him by plunging the small blade into his right cheek. He had really been going for the neck, but something stopped him. Maybe it was bad aim, maybe there was some part of his brain that really didn't want to kill anybody, even somebody who seemed quite intent on killing him.

The man cried out in pain and shoved Brown fully into the green light, freezing him as surely as if he had been dipped in plaster of paris and left to dry. The tall man stepped close to him, apparently unaffected by the light's freezing power.

"That was not necessary," the man said, as blood gushed from his cheek.

A flap of his skin hung down from his jaw, like wrapping paper dangling off a half-opened gift. Brown saw what appeared to be green scales underneath.

"What are you?" he wanted to ask, but his mouth wouldn't move.

The other man also stepped forward, and the thinner man clapped a hand to his cheek, covering the hole back up.

"Not good," the other man said. "You'd better let Hern take a look at that."

The thin man nodded, keeping his hand on his jaw.

"Ready?" he asked.

"Ready."

The green light flicked off, and Brown could move again, for all the good it did him. The other man was holding some kind of silver stick, and suddenly Brown saw more lights, these brighter than anything else, but they were all in his head. He felt strong arms catching him before he tumbled head over heels into the black abyss.

He awoke in what seemed like some sort of greenhouse. It had a large, vaulted roof but didn't seem to have any plants, only tall, blonde-haired men walking around, looking worried. He tried to move an arm and found that he was frozen again. He heard heavy footsteps, and then voices in English.

"We found another one lurking about, sir," said a voice, and then the heavy face of a man peered in at him.

The man's forehead was crisscrossed with scratches and bruises. Unlike the others, his blonde hair stuck straight up off his forehead.

"He was spying on us from a cliff. He saw us working."

Brown recognized the voice as that of the stockier of the two men who had accosted him.

"Any unusual physical characteristics?"

"No, sir. He has very little hair on his head, but that is not uncommon for his species."

"I know that," the broad-faced man said.

Brown did not think it fair that someone would comment on his baldness without giving him a chance for rejoinder, but his lips refused to budge.

"So what shall we do with him?" said the voice of the unseen man.

The broad-faced man shrugged.

"I suppose we will do like we did with the other. We'll let Luther Gumpson shoot him."

FIFTEEN

"You are bleeding very badly," Hern said. "I believe it will be necessary for you to revert to true form so I can work on your body."

"I do not have time for that," Bjorn said. "Can't you just sew it up? It's really not that bad."

They were situated in Hern's medical room, which was a good forty paces off the central command room of the ship. Its wall screens were full of depictions of the various tubes, pipes and rounded objects that made up the bodies of human beings. Bjorn knew that the Swedes found those bodies quaint and lacking in the structural symmetry that made up their energy forms; Hern kept them on the walls as much for the crew's amusement as for reference material.

Hern peered at the bloody flap of skin, which Bjorn was holding close to his face.

"Sewing that up is a rather crude method, one that may leave a scar on your face."

"I'm just trying to emulate our captain," Bjorn said. "If it's good enough for Art Kan, it's good enough for me."

Hern put a hand to his mouth to stifle a laugh. He gave Bjorn a mischievous look.

"Now, don't go saying things like that or you'll get us both in trouble."

Hern was not the ship's physician. Fredrik had that job, but Fredrik was more knowledgeable about gaseous

Swede bodies. Hern knew more about the physical Earth bodies, so he bore the unenviable task of trying to keep Kan in some kind of presentable shape, as well as tending to the scrapes and cuts borne by the rest of the crew.

"I can't sew it up if you won't take your hand away," Hern said, and Bjorn frowned.

"Can't you just work from side to side? I'll hold it up as you go along."

Hern frowned in obvious exasperation. One advantage that physical bodies held for the Swedes was that they were much more nonverbally expressive.

"I *could* do that, if it had already been cleaned underneath. But you've got caked blood under there, and probably dirt from outside, and who knows what else. Your face could start rotting off, and the captain would not like that at all."

"Well, he's always bloodying himself up."

Hern nodded.

"But *he* is the captain, and you are not. That is the key difference."

"Well, all right," Bjorn said. "But let me wash it, and then you can sew it up."

He reached for the vial of clear cleansing fluid that Hern had set out on the table for that purpose. He misjudged the distance and nearly knocked the bottle off the table, and then lunged for it with both hands. If there was anything Kan hated more than crewmembers with rotting faces, it was wasted supplies. Bjorn caught the bottle just before it hit the ground, finishing the catch with a neat little dip that took into account this planet's gravitational pull and provided just the right amount of correction to keep all the fluid in its container.

"There," Bjorn said, putting the bottle back in its place.

Hern stared at him fixedly. Bjorn felt blood rush to his face when he found himself being stared at so openly. He reached to put his hand back to his cut, and felt that the flap of skin was hanging down.

"You are an intruder," Hern said slowly. "You are a *lizard.*"

"That is not what we call ourselves," Bjorn said, his voice a near hiss. He lunged at Hern, but Hern was fast and agile, like most Swedes, and managed to twist away. Bjorn did a running dive after him, grabbing his heels and sending Hern crashing to the floor on his sizable chin. Hern huffed in pain but kept crawling for the door, and Bjorn could do nothing to stop him from pulling his head through the doorframe and shouting, "Help!"

Bjorn let go of Hern's ankles and reached for a better hold, but Hern gave him a kick and managed to stagger to his feet and make it into the hall.

"Help!" he shouted louder, a shout that carried far.

Bjorn pounded his fists on the floor in frustration. He had not intended for it to end this way. He had trained hard for this mission, had taken the time to get to know his fake human body, the best facsimile that his people could produce. He had learned the ins and outs of Swede society, learned their destructive philosophy and self-centered ways. All of that was wasted, all because of one careless move on a dark Earth night, all because of one human and his archaic weapon.

Bjorn still had a role to play. He scrambled to his feet and bounded into the hallway, as if still pursuing Hern, as if he still thought he could catch him. He ran at full speed into the control room, where Kan and several other members of the crew were staring at Hern, who had just made it to Kan's side, holding his chin and breathing hard.

"Him," Hern said, pointing back at the advancing Bjorn. "He's a lizard!"

The Swedes stared in amazement at the torn flesh that flapped at Bjorn's cheek, and the green scales that shone through the blood underneath it. A follower of Mother Naga, here in the very middle of their ship!

"Lizard!" said Lasse. "How dare you insult us with your presence!"

With a furious look twisting his face, Lasse snatched a small metallic wand from his belt. It was the standard Swede multi-purpose tool that had no English name, so for the purposes of this trip the Swedes had decided to call it the Multi-Purpose Tool, which showed their general level of imagination. It could be used to suspend subjects for study by enveloping them in a green gas that was not unlike the energy bodies of the Swedes, or it could be used to compress subjects, to squeeze them down to miniature form.

"No!" shouted Art Kan, when he saw what Lasse was doing, but he was too late.

The tool was recommended only for shrinking inanimate objects. When used on living subjects—one exception being the energy bodies of the Swedes—it was invariably fatal. Bjorn knew that his fake outer body was designed to withstand the shrinking, but his true form was not. Just for an instant, Bjorn saw the look of hate on Lasse's face replaced by a look of intense sorrow, and then the green cloud enveloped him and he saw nothing else at all.

SIXTEEN

Bjorn thrashed in the grip of the green cloud for an instant and then disappeared, to be replaced by a small, motionless shape on the floor.

"Lasse!" Kan shouted. "Give me your Multi-Purpose Tool!"

His face still twisted by rage and disgust, Lasse did as he was told. Kan manipulated the tool and turned it on again, bringing the form of Bjorn back to full size. It was, of course, far too late. He was obviously dead. Blood poured from his false nose, ears and eyes, testifying to the grievous damage done to the real body within. He looked like a dead Swede except for the bloody patch of lizard cheek showing through the open flap of skin. That small tear was enough to reveal him as a Nes, as the followers of Mother Naga preferred to be called. The other Swedes made similar faces of disgust as they stared at his motionless body. A scowl even crossed Kan's face as he handed the Multi-Purpose Tool back to Lasse.

"The desperation of the lizards never ceases to amaze me," he said after a pause. "Lasse, I can understand what you did, although I wish you hadn't done it. We could have learned something by talking to this Nes, but now we do not have that opportunity. I would like to have known what they were up to."

"I am sorry," Lasse said. "I was overcome with disgust at his presence."

106

"I said I understood. I mean no insult to anyone, but we must make sure he is not the only lizard aboard. I want Hern and Fredrik to monitor that everyone on the ship can leave their flesh bodies and display their true energy forms, and then I want everyone else to do the same for Hern and Fredrik. We will do this, a few at a time, in Fredrik's office. To make it fair, I will go first."

Earth Reclamation Unit 17 had entered the main room. After eyeing the dead Nes for a minute, he turned his attention to the motionless captive. The man named Luther Gumpson was in another of the red-light chambers, which was currently sealed so he could sleep.

"Sir, before you do that, I think you should know something," Unit 17 said.

"What is it?" Kan said, forgetting Lasse and his transgression for a moment.

"What are you planning to do with this man?" he said, indicating the bald captive.

"I thought we could reserve him as needed and then use him to distract the humans. They seem to get excited over incidents of gunplay, so I was thinking Gumpson could shoot him."

"I don't think that's a good idea."

"And why not?"

"Because I saw this man, outside. He's the leader of the scientific mission that is working in the rocks."

"So?"

"So his death will be noticed much more than the death of the other man Gumpson shot."

Kan shrugged.

"That is exactly the purpose."

"But this man heads a large party. I am familiar with some of Alf Swenson's reports from his trip, and it seems that these expeditions are funded by residents of the large cities in the eastern part of this country."

"Meaning?"

"Meaning that if this man is shot, not only his fellows

will come looking for Gumpson, but quite likely law enforcement people will as well, at the behest of those residents of eastern cities, and we'll have more people out here looking for him than we do now."

Kan frowned and studied the immobile face of his captive.

"If I may, sir," Lasse said, "it seems sensible to release this Gumpson instead. He is the one all of these people are looking for, and if they get him they will all go away."

Kan inflated his cheeks with air, and then expelled it in a gust, a motion that secretly repelled Lasse.

"Oh, I hate to do that," he said. "Even if keeping him around increases the risk to the mission. We finally have him where we want him. We have a warrior whose physical skills make him the perfect competitor in his environment, and we have the means to control those skills completely."

"But, sir, we could always wait until we get home and replicate him there, as Earth Reclamation Unit 17 well knows. Luther Gumpson could become Earth Reclamation Unit 18."

Kan shook his head.

"You don't understand. We don't go around on our world controlling each other by firing shaped metal into our bodies. That is how they do things here, and that is what Luther Gumpson is especially good at doing. He is a warrior in his environment, and that is where he should be studied. Or rather, observed. I am not a scientist, and I do not study things. I observe them. I want to watch Luther Gumpson operate in his own world."

"There is one thing we could do with this other man," said Hern, whose hands were still trembling from the shock of having been attacked by a Nes. "I could implant a memory revoking unit into his head. It periodically erases short-term memory, and we can set it to do that as often as we want."

"That's a good idea," Earth Reclamation Unit 17 said. "It's morning outside now. If you can do that quickly, we could have him back to his camp and nobody would know the difference. He hasn't been gone that long. We'd be right back where we were, with no harm done."

Kan gave a swift, imperious nod.

"I would prefer that you leave to me the judgments about which ideas are good and which are not, but I must say this makes sense. This way I keep Luther Gumpson and we attract no further attention, or at least not until we actually want to attract it. Hern, how long will this implantation take?"

"No time at all."

"Then do it. We'll get started on the lizard hunt with Fredrik in his office, but you go ahead with this. Then I'll need someone to take this gentleman outside and send him on his way."

"I'll do it," Lasse said, chiming in before Earth Reclamation Unit 17 could speak.

Kan gave him a quizzical gaze.

"You are a warrior," he said. "I would not think killing is difficult for you. You should not need a break."

"Actually, I am signed onto this trip as a scientist," Lasse said.

"Very well. You have earned a short trip outside. Just take him to the far edge of the trees and we'll do the rest from in here."

"Yes, sir."

SEVENTEEN

"All done," Hern said.

He leaned over the bald Earth man, who was now unconscious on a white table in Hern's office. He wiped a little blood away from the man's forehead with a cloth tissue and then tossed it into a hole in the wall. There was a whooshing sound and it was instantly destroyed.

"I will go and tell Kan that I am finished."

"There's no need for that," Lasse said. "I've already got my Earth clothes on. I think I should go ahead and take him outside."

"I believe Commander Kan would like a progress report. Please get out of my way. By the way, Lasse, have you had your lizard test yet?"

Lasse smiled.

"You know I haven't."

He was carrying the pistol that Luther Gumpson used to gun down his opponents. The Swedes, in their natural state, did not know the meaning of the term unconscious, because they never were. While wearing human bodies, however, they were subject to experiencing anything humans might experience, including the state of being asleep. Lasse knew that state could be induced by the force of a gun butt being applied to the base of the neck or the side of the head, so he decided to try it. Hern was quick, and Lasse actually had to apply the gun butt to both places before Hern collapsed in a heap.

His blood racing through his body—actually, through both his bodies—Lasse dragged the snoozing Earth human off the table and carried him down the hallway. He peered around the wall into the main control room, ascertaining that no one was there. The others were in Fredrik's office, going through the lengthy process of peeling off their Earth bodies. This was his chance. He made it across the vast room and into the hall headed for the exit tube when a thought occurred to him. Why not take Luther Gumpson as well? Gumpson appeared to be a rather vile specimen of his kind, but all the same Lasse hated to see him operated as a puppet by the likes of Art Kan. It was perhaps within Gumpson's rights to be able to kill his own kind, but it was certainly not right for Art Kan to make him do so.

He let the other human slump to the ground while he walked back to Gumpson's room. He waved his hand near the wall, and the buttons that controlled the red room appeared as if from nowhere. The Swedes did not like to have buttons and controls cluttering up their space vehicles, so they hid them whenever possible. He pushed one of the buttons and the wall slid open, revealing the snoozing Gumpson. A push of another button brought Gumpson's eyes fluttering to life.

"Now what?" Gumpson asked, appearing irritated.

It would take too long to explain things to him, so Lasse decided to give him encouragement to move in a way he could better understand. He waved Gumpson's own pistol under his nose, and then backed away, motioning for the man to follow. Gumpson did as he was told. He probably would have made a better fight of it, but Lasse had overheard Hern saying earlier that prolonged time in the red room made Earth people sleepy.

"What are you doing?" Gumpson asked, but Lasse merely poked him in the back with the pistol and prodded him down the hallway.

"Pick him up," he said when they came to the body of the other man, who was now snoring.

"He's big," Gumpson complained. "I can't carry him."

"Carry him or you'll die," Lasse said, his desperation making his voice sound truly menacing.

"Maybe I can wake him up."

Gumpson knelt at the other man's side and began slapping his face, hard. Lasse worried that he was more likely to knock him even further unconscious than he was to wake him up, but after three ringing slaps the other man moved his head of his own accord and moaned.

"What?" he said.

"Get up, brother," Gumpson said. "There are some strange things going on around here."

The other man blinked but couldn't seem to focus his eyes, but that didn't keep Gumpson from hauling him to his feet. The man was able to stand after all.

"Now *move*," Lasse said. "We don't have much time."

They made it to the lift tube and Lasse waved them into it. It was not really designed to allow three human-sized objects to ride in it, but Lasse had no choice. Gumpson was fast with his hands, Lasse knew, but those hands were currently occupied with helping the other man stand up. Plus, Gumpson seemed pleased to be heading back in the direction of the surface.

"Are you going to make me shoot this man?" Gumpson asked as they rode up.

"Yes," the other man said, his voice now stronger and more clear. "He is. I heard them talking about it."

Lasse kept the gun pointed at the bald-headed man's chest. The projectiles it fired could probably pass through the tissues of both of their bodies, and they seemed aware of that fact.

"I am not," Lasse said. "We are leaving this ship."

"This is a ship?" the bald man asked. "What kind of ship?"

"A ship for flying through space and time," Lasse answered. "Beyond that I cannot explain, because you will not understand."

"If you're with this crowd, why are you breaking us out of here?" Gumpson asked.

"I'm not with this crowd, as you say," Lasse replied. "I was spying on them, but I now have to escape, and I wanted to take you both with me before they do something horrible to you."

"Let me ask you something," the bald man said, looking closely at Lasse's face. "Do you happen to be some kind of lizard, dressed up in the skin of a human being?"

Lasse nearly dropped the gun.

"How do you know that?"

"You mean it's *true*?" Gumpson asked, leaving his mouth gaped open after he finished speaking.

Lasse weighed the pros and cons of answering what he was being asked, and then had what he supposed was a very human thought: what the heck.

"Yes. I am. I am a Nes from the planet that is called Nesi. I am a follower of Mother Naga and an enemy of the *Hrvoi*, who call themselves, in your language, Swedes."

The bald-headed man seemed to slump.

"I'll be damned," he said, seemingly speaking only to himself. "She was right. The crazy lady was right."

"You're an enemy of Harvey?" Gumpson asked.

"Hrvoi. They are here on a mission that will defile Mother Naga for their own purposes. I managed to get on board for the trip along with one of my fellow Nes, but he is now dead."

"What happened to him?

After a long pause, Lasse found the courage to say the words.

"He was discovered. I was forced to kill him."

"This sounds like a complicated story," Gumpson said. "If you're willing to kill one of your own kind, from—from another planet, did you say? Jeez—how do we know you won't kill us?"

"You don't."

There was a crunching noise from above, and a view of the surface appeared. They were nearly to the top, and then the tube stopped moving.

"What happened?" Gumpson shouted.

"They may have noticed we're leaving," Lasse said, and just at that moment the tube started down again. He jammed a finger on the button and it held still. "We have to get out. Now."

The tube was about three feet above the top of the surface, providing just enough room for a man to climb out.

"So who goes first?" Gumpson asked.

The tube shaft bucked and descended six inches.

"They're going to work around the switch," Lasse said. "We have no more time."

"Shoot it," the bald man said.

"What?"

"It works from this switch by wires, doesn't it? Just shoot it."

"*Wires?*" Lasse said. "No, it uses waves."

"Just shoot it anyway!" Gumpson chimed in.

He did, which forced him to turn his back on his captives, which he was sure was not a good idea, but they did nothing to take advantage of it.

"How does this thing work?" Lasse asked after a second, and after the tube descended another inch.

"You don't even know how to shoot it?" Gumpson asked. "Give me that."

Gumpson snatched the gun from Lasse's grasp and fired at the switch, narrowly missing Lasse's finger. There was a deafening explosion and a sudden blinding stench, but the tube stopped moving.

"Now go," Gumpson said to the other man, who scrambled up onto the surface of the Earth with the help of a shove from Gumpson and Lasse.

"You next, lizard man," Gumpson said, and Lasse did not argue.

"Well come on, then," Lasse said once he and the other man were on the surface.

Gumpson was still in the tube, only his face and shoulders visible.

"Naw. I thought I'd wait for them to get their switch fixed, take me a ride down and blow those bastards all to hell," Gumpson said.

Lasse suddenly wished he had kept the pistol.

"I really don't think that will work."

"They keep me in that little booth of theirs, with damn red lights in my eyes, and then they jerk me all over the place and make me shoot people I don't have any reason to shoot," Gumpson said. "That warrants some killing, in my book."

"How many projectiles do you have in your weapon?"

Gumpson looked down and manipulated the pistol.

"Four."

"There are six of them left down there."

"Well, I'll shoot four and beat up the other two."

"Actually, shooting them won't kill them."

"They are from some other planet, too, huh?" Gumpson said.

"Yes. You can't kill them, not that way."

"Well, hell."

He dragged himself through the opening, just as the tube shook itself free and continued down.

"All right, lizard man, what now?"

"We have reached the end of my plan. Now we run."

"I don't understand it," Art Kan said, scowling at the images of Lasse fleeing with the two humans, both of whom were running away with some very sophisticated and expensive Swede equipment. "What does he think he is doing? Does he fear punishment for killing the lizard?"

Earth Reclamation Unit 17 watched them go with a trace of envy. They were out in the wide open sky, and here he was back in the confines of the ship.

"I don't believe that is his motivation, sir," Unit 17 said. "I believe he may be a lizard as well."

It took a moment for Kan to digest this news. He was not given to very flexible thinking.

"That is amazing," he said at last. "He killed his own kind to avoid detection, and I let him get away with it. Amazing."

"They are quite dedicated," Unit 17 said.

"Indeed. If they were not so wretched, you could almost admire them, from a military standpoint."

The three fugitives had disappeared from the view of the lift's camera.

"Hern, did you get all the equipment installed in our former captives?"

"Yes, sir."

"Is it working?"

"Obviously we didn't get to test it, but I believe so, sir."

"Fine. What is its longest range?"

"About two miles, depending on topographical conditions."

"They haven't been gone long, so that should be enough. Set the equipment so that Luther Gumpson feels the overwhelming urge to kill the nearest human to him, say, every ten Earth seconds."

Hern frowned.

"I believe the quickest we can get it to do automatic reset is every thirty seconds."

"Do that, then. And program the memory revoker to operate every thirty seconds as well. So Luther Gumpson will have the irresistible urge to shoot someone twice a minute, and the other man will forget everything he's been doing at the same time, assuming he lives that long. That should slow our fugitive band down. Earth Reclamation Unit 17?"

"Yes, sir?"

"Are you up to another visit to the surface?"

"I believe so."

"Good. Go and find them. It shouldn't be hard. I can't imagine they've made it very far."

It was now well into the morning, and the man who introduced himself as Barnum Brown realized that they could not take the easy way to his camp.

"There are probably hundreds of men out here, all looking to shoot Luther Gumpson. We need to go back around behind that ship, as you called it, and skirt behind the rocks. Otherwise they'll just blow him away as soon as they see him."

Gumpson was surprised by the news that he had been so popular.

"There are people out here looking for me? How did they know I was out here?"

"I don't know, but they do," Brown said. "There's a bounty on your head, and an awful lot of people out here looking to collect on it."

"So that's what was going on," Gumpson said. "You know, they've had me outside that ship twice, and I think I shot some people. It all seemed like a dream."

"It was no dream," Lasse said. "They are impressed with your shooting ability. They wanted to use it to their own ends."

They were hiding behind a smallish ridge of rocks, looking across an open patch of land to a clump of trees that looked like they would provide more shelter. From there it was an easy climb to the edge where the sandstone cliffs began, and it would be easy for three men to hide in there and pick their way around to Brown's excavation. They had not planned things out beyond that; simple survival was the number one priority at the moment.

"I still don't know why we're going to where your men are digging," Gumpson said. "If these alien blonde people know who you are, they know where you'll go."

"That's true," Brown said. "But they'll find me with a dozen men to help me."

"And they may not come, anyway," Lasse said. "Part of their mission is to be unobtrusive. They try not to go around in daytime."

"I still don't think it's a good idea," Gumpson said. "I would like to get out of here and head for California, but I'll stick with you in the meantime."

"Good idea," Lasse said. "It looks clear now."

As time went on, the men in the wagons were apparently getting lazier and lazier about patrolling the territory, which was good for any actual fugitives trying to get across it. Lasse started to step from behind his tree into the open space when Luther Gumpson pointed his pistol at his back and pulled the trigger. The hammer clicked on an empty chamber.

"Damn it!" Gumpson said.

Lasse whirled and tackled him, and Barnum Brown dove for the pistol.

"What are you doing?" Lasse asked through clenched teeth.

Gumpson looked at him curiously, and didn't put up much of a fight.

"I don't know, I swear," he said. "I felt this strange urge come over me. I felt I had to kill you. Good thing for you I only have four bullets."

"You're about to have no bullets," Lasse said.

He remembered hearing something about equipment being planted in this man's brain; it apparently enabled the Swedes to take control of his body. They never stopped. Their willingness to invade the sanctity of any body they came across never ceased to disgust him.

"How do you feel now?" Lasse asked.

"Normal. I don't feel the urge to kill you."

Lasse cautiously let Gumpson up.

"I think, just to be safe, I will hang on to the gun."

Gumpson, looking confused, nodded in agreement.

Lasse looked at Barnum Brown, and he looked even more confused than Gumpson.

"Who the hell are you people?" Brown asked.

His companions stared back at him.

"How did I get here?" he asked. "Oh, by the way, mister, you dropped this gun."

Brown handed Gumpson the pistol. Lasse stepped in to stop him, but Gumpson whirled and shot him in the stomach.

"Hey!" Barnum shouted. "What are you doing?"

Lasse clutched the wound. It had penetrated his earthly body, but had not gone through his Nes skin underneath. He would be fine, but his Earthly disguise, which consisted of actual living tissue, would probably now die and eventually rot away. Soon his disguise would be useless, but he didn't have time to worry about that now. He backhanded Gumpson across the face, knocking him flat on his back.

"I can't help it!" Gumpson shouted. "I don't mean to shoot you!"

Lasse flung himself on Gumpson, pinning his hands together. Gumpson did indeed have very good motor control—despite the fierce pressure applied by Lasse's fingers, he did not let go of the gun. Lasse reached into the inner pocket of his jacket, part of the costume he was required to wear when going outside in daylight. He was wearing his Multi-Purpose Tool, but it was on his belt under his clothes, and he would likely be dead before he could reach it.

But he had something else. For this trip, he had brought along some rope, which he had thought could come in handy if they had to climb any rocks. Now he could see another, even more practical use, that of keeping Luther Gumpson from killing him. He started looping it over Gumpson's wrists when suddenly Brown kicked him, rolling him over onto the ground.

"What is this, some kind of robbery?"

Brown extended a hand to Gumpson, to help him up. Gumpson responded by whipping the pistol up to aim at him. With a speed he wasn't sure he possessed, Lasse managed to whip out the Multi-Purpose Tool and freeze both men where they stood in its green cloud. Once that was done, he lay back on the ground and took a breath. His outer body ached where the bullet still lodged in it, and the ribs on his left side throbbed from Barnum Brown's kick. He toted up the damage so far: Bjorn was dead, by Lasse's own hand; Art Kan knew they had been aboard; Art Kan's ship was his only way home; his human body was wounded and probably dying; Luther Gumpson's gunshot was probably even now drawing a bloodthirsty crowd to this very point.

The only bright spot he could see was that he had managed to beat Luther Gumpson to the draw.

EIGHTEEN

"Hey, Barnum. You don't look so good. You feeling all right?"

Brown looked up to see a middle-aged man who was looking more like an old man, but who wore a clean shirt and a nice smile.

"Digger Phelps," he said, standing to shake hands with his visitor. "It's been quite a while."

"It sure has, Mr. Brown."

"Barnum, please. Take a load off, there, Digger. Not much to look at but these rocks make pretty good chairs. Like some coffee? It's late in the day for it, I know, but coffee's pretty good anytime."

"I would, actually."

They were in camp, which was situated at the base of the cliff, against the rocks which cut the wind. This meant they had the best fire of anyone in the area, which also meant they had the hottest coffee. Brown poured a tin cup full for Phelps, who accepted it gratefully and blew gently across it.

"Digger, if you want to put something in that coffee, you go right ahead," Brown said. "You used to like that, as I recall."

Phelps gave him a long look, and then finally shook his head.

"To be honest, Mr. Brown, I want to, but I've been traveling here with a man who doesn't care for it, so I

121

finally cut down a lot just to keep him from complaining. Fact of the matter is, I feel better than I have in days. I have me a little snort to help me get to bed, but that's it."

Brown nodded along with him.

"That's good to hear, Digger. You were getting quite enthusiastic about drink a while back with us, and I've heard that didn't stop after we left."

"I won't lie to you, Mr. Brown, I was. But I feel better now, like I said. I've delivered the man here and now I don't have much to do, and was wondering whether you might take me on again. I could handle the horses and transport the bones, or dig fer 'em, whatever you need done."

Brown looked up the hill to where his men were spread out along the ridge, digging more of S.L. Burgess's find and looking for something to rival it.

"You can see I have a pretty good team up there, Digger."

"Yeah, I can see that, but I heard you're not feeling too well right now, and so maybe you could use some help."

Brown nodded and ran his fingers along his left temple, as if trying to loosen a lump there.

"What happened to you, anyway, if I may ask? I don't remember you being sickly at all."

"I'm not sick," Brown responded, maybe a tad too quickly. "It's hard to explain. I went for a walk the other night, which was a dumb thing to do because it was really dark, but I didn't feel like sleeping so I thought it would be okay. I'm not clear on what happened next. I must have fallen down and hit my head. I had these very strange hallucinations, like I was inside this strange room that was all red, but nothing seemed to make sense. I dreamed I saw a man who turned into a lizard, and then suddenly I was outside again, and I remember these two men fighting, but I don't know who they were, and then the next thing I know I was back at camp. A man who was passing through had found me wandering around."

"That's quite a bump you took," Phelps said with a laugh.

"I know. I still don't feel right. I feel like there's some kind of cloud in my head."

Phelps stared at his head, and Brown swiveled it on his neck to give his visitor a good look.

"The funny thing is, I don't see a bump anywhere on you," Phelps said. "You ought to have a bruise, anyways."

"Especially since I don't have any hair to hide it," Brown said, chuckling to show Phelps he meant it as a joke.

"It's very strange," Phelps said, and resumed sipping his coffee.

They sat there in silence for a long time, listening to the sound of the picks above and the breathing of the horses to their left.

"Say, Digger, do I recall you mentioning that you were out here in the field with O.C. Marsh back in 1876?"

Phelps squinted and rolled his left eye around, as if he had the answer written on the top of his skull and was trying to read it.

"Yes, sir, I was."

"That was the same time Mr. Cope was out here, if I'm not mistaken."

"Yes, sir. Couldn't forget that. Like getting between two coyotes fighting over a piece of meat."

Brown took a long sip of his own coffee. He was not sure how to broach this.

"Digger, you don't happen to recall running afoul of any creatures from outer space, one of whom happened to be a lizard disguised as a human being, do you?"

He sipped his coffee again, leaving Phelps to stare at him.

"You would remember something like that, wouldn't you, Digger?" he asked, after Phelps failed to respond.

"Yes, sir," Phelps finally said.

"You mean, yes, sir, I saw a lizard man from outer space?"

Phelps shook his head, as if to get his speech gears moving again.

"I mean, yes, sir, I would remember something like that," Phelps said. "And I most assuredly did not see anything of that sort."

"Do you remember a young man in the party named Al Stillson?"

"Vaguely," Phelps said. He still looked a little stunned, which Brown could well understand. "He was a little fellow if I recall correctly."

"How well did you know him?"

Phelps rubbed his chin. He seemed to require physical sensations to start his memory.

"Not very well. He was around. If I recall correctly, Mr. Marsh used him to spy on Mr. Cope."

"Did he seem a trustworthy sort?"

"Not particularly, but everybody seemed to like him. I believe he took to spying for both men."

"You knew he was really a girl, didn't you?"

Phelps seemed genuinely surprised.

"Yes, he was," Brown continued. "In fact, she has a son up there working on my team right now."

He thumbed in the direction of the crew, and could just make out S.L. Burgess's back.

"That is amazing," Phelps said. "I had no idea."

"Well, it's true. Tell me, Digger, do you ever have memories—or maybe memories is not the word . . . dreams—do you ever have dreams of being trapped in a small room, and you can't move, and there is nothing but red lights in your face?"

Phelps fell silent again for a long time. He didn't roll his eyes around or manipulate his chin, but he finally shook his head.

"No, Barnum, I don't. May I ask, why do you ask?"

"Well, Al Stillson—whose real name was Alice Stillson—wrote up a long story about her time out here with Cope and Marsh. One of those Wild West magazines published it. I've been reading it today since I'm not working. She has all kinds of wild things in there, and one of the things she says is that you got caught up in some kind of red room in a ship that had come from outer space."

Phelp's eyes opened wide.

"She wrote *that*?" he said.

"Yes, she did."

He downed his coffee in one gulp, even though it was apparently so hot it brought tears to his eyes.

"I can't believe she wrote that! Did she use my name and all?"

"Either that, or she has some fictional character named Digger Phelps. I guess he was fictional if you don't remember that."

"I can't believe she wrote that. I didn't get paid for it or nothing."

They sat in silence again. The sun was making its way down, turning Phelps' face into a mask, filling in the eye sockets with luxurious shadows, adding a golden glow to his cheeks. Brown thought it was a little sad that it made Digger look better.

"So you don't remember anything like that," Brown said at last.

"I swear I don't. You've been reading that all day, you say?"

"Yes. The men didn't want me to work after my fall and I didn't have much else in the way of entertainment around here. Some fellows stopped by a little while ago to chat and ask what we were doing, but aside from that you're the first company I've had, so I had plenty of time to read."

"Was it a good story, overall?"

"Not to my usual taste, but not bad."

"Well, if I may say so, Mr. Brown, it seems like maybe reading that story is what caused your dreams. You knocked your head last night and you read that story today, and you must have dozed off a time or two and got them all mixed up."

Brown nodded his head slowly.

"I suppose so, Digger. I just wanted to check with you and make sure it wasn't real."

Brown watched as Phelps finished off his coffee with a noisy glug. His gray hair, paunch and impressive collection of wrinkles showed that he was now an old Digger, but all the same his hands weren't shaking and he looked a little more stable than the Digger of old.

"So," Phelps said after a bit. "Were you able to think a little bit more about my offer? I'd be a good worker, and it looks like you could use an extra hand."

He couldn't, really. The stranger who had found him wandering around had proven quite knowledgeable about fossils, and displayed no eagerness to be on his way, wherever that might be. He had offered to help work today, to fill in for Brown, and had put in a good day of it, by the accounts Brown gleaned when workers came down for occasional breaks. He did have a considerable appetite, taking enough for lunch for two men, eating by himself out of sight somewhere on the cliffside. That was, in fact, the only time the stranger wasn't in the thick of things. He seemed to crave company, and treated Brown's crew as if they were a gang of his oldest friends, with whom he had been reunited by fortunate fate.

"It's not going to be easy work, Digger. I'll need men I can trust, men I can depend on. I can't use men who might work a little here and a little there and then quit when the going gets tough."

Phelps sat up straight and looked Brown straight in the eye.

"I won't be like that, Barnum. I'll work harder than you remember me working a while back, and I'll even work harder than I used to for Mr. Marsh."

He looked like he meant it, too, and it would be a

task to get those bones down from the cliff, if the find turned out to be as good as Brown hoped.

"I swear I'll work even harder than I did for Mr. Marsh. You're a better scientist than he ever was, anyway."

Brown laughed.

"Now, Digger. No need for flattery. I like to think I can sense when a man is being sincere, and I think you are. If you promise to work hard, I'd be honored to add you to the crew."

Phelps rocked back and forth on his haunches, smiling so broadly his cheeks nearly touched his eyebrows. He hopped up and Brown steeled himself for a bear hug, but Phelps pointed off toward the road.

"I'll bring my wagon over here," he said, and started off, showing more speed than Brown would have thought possible. In an instant, he was back. "Say, Mr. Brown. The fellow I brought over here is a preacher, and he was surprised to find that Jordan's not much of a town. He's been sort of sleeping in my wagon. Do you suppose—"

"He can stay in your wagon, here in the camp," Brown said. If he couldn't be up on the hillside digging for Tyrannosaurus rex, he could at least sprawl here and dispense favors. "Maybe he'll keep some of the men out of trouble."

NINETEEN

Lasse had scarcely believed his eyes when he saw what the men had dug partway out of the rocks. Its hind claws, the curve of its spine, the gape of its mouth, had all proclaimed the truth: It was a creature whose sacred name was unpronounceable in this coughing, spitting language; it was a sacred guardian of Mother Naga, a sign that this small planet was indeed the origin of his very species.

"What are you talking about?" said Luther Gumpson, who was tied to a boulder high up on the north side of the cliff face, his legs immobilized thanks to the green emissions of the Multi-Purpose Tool.

"One of our people came here three of your Earth decades ago. He was trying to dig up some of the fossilized bones of what you call dinosaurs, but he had some competition. A Swede scientist was also here. They had a battle before they left the planet. Our person's ship was damaged, and it crashed when he finally made it home. His records indicated that this planet is our place of origin, but we weren't sure. Now I think he was right."

Lasse did not like telling Gumpson all of this, but he found it helpful. The followers of Mother Naga did not like to be alone. He could not imagine how one of his kind had come here by himself; it must have been torture. Just as he had this thought, Lasse realized that he was

128

in exactly the same shape. Not only was he here alone, but he had personally killed his companion. He had done it according to plan, had done it through training, almost without thinking, and it had surely saved his life thus far. He still could not shake the guilt and the shame, and he had to pause to collect himself while an angry Gumpson asked for more information.

"If you came from here, why didn't you stay here? Why did you leave?"

Lasse had brought Gumpson his dinner, only the second time in the day he had visited him. Gumpson had demanded to be untied the way Brown had been, but Lasse explained that he wasn't sure of the range of the devices that had been implanted in his body. Brown only forgot things, he pointed out; the devices Gumpson had inherited made him a little more dangerous. Enraptured by the sight of the guardian of Mother Naga appearing from the hillside, Lasse had set to work with Brown's men. Brown had rested below, which meant Lasse had been unable to determine if his memory was still being manipulated by Art Kan, which in turn meant he was extremely reluctant to untie Luther Gumpson.

"What did you say?" Lasse asked, having heard Gumpson speak, but not the actual words.

"I said, if you came from here, why didn't you stay here? Your people, I mean. Why did they leave?"

Lasse took a deep breath, and then let it out.

"The sea dried up. There was once a great sea here, you know, on this very spot. Our forebears depended on it for survival. When it began to dry up, they were forced to leave."

Gumpson chewed on that idea for a while as he chewed on his dinner, which was chicken and potatoes.

"I don't know much about dinosaurs," he said after having noisily masticated a big bite. "But I was under the impression they weren't all that bright. You mean they built a *spaceship* and took off from here? We just now got airplanes and automobiles, and your folks could build spaceships way back then? If they could do that, why not just fly to another ocean? Why go all the way to where you're from?"

He knew it would come to this, and he knew the human would not understand. Their own beliefs spoke of what they called miracles, which they accepted without question, but when it came to someone else's miracles they were suddenly skeptics.

"They did not take a spaceship. They were not as developed then as we are now. They were closer to nature, closer to the true form of Mother Naga."

"And who would that be?"

Gumpson was grumpy, for which Lasse could not blame him. He had been tied up all day, not to mention being immobilized by the Multi-Purpose Tool. Now he would have to remain that way all night, until Lasse could speak with the man named Barnum Brown, to see if he, too, was still being affected. Only then would he release Gumpson. This was clearly not pleasing to his captive, but on the other hand he got the impression that Gumpson would have done the very same if the situation was reversed, and that to some extent Gumpson even respected him more for doing it.

"It is easier for me to show you Mother Naga than to tell you."

He stood up and advanced to Gumpson, who had now finished his chicken. He reached out his hands toward Gumpson's head. Gumpson steeled himself, as if he was about to be struck by a snake. His fingers twitched, and Lasse realized what he was about to do—put his arms within grabbing range of the fastest gun in the west.

"Excuse me," he said, and withdrew the Multi-Purpose Tool.

"Oh, come on," Gumpson said, but Lasse ignored him and deftly immobilized his hands with a narrow beam.

He then put the tool back in his pocket and reached out his hands.

It always amazed him that the gift of putting pictures in the mind could work even through the disguise of a fleshly body, but it did.

"Here is Mother Naga," he said, resting his palms on Gumpson's temples. Gumpson closed his eyes.

It was a feeling of immensity, like being a flea staring at a mountain. Not a mountain, but a mountain range, a ridge of rising peaks. Not a mountain range, not a ridge, but a spine. A spine of a beast so immense it could coil around the sun, rest its head on the Earth and lick the moon. He saw only the rear of its massive head. He thought he caught the bursts of fire which were the eyes, and was glad he could not see all their fierce brilliance. He saw the head move, heard unearthly sound that came from the abyss that must be the mouth, and shuddered. The sky then started to go dark. It was an eclipse, so rapid it was like the blink of an eye. The vast creature was moving what could only be wings, wings so tall they reached to infinity.

"Stop it," Gumpson said, softly at first, and then louder: "Stop it!"

Lasse removed his hands and stopped his thoughts, for fear that Gumpson's cries would attract attention. Gumpson slumped in relief as Lasse's hands moved away, and then he noticed that he had released a stream of urine during the vision.

"Aw, now look what you made me do!" he said, his face twisted in disgust, his lingering fascination from the vision fading instantly. His legs were immobilized, and the puddle was soaking into his trousers. "Turn off this damn green soup of yours and let me move my leg!"

"Mother Naga is impressive, is she not?" Lasse asked as he reached for the Multi-Purpose Tool.

"Yes, yes, yes," Gumpson said. "Now come on and help me!"

Lasse released his legs long enough for him to shuffle a few feet to the side, to a drier spot under the rock overhang that hid him from view.

"This is going to stink all night," Gumpson complained.

"I could let you go and you could get yourself shot," Lasse said, and Gumpson snorted.

"Hah," he said. "You could let me go and I could get away from these morons and get to California."

Lasse ignored him.

"I have not told you the rest of my story. My forebears did not need a spaceship. They were carried to their new home—my home—by the mighty wings of Mother Naga."

Gumpson was scowling at his stained trouser leg and did not appear to be paying attention.

"I said, Mother Naga carried them with her mighty wings."

"Yes, fine," Gumpson said.

"Do you doubt that she could do such a thing?"

Gumpson gave up his leg inspection with a sigh and seemed to resign himself to Lasse's questions. Lasse was always fascinated by the response to Mother Naga from those who had never contemplated her before.

"Do you?"

"No," Gumpson said. "She looked pretty damn big. So where is she? Is she living on your planet somewhere, stomping around? Why don't you get her to come eat that spaceship that all those blonde-haired people are in if they're giving you such trouble?"

"Mother Naga does not manifest herself that way. Although sometimes I wish she did."

"So that wasn't a picture of her?"

"No. Not a literal image. That is how we are taught to imagine her."

Gumpson stared at him.

"What if you're wrong? What if she doesn't look like that at all? You could just make up anything and no one would know if you were right or not."

Lasse scowled at him.

"It is a true image," he said, harshly enough that Gumpson didn't continue to argue the point.

They sat in silence for a moment. Lasse thought Gumpson's attention had shifted back to his wet leg, but he suddenly said, "Tell me something. If your ancestors or whatever were taken away from here a long time ago, why did you come back? Why stow away on that ship?"

"It's a little hard to explain," Lasse said.

"I can't imagine that."

"Before she left us, Mother Naga dictated a holy book. In the book, it says that when all her bones are gathered together again, she will return."

"So?"

"So our people have gathered our bones together since before we can remember. When one of us dies, we preserve the bones."

"That must be a lot of bones," Gumpson said, but Lasse ignored him.

"We decided that Naga's command included the bones of those who went before, so we have tried to regain them. We are very poor. It is hard for us to come here. The mission undertaken three decades ago was a failure, and we could not afford to mount another. When we learned the Swedes were coming back, we decided to sneak aboard. It was very hard. I have been away from my family for many years to accomplish it. I do not wish to fail this time."

He felt his human eyes misting up at the thought of all he had undergone. He had to wear his monkey skin, and get into training with faked documents. He had to leave his people and live among the Swedes, aware that at any moment his disguise could be penetrated. Only his faith in Mother Naga and the presence of Bjorn had pulled him through, and now he had lost Bjorn. Correction: He had killed Bjorn.

"Your answer sort of makes sense," Gumpson said. "But why do these blonde types want your bones? What do they care?"

"They were here at the same time my forebears were," Lasse said. "They claim that it was they who created us, but it is a vicious lie. They want the bones because they fear we will succeed, and Mother Naga will destroy them."

Gumpson nodded. Having seem the face of Mother Naga, certainly he could understand their fear.

"Your buddy died in that ship, right?" Gumpson said. "I didn't see it, but that's what you said."

"Yes."

"So you need his bones, too, don't you?"

Lasse drew in a long breath. That was not something he was looking forward to, but there was no way around it. Mother Naga's book said so.

"Yes. I was hoping you could help me with that."

"What, you mean go back in there?"

He did not look overly excited at the idea, and Lasse wasn't so happy about it, either.

"I am not sure yet. That may not be necessary," Lasse said, and Gumpson relaxed.

"I should go to the camp now," Lasse said. "Soon it will be completely dark. You have the heating unit I left for you?"

"Yes."

"Good."

"I would be happier if you would leave my gun with me," Gumpson said. "What if some animal gets up here tonight?"

"Your urine-soaked leg will deter them."

"Very funny."

"Don't worry. If all is well, I will release you tomorrow. If you will help me."

Gumpson said nothing. Lasse turned to head out of the small cave, picking up Gumpson's tin plate on his way out. Then an idea came to mind.

"There is something else. I think I will need you to help me steal something."

Gumpson smiled.

"Theft? I'm your man."

TWENTY

For several minutes, Digger Phelps thought that perhaps the preacher Parnassus had run off with his wagon, which would not really have surprised him too much. He had met numerous preachers roaming the west, and many of them appeared to be quite well acquainted with the sins they were always raving against.

He was already irritated. Phelps was glad to get another job so soon, but he was annoyed that Barnum Brown had grilled him about his drinking. Brown must have believed that he was already well in the bottle when he had come to visit. Why else would he ask him about all that crazy stuff, about a lizard man and the red room? He just wanted to hear Phelps admit to believing them, so he could lower the boom on him and fire him before he ever hired him.

Those strange things had happened, but that was so long ago he could almost imagine he had invented them in his mind. Certainly Marsh and Cope had never made so much as a peep about them, and if they hadn't seen fit to, he certainly wasn't going to, either. Brown had tipped his hand when he mentioned that little Al Stillson had written the whole thing up for anyone to see. Al Stillson, a woman; he couldn't imagine it. Brown had just read whatever she wrote and decided he would stick Digger with it, but he wouldn't let him, no sir. He had his promise of a job and he was going to stick with his story.

He was just about to give up on the search for the wagon when he spotted it, tucked between two other wagons that appeared to have seen much better days. There were so many wagons out here these days you would almost think the government was giving away land again.

Phelps had bought his wagon years ago, when he actually had some money, and it was both his pride and joy and his smartest investment. It was, more accurately, the only thing he had that was worth anything at all. Othniel stood at the front of the wagon, still tethered to it. Parnassus was so intent on saving souls that he couldn't even be bothered to untie the horse properly, but fortunately for him and for Phelps, Othniel was so lazy he wouldn't wander off even if there was a string of carrots before him, leading to the horizon.

Othniel was his other great investment, although he was so old he probably had one hoof in the grave. He had done well to get Phelps and Parnassus out here, but the effort had clearly exhausted him. Phelps had named his horse after the great paleontologist Othniel Charles Marsh, his former boss. He didn't really intend to make fun, although it was certainly an odd name. Seen from certain angles, the horse actually resembled the great scientist. He was pale and had patchy hair and a poochy belly. He was also always fluttering his eyelids, as though squinting at his surroundings. Marsh used to do that, too; he was nearsighted but hated to wear his spectacles. He should probably keep the horse's name a secret from Barnum Brown. Brown might see the name as poking fun at one of Phelp's former bosses, and might surmise that a future equine purchase might someday bear his name. Phelps decided that he would simply refer to the horse as "O" whenever Brown was around.

"Hey boy," he said as he approached the wagon. "How are you? That rotten preacher has kept you tied up, hasn't he?"

Othniel lifted his white head and fluttered his eyelids at the sound of the familiar voice.

"I'll be damned, if it isn't Digger Phelps," said a voice, and for a second Phelps thought Othniel had somehow gained the power of speech.

Then he turned to one of the wagons near his. It was a flea-trap affair, unlike his own well-maintained rig. Its canvas top was tattered, the metal bands on its wheels appeared ready to pop right off, and the wood of its body was so frayed that it appeared almost fuzzy. Paint was no doubt only a distant memory for it.

"You are Digger Phelps, aren't you?" said the voice again.

A face appeared from within the darkness of the wagon. It was a familiar face, but at first he couldn't place it.

"Are you pretending you don't know me because you owe me money, or something?"

Then the face came into focus in his memory. The red hair had long since turned silver, and the round face had started to droop somewhat, but the speaker was clearly Sam Sharp.

"I'll be damned," Phelps said, Sharp's phrase seeming an apt enough one to use back at him.

Sharp had been part of Othniel Marsh's team, too, thirty years back, and if the intervening years had treated Phelps badly, they had treated Sharp worse. His skin was puffier, his eyes duller, his teeth, what few had managed to remain in his jaw, were dirtier. When he got to feeling sorry for himself, Phelps liked to say to anyone who would listen that life had beaten him up. If that was true, then he had gotten off easy. Life may have roughed him up, but it had damn near killed Sam Sharp.

Sharp managed to scramble his way to the front of the wagon, and he extended a shaggy paw for Phelps to shake. The hand was big and soft as a pillow. His welcoming smile carried with it the powerful fumes of what smelled like pretty bad whiskey, which only made Phelps regret his sudden abstention.

"Digger, what brings you out here? Like I need to ask."

He brought around a small jug with a big crack in it and took a sip of brown liquid that probably had some passing relation to whiskey. He offered it to Phelps, but Phelps shook his head and Sharp didn't press the point. More for him.

"Oh, this and that," Phelps responded. "How the hell have you been, Sam?"

"I been better," Sharp said. "I would say I've been worse, too, but I'm not so sure that's true."

"Times are tough," Phelps said, and Sharp nodded his silvery head. "Not like it used to be out here."

"Used to be, you could get out here and make a dollar some way," Sharp said. "Now there's too many fellows ahead of you, and too many fellows coming up behind you."

Phelps started to tell Sharp about Barnum Brown, since Sharp was an old bone digger himself. He had worked on the crews of both Marsh and Edward Drinker Cope, something few people could claim. Then he thought better of it. His own job was tenuous enough, but it would be endangered indeed if Sharp decided he wanted to try to come along, too. He wasn't so sure that Sharp would try; the lure of possible money associated with shooting this outlaw would be a bigger attraction than the sure, but smaller, amounts that Brown would pay. Brown would require hard work for his meager paychecks, whereas the hunt for the man named Luther Gumpson seemed to require nothing more arduous than sitting around all day and drinking half the night. Then again, Sharp had enough knowledge about dinosaurs that he might want to try, and Phelps didn't feel right about saddling Brown with two sodden old drunks rather than just one.

"Say, Digger," Sharp said. "I hate to ask, but I wonder if you might be able to make me a little loan for a week or two. I know I haven't seen you in a good while, but it seemed to me like we used to be pretty good friends. I do not recall really seeing any worse days than these. That's why I'm out here with all these other fools trying to put a bullet through that bank robber. I sure could use it, Digger."

Phelps suddenly felt bad that he had not shared his good fortune.

"Sam, I hate to tell you, but I really don't have it. I brung a man out here with me but he hasn't paid me yet, and I'm not sure when he's going to. I'll tell you one thing, though. Barnum Brown is out here. He's said he'll take me on, and maybe he'll take you on."

"Barnum Brown?" Sharp asked. "Is he running some kind of circus?"

"No. He's a paleontologist, Sam, just like old Cope and Marsh, only he's not as crazy as them. He's digging up some more bones. I've signed on to help him. It could be like old times, Sam."

Sharp leaned back, as if Phelps had just drawn a knife on him.

"What are you talking about? For God's sake, Digger, have you forgotten what happened out here with those damn fool bone diggers?"

"Well, no, but . . ."

"There were weird creatures out here, Digger! Don't you remember those little men and that tall man with the blonde hair and the ghost wall that we couldn't see but we couldn't get through? Don't you remember any of that?"

He had pushed himself back from the front of the wagon until he was very nearly inside it, with only his head sticking out, showing his wild eyes, open wide.

"You couldn't pay me enough to do that again," Sharp said. "Only reason I came back here at all is I need the money and was passing nearby and thought I might get lucky. But dig bones? Damn it, Digger, have you lost your mind?"

Phelps did not care to have his sanity questioned. He

had wrestled with the events of three decades before, and decided the answers were beyond him.

"Sam, I've been digging with the Sternbergs some, up in Canada, and we haven't seen anything like what you and I saw back here. Nothing. Nothing weird at all."

"But have you been back here doing your digging?"

"No, but we aren't where we were back then. Not exactly."

"Close enough, though. Close enough. Too close, if you ask me. You might as well not sleep at night, Digger, because he's going to be after you."

Phelps snorted. Talking to Sharp was like talking to a badger, the way he stuck his head out from his wagon cover. Now he was glad Sharp had turned down the possibility of working with Brown.

"Who is going to be after me, Sam?"

"That blonde-haired man, that's who."

Sharp's eyes seemed to grow even bigger, if that were possible. He was looking off over Phelp's shoulder, and suddenly he pulled his face inside the wagon so Phelps could see nothing of him at all.

"What are you doing?" Phelps said.

"Look behind you, Digger. I told you."

Phelps turned and squinted in the direction Sharp's eyes had been looking. He saw two men walking in the road, taking their time, glancing from wagon to wagon. They did not particularly appear out of place, except one was tall and had blonde hair. The other man was shorter, but there was something strangely familiar about him.

"Look! Digger! I told you!" Sharp's frantic voice rasped from inside the wagon. "He's come back for you!"

"Oh, he has not," Phelps said, and it was true. "That's not the man who was here before. That's some other man."

"It's another one of them! Look at him. Tall. Blonde. Long hair. What more do I have to say?"

Phelps wanted to retort that there were any number

of tall blonde men walking around in Montana, but he wasn't sure it was true, and anyway the man did sort of give him the creeps. He did look a great deal like the man who had called himself Alf Swenson from Sweden, and who had turned out to be from somewhere much, much further away. Still, he couldn't be sure, and he didn't want to give up all sense of dignity and hide the way Sharp had. Phelps heard the slosh as Sharp took in a good mouthful of liquid courage. He didn't seem to have enough in the bottle to get him to stick his head back out.

"He's after you, Digger."

"He's not even looking at me."

Phelps leaned on the wagon, nonchalantly, as though it was his. The men made their way up the road, nodding at the grizzled men who watched them pass. When they came alongside him, Phelps nodded pleasantly. The blonde-haired man gave him a slight smile and then looked past him, but the shorter man looked him up and down, as if struggling to place him. Phelps was struggling to place him, too. There was something oddly familiar about him. Phelps had a good memory—he had pulled Sam Sharp's name from the depths of his mind after thirty years—but this man he couldn't quite place. He heard a sharp intake of breath from the wagon.

"Digger!"

"What?"

He whispered, afraid that the men would turn and look at him.

"Digger—that was you!"

Sharp must have been dipping into the bottle more than he thought.

"What do you mean, that's me?"

Sharp stuck his head back out through the wagon cover, but he wrapped the cloth around his neck so that he resembled a demented old lady trying to ward off nonexistent cold.

"Didn't you see him? That was you!"

"I was right here, Sam. You were talking to me."

"No, Digger." Sharp's face was grave. "You don't realize it. That man—that's what you used to look like, thirty years back. That man was you."

"I didn't look like that," Phelps said, but even as he spoke the words he realized they weren't true. He was about the same height as the man, and thirty years ago he had as much hair as the man.

"I don't know how it happened," Sharp continued. "Did that blonde-haired man do something strange to you, Digger? Did he make some kind of copy of you?"

The thought nearly made his knees buckle. He thought back to the very thing Barnum Brown had been asking him about. Swenson had put him in some kind of hole in the wall, where he couldn't move and where a red light seemed to invade his whole body. It didn't hurt, not exactly, and after he got out he felt fine, so eventually he thought little of it.

"Stay here," he said to Sharp, and set off down the road after the men.

"I intend to," Sharp replied.

Phelps saw the men down the road, just heading around a bend that skirted the lower part of the rock formations. Phelps was relieved; that part of the road led across some relatively featureless flatlands, disturbed only by occasional rock outcroppings or copses of scrubby trees. They were making surprisingly good time, but at least he couldn't lose them there. Or so he thought. When he rounded the corner, they were nowhere to be seen. Two sets of footprints led off across the packed dirt to a nearby stand of trees, and Phelps followed them as best he could, but tracking was not his best talent and before long the tracks just seemed to vanish, as if a great bird had flown over and snatched the men up into the air.

TWENTY-ONE

"So how does it look, Earth Reclamation Unit 17?"

Art Kan had been focused on acquiring the bones in the immediate area of the ship, and had not been stomping around very much. Consequently, his forehead was sporting no fresh scars or bruises. It actually made him look a little bit younger, Eric, as he would have preferred to be called, thought, although age really meant very little to the Swedes—at least when they were in their true forms.

"They have done a fair amount of work on it. Many of the bones have been revealed."

Eric was making his report along with Mikael, who had quickly passed his impromptu physical and had been outfitted with Earth clothing and ordered topside.

"They aren't nearly done, are they?"

"No. Their methods are very crude. They are literally picking at the rocks around the bones. At some point they will blow up part of the rocks, bringing the bones down with them. They will then cart them to a nearby railroad and send them to New York City, where they were be completely chipped from the rocks, cleaned and mounted in a semblance of the way they would have been arranged in life."

Kan nodded thoughtfully.

"Appalling. How very crude. You say only the bones are displayed? There are no attempts to try to replicate the way the dinosaurs lived in life?"

"They do not have that sort of technology. They are not even close."

"So they just line up the bones and look at them?"

"That would appear to be the case."

They stood in the command room, the central atrium of the ship. An exploring vessel would devote this room to cataloguing the bones that were being found, but this was not an exploring vessel and Kan was not interested in such scientific frippery, so the room contained very little of anything. This was not a scientific mission, Kan kept reminding them. Get the bones, and get out. The current site had been played out, according to the sketchy maps that Swenson had made of the area when he flew over at the start of his mission three Earth decades before. It was time to move on to some significant bones nearby, but there was one problem: the man who had introduced himself as Barnum Brown had found them first.

"Tell me, Unit 17, how do you know all this?" Kan asked. "This is not the sort of information you can pick up with a camera from a distance."

"No. We saw the leader, whose name is Barnum Brown. We spoke to him."

Kan's eyes widened slightly, and his forehead dissolved into the usual sea of concerned wrinkles.

"You were taking a chance, weren't you? What if he had recognized you?"

"Sir," Mikael said, "we decided to risk it. If he did remember his time here, we thought perhaps he would be frightened enough to leave the area. As it was, Hern's devices apparently functioned properly. The man did not seem alarmed at all to see us, so we spoke to him. We alleged an interest in his field, and he was quite happy to talk about what he was doing."

"I see," Kan said. "In a way, it's not good that he does not remember. Like you said, perhaps it would have convinced him to do his business elsewhere."

"I doubt that," Eric said. "He seemed quite interested

in what his team is doing. He does not seem to be the type to be easily dislodged."

"Plus, we didn't quite push things as far as we might have," Mikael said. "We didn't take off our hats. He didn't see my hair. That might have triggered a memory. Perhaps I should have."

Kan shook his massive head.

"You may have your chance yet. Unit 17, are the bones indeed those of the predator type we are seeking?"

"Yes, they are. I scanned the area while we spoke to Mr. Brown."

"Let me see."

Eric walked near the wall and activated his camera. This was an old ship, without the latest equipment. The new ones would let him send his display signals from across the room, but in this one he had to stand close by or the picture was fuzzy.

"Enlarge it," Kan said once the image of the bones in the hillside appeared on the wall monitor.

Eric did so, and the monitor showed what was clearly the skeleton of a large carnivore. The rocks still held most of the remains of the beast, but the length of the spine was clearly visible, as were the massive hind legs and the awesome skull, nearly as long as a man. The bones appeared largely intact, although the head was some three feet beyond the end of the spine and the tail was not visible at all.

"Can we see the front limbs?"

"I don't think so," Eric said.

"Why not? Aren't they there?"

"I don't know. There's no way to tell from this. They could still be in the rock. They may not be there at all. Swenson said they tended to wash away quite a bit. They were very small, you know."

"So this is what we are looking for? The one with the very small forelimbs?"

"It looks like that."

Kan stared at the image.

"Good. We must get as many of these as we can. This, more than any of the others, shows the decadence of our ancestors."

Those watching along with Kan maintained silence and knitted their brows. It was not permissible to criticize those who had gone before, even if you were the commander of a Swede ship. Seeming to realize his error, Kan quickly added, "But of course they were great and honorable."

The assembled Swedes let that comment hang in the air.

"So how should we proceed, sir?" asked Hern, who had come into the chamber while the bones were being displayed.

"Has everyone been checked?"

"Yes, sir. Everyone is clean, except of course for the dead Nes and Lasse."

"Do not refer to him again by a Swede name," Kan ordered, his voice regaining its steely edge. It was clear that he expected his gaffe to be forgotten, and quickly. "He is henceforth to be known as the escaped lizard, or simply as the lizard, as he is the only one of them remaining here. I will take this up with the council when we return. It is idiotic to continue this policy of having us inhabit our Earth bodies for so long prior to a mission. That allowed not one but two of the vile Nes to sneak in here, and that cannot be allowed to continue."

"Sir, we are done with these bones. We have everything in the immediate area," Mikael said, getting Kan back on track. "How do you want us to proceed?"

"We need *those* bones," Kan said, pointing at the monitor image of the predator.

"The scientific team is there," Eric said. "They camp below the rocks at night. They would see us."

Kan stared at the monitor. He seemed to find thinking difficult when clad in his flesh body.

"I do not care, at this point. We need that skeleton.

We did not come all this way to be nice to everyone. We will kill them all if we have to, but we will get those bones, and we will get them tonight."

Eric switched off the monitor, which now displayed the image of a man wandering around outside the ship, looking down at the ground.

"I see you did not return without some company," Kan said in an irritated voice. "Why don't we just put up a flag showing where the ship is and invite everyone in for a drink?"

"We didn't see him, sir," Mikael said. "We thought no one was behind us."

Eric stared at the man's image. He remembered seeing him earlier, leaning on one of the wagons. He remembered staring at the man, because there was something peculiar and familiar about him, although he could not remember what it was. Eric could almost swear he had seen him somewhere before, although of course that was not possible.

"What shall we do with him?" Mikael asked.

"Kill him," Kan replied. "Although we should not kill him directly outside the ship this time. That only brings more of them around. That same mistake cost us a significant amount of time."

"Sir, don't forget that we do not have the Earth person Luther Gumpson here to do the shooting," Hern chipped in, which only made Kan's irritation grow.

"I am fully aware of that, Hern, you didn't put one of your memory erasers in my body, or at least you better not have."

"Of course I didn't," Hern said, wanting that on the record.

"I thought we could just use a Multi-Purpose Tool to shrink him," Kan said. "It's not elegant, but it works, just like it did on that lizard. In fact, we could just leave him shrunk down, and we wouldn't have to bury him. Speaking of the Nes, Hern, what did you do with him?"

"He's in my laboratory, reduced in size," Hern said. "I recovered the physical body he was using as a cover so we can study it and determine how they managed to build one that was so effective. It is fascinating. It seems to be composed of living tissue that actually survived the shrinking with little damage, although the Nes inside obviously did not. We didn't know they could build a body that good, and it warrants further study. I don't need the Nes, though. Should I just throw the lizard out?"

"No, I guess we should take that back, too. We're here to remove traces of our presence, not to leave new things. We'll just kill this man, leave him shrunken so no one will find him, and move on."

Eric felt sweat breaking out on his forehead. Something inside told him he did not want this man to die.

"Sir, I have a suggestion. Even if we kill him and no one can find him, he probably has friends and they will probably come looking for him. I am concerned that they will assume that Luther Gumpson has killed him, and will come here in great numbers again."

Kan frowned at him.

"That's always a risk, but perhaps you're right. We should kill him, move his body to draw their attention away, bring it back to normal size and let him be found. Good idea, Earth Reclamation Unit 17."

That was not what he had in mind.

"Sir, if I may. The damage that will be done to his body by the Multi-Purpose Tool will not look remotely like anything that would be done by Luther Gumpson. Gumpson would just shoot him, leaving a hole in his body. Using the Multi-Purpose Tool will crush him."

"Then they will assume perhaps an animal got to him after he was shot."

"There are no animals on this planet that crush their food like that," Eric said. "Sir, I think it would be better if I just went up and talked to him and asked him to go away."

"What will you say? Please, sir, you're walking over our spaceship and we would like for you to stop? I don't think that will work."

"I will think of something, sir. It will hone my interpersonal skills on this planet. I think it is worth a try."

Eric knew full well that Kan cared nothing about his interpersonal skills, but he also knew the captain was a stickler for efficiency and would be glad to get some use out of his reclamation unit.

"All right," Kan said at last. "But if he gives you any trouble we will use the Multi-Purpose Tool on him, or you can just do it yourself. In fact, if he sounds the slightest bit suspicious, you should use it."

"I will," Eric said. "I will also take the opportunity to talk to him about the situation here, and find out more about what is going on."

He might as well have announced that he was going to stand on his head for the rest of the day, for all it seemed to mean to Kan.

"As you wish. Now go."

Digger Phelps heard the man's footsteps behind him, but he hadn't heard him approach.

"This is a dangerous place," the man said in his familiar voice. "A man was shot here not long ago. You are not armed. You should not be here."

Phelps whirled and gave the man the same curious stare he had given him before, when he had passed by on the road.

"Hello," Phelps said, and when he heard his own voice following in the air so soon after the stranger had spoken, he knew that what Sam Sharp said was true.

"You seem very familiar to me," Phelps said, unsure of how to proceed.

"I am sure we have not met."

He reached out a hand, and the man stared at it for a moment before shaking it. Then the man gently grabbed him by the arm and began leading him back toward the road. The man seemed eager to get him away from here. This is probably where the spaceship is, Phelps thought, but he didn't think he should mention that.

"I am not kidding about this place being dangerous," the man said.

Phelps stared openly at the man's face. It was uncanny. It was the face he had seen so many times in the shaving mirror, only his own face hadn't looked like that in a long time. He had a tiny scar above his left ear, just below where the hair began. This man had it, too. It was shaped like a semicircle, and was almost invisible—unless you knew where to look for it.

"Where did you get that scar?" he asked the man.

"What scar?"

"Above your ear. There," Phelps said, tapping the side of his own head, just above the ear.

The man ran a finger over the scar, but didn't seem to be able to feel it.

"That is not of your concern," the man said.

"It's from a bar fight, isn't it?" Phelps said. "In Carson City. When you were eighteen. You got hit in the side of the head by a beer bottle thrown by Skeeter McAllister, didn't you?"

The man seemed stunned by Phelps' words. He actually staggered back and held his forehead, like his head was going to explode. He would have then lost his balance altogether if Phelps hadn't hurried to hold him up.

"Are you okay, mister?" Phelps asked.

He guided the man over to a rock beside the road. The man sat down and held his head in his hands.

"I remember," he said, over and over. "I *do* remember that."

He finally looked up at Phelps, and extended a hand again. Phelps thought he wanted help to stand up, but instead the man just shook his hand.

"My name is Eric," he said. "What is yours?"

"Digger. Digger Phelps."

"It's nice to meet you."

The man looked at him without speaking for a long time.

"What else do you know about me, Digger Phelps?"

Now was his chance to find out the truth, once and for all.

"Everything. I think."

Eric nodded, as if that was the answer he was seeking.

"You're me, aren't you?" Phelps asked.

"That appears to be the case."

"You have a spaceship around here, don't you? Back where we were standing."

Eric looked around, as if making sure they were far enough away from it, and nodded.

"It was that room, wasn't it? That room that Alf Swenson put me in. I remember it felt very strange in there. He was making some kind of copy of me, wasn't he?"

"Yes," Eric said.

"And the copy is you."

"That would be me."

He smiled at Phelps, and Phelps couldn't help but smile back. It was like smiling at a son, except the son was actually him.

"Sit down next to me," Eric said. "I'll make some room. Let's talk."

He scooted over on the rock, which had a broad, flat top, suitable for sitting. It had been used for that purpose in the past, judging from its smooth top. Travelers had probably rested there, at the end of the road, before heading out into the roadless wilderness that lay beyond.

"Please tell me what happened," Phelps said.

Eric frowned. He looked into Phelps' eyes, and his own eyes reflected discomfort.

"I am not supposed to."

Phelps leaned in until their foreheads almost touched.

"Buddy, this is *me* you're talking to. Nothing wrong

with that. It will be like talking to yourself. In fact, you *are* talking to yourself."

"What other memories of mine do you have?"

"You mean you don't remember anything?"

Eric shook his head miserably.

"No. They gave me enough memories to know the ways of Earth and to speak English, but everything else is gone. I can feel the memories, almost, somewhere in my mind, like they're ready to come out. But I can't remember. What memories do you have?"

"All of them," Phelps said, and then he laughed, hoping to lighten the gloom his younger self was showing. "At least, all of them except for certain nights when I may have had a little too much to drink."

"Tell me another one."

"You tell me something first."

The young man was headstrong when he had to be; or rather, *he* was headstrong when he had to be, Phelps thought.

"I have to know," Eric said. "I have to be sure."

Phelps nodded. He had plenty to spare. Surely there would be no harm done.

"Okay. Do you remember seeing the sun behind the rocks in Arizona? In Monument Valley? Do you remember how the rocks looked like the gates to some other world?"

Eric squinted, as if that would make the memory come into focus.

"It's your favorite place in all the world," Phelps said. "It's so beautiful. You've always thought so."

Eric squinted for a few seconds more and then stopped.

"No. Nothing."

"Here's something," Phelps said. "Let me see your left hand."

Eric proffered the hand. Phelps turned it around like he was going to do a palm reading, but instead he found another tiny scar near the tip of the thumb.

"Here," he said, making sure Eric saw it.

"I never even noticed that," Eric said.

"You were bored. You were whittling one night, the first night you camped in Monument Valley. You started watching the sunset. It was so beautiful that you stopped looking down. You were beheading the little man you were whittling and you cut your own thumb."

The eyes that had so recently been filled with doubt were now filled with tears.

"You're right. I do remember that. I remember camping there. I remember looking at the rocks in the daytime, thinking of how great they were, then after a while I got bored and quit looking at them. Then I remember having a few drinks and fooling around with the knife and then I just looked up and there they were again, beautiful all over again, like I had never seen them before."

His voice faltered and he stopped talking and took a long swallow. Phelps felt his own eyes tearing up at the memory and at the effect it had on his younger self. He gave himself time to recover, then moved in to complete the bargain.

"Okay. Now you. I mean me—how did we come to be?"

"You must tell me a few things first. You did meet Alf Swenson?"

"If that was his real name, yes."

"It wasn't his real name, not exactly. But you were on his ship?"

"Yes. He caught me in this green cloud and put me in this little cell or room. It had a lot of red lights in it. It made me tingle all over."

Phelps' younger self nodded.

"What he did was make a copy of all your biological data. It was sort of a blueprint of your whole body and even your mind. Later it enabled our scientists to create me."

Phelps gave him an exaggerated lookover.

"And a fine job they did. But if Swenson made a copy of your mind, why don't you have my memories already? Why do I have to bring them back to you?"

Eric's face took on a pained expression.

"Our scientists considered it useful to have me come back here with intimate knowledge of how your society operates, but they thought it would be dangerous to just send me back with all my memories intact. They thought I might forget what I am and think I am human, and somehow endanger the mission."

He looked at Phelps, and his face broke into a grin.

"You look like you have a lot of questions."

Phelps returned the smile.

"Brother, I haven't even started."

"I have limited time. Art Kan will be impatient. Ask them as rapidly as possible and I will attempt to answer them the same way."

"Okay. I don't know who Art Kan is but right now that's not the biggest thing I want to know. Here goes: If you were created thirty years ago, why aren't you older?"

"I wasn't created thirty years ago. I was created just for this mission, which began about ten Earth years ago. For the trip here, we slept in special chambers that kept us from aging."

"Who are your people and what is this mission you mentioned?"

"They are an ancient race of aliens from—I don't know how to explain that to you."

"Skip that part, then. I'll trust it's far away."

"Very. They are ancient, like I said, and they have traveled all over the universe since ancient times. They sort of had colonies everywhere, including here, on this planet, millions of years ago."

"Millions?"

"Yes. They used to take great interest in the local life forms, and would experiment with them. They did so with your dinosaurs. They bred them and tinkered with them. They left here after a huge asteroid hit the Earth and wiped most everything out."

"It did?"

"Yes."

"I never heard anything about that."

"You weren't here. Please let me talk, I don't have much time. They were once physical beings—like us— but over time have redeveloped themselves into beings of pure energy, sort of like clouds of gas. They are trying to position themselves among the other races in the universe as being one of the more advanced races, but they're having trouble. They are not well-liked. Their colonization has been pretty clumsy, and they are generally resented for the experiments they performed on virtually everything they came across. There is sort of a governing body of the more advanced civilizations— you'd call it a council or something—and they are appealing to it to be allowed to join the top people, the elite, the . . ."

"Cream of the crop?"

"Yes. Good phrase. To help their case, they are trying to downplay the experiments they performed. They are sweeping the universe now, going to their old haunts, trying to get rid of the evidence, you might say. Teams from the advanced civilizations' governing body will be going through to check on their claims, but they want to try to clean everything up a bit first."

Phelps stroked his chin. So far, he was actually understanding this. So far, none of these aliens sounded all that advanced to him.

"So these lizard people are the ones checking up on your people?"

His younger self blinked in surprise.

"You know about them, too?"

"Your advanced races are not as stealthy as you seem to think."

"Apparently not. No, the lizard people are not those

aliens. The evaluation team will be made up of aliens that don't look like anything you'd recognize. They are little and have big heads and are gray all over. They aren't here yet. I don't know when they'll get here."

"That gives us something to look forward to, I guess. More company. So who are the lizard people?"

"When the Swedes left this planet, they took some of their dinosaur experiments with them. Eventually they evolved the lizard people, although the lizard people refuse to believe that. They were put on a barren planet and they continued to develop there, and eventually there were several wars between them and my people. In fact, they never really stopped warring. The lizard people want the bones for religious reasons. They believe if they can assemble all the bones of their people in one place, this giant lizard god they worship will come and destroy their enemies."

Well, he *had* been understanding this, up until now.

"So what are your people called?"

"They call themselves the Swedes."

"Why? That sounds like what we would call them."

"Well, you have to understand that they don't really use a spoken language in their real bodies. When they come to a planet like Earth, they are able to inhabit bodies made of flesh that look like the people here. They have developed stocks of bodies they use for different places. Most of the ones they use for Earth are tall and blonde-haired, just because they like the look. They noticed that the bodies look like the residents of Scandinavian countries, so for the purposes of coming here they call themselves Swedes. They also picked Earth names that they thought sounded sort of Swede, although they probably aren't."

"And what do the lizard people call themselves?"

"They do use a spoken language. They call themselves Nes."

He ended the word with a kind of low whistle, so that it almost sounded like he said "next."

"Why do you call yourself Eric?"

"It's a shortening of what they call me. They call me Earth Reclamation Unit 17, because I am a copy of one of you. Of you, in fact."

"Number 17? Does that mean—"

"Yes. There have been others. There will be more. I could call myself Digger, if you'd rather."

Phelps ran the thought through his mind—Digger Phelps, Jr., except he wouldn't really be a junior.

"Maybe not. Eric is fine. It's a good name."

His younger self seemed pleased at the praise. Phelps paused, but not because he was out of questions. He was just out of breath, and was trying to sort out what to ask next. He wiggled his rear end, trying to get a more comfortable spot on the rock.

"My turn, and then I must go," Eric said. "Why are you here? Have you been here the whole time, since I was copied from you?"

"No. I just came back here by accident. I've just signed on to work with Barnum Brown, digging up one of those dinosaurs that everybody in the universe seems to be after."

He started to laugh at his own joke, but Eric grabbed his arm and stood up, forcing him to stand, too.

"Are you serious?"

"Of course."

Eric stared into his eyes, causing Phelps to take a step back.

"Get away from there. We're going in there tonight. Art Kan is serious about getting that skeleton in particular. He will kill anyone and everyone that stands in his way. You have to get out."

Phelps gaped at Eric. How did his younger self get involved with such a rough crowd? Weren't they supposed to be an advanced race?

"I can't just run away. I don't want Barnum Brown or any of the others to be killed. You've got to stop your boss."

"I can't stop him. He didn't want me along on this trip anyway. You've got to do something."

"But what?"

His younger self paced around the road, trying to think.

"Is there some way you can get everyone off the side of the hill where they are camped? Maybe take them somewhere, just for the night?"

"So you can get in there and get the bones? Can you do it in one night?"

"Usually, yes, if they are as exposed as that skeleton is."

Phelps whistled in astonishment. Brown's crew had been working on that dinosaur for days, with relatively little to show for it.

"Mr. Brown will be very angry to find it gone," he said.

"Better angry than dead."

It was hard to argue with that.

"I don't know what you need to do, but you have got to get those people away from their camp *tonight*. Keep them away all night long, otherwise they will disappear and they will never be found. Now I have to go. You have been warned. Please go away tonight."

The two versions of the same man, decades apart, stood in the road and looked at each other.

"How—how long will you be here?" Phelps asked. "Can I speak with you again?"

Eric's emerging smile pushed the look of worry off his face.

"I'd like that."

Phelps extended an awkward hand for a shake, but Eric pulled him into a bear hug. Damn, Phelps thought as he felt Eric's arms tighten around his shoulders. I was a strong bugger back then.

TWENTY-TWO

"This is not going to work," Luther Gumpson whispered. "That is a solid wall of rock."

"Rock is not as solid as it seems," the man named Lasse replied. "Not when you have the right tools."

"Oh, right. I forgot about you and your stick. You're going to dig out this whole skeleton with that."

Lasse held the silver stick before his face. It glowed a faint green around the top, shedding just enough light to allow them to see the faint outline of the dinosaur bones.

"Allow me to correct you. *We* are going to dig it out with this."

"Whatever."

He should be on his way to California by now, money in his pocket and dreams in his heart. Instead, he was forced to help a monster from outer space dig up the skeleton of a creature that had been dead and safely buried for who knows how long.

"Just my luck," Gumpson said. If he had been luckier, one of those fools out there in the wagons would have already killed him by now.

Lasse motioned for Gumpson to take his place at the far end of the rock wall. Gumpson's feet were still bound by rope, but it was just loose enough to allow him to walk in baby steps.

"I still don't see how this will work."

160

"It will work a lot better when you stop talking."

"And you'll give me my gun back when we get this out?"

"Yes. I'll give you your gun back."

"Well, let's do it, then. I can't walk very well, you know."

"I know. I just need you to look and make sure I'm not hanging it up on anything. The Multi-Purpose Tool will do the rest."

"That's a very catchy name for your gadget."

"Don't blame me. The Swedes thought that one up. My people refer to it as ———."

He made a sort of grunt that ended in a whistling sound, and Gumpson decided not to pursue that line of questioning any further. For a creature from a supposedly advanced civilization, Lasse was not much of a conversationalist.

"How does it work?"

"I don't know. It just does. Do you understand all of the science behind how your primitive projectile shooter works? I didn't think so. Now please be quiet, I'm trying to concentrate my thoughts."

Gumpson actually did understand how his pistol worked, but he decided to just shut up and let this alien go about its business. Lasse stood before the rock and seemed to adjust something on his silver Multi-Purpose Tool. It glowed a brighter green, and then the green light jumped to the rock face, forming a rectangular frame of light around the green bones.

"Geez, why don't you just send up some fireworks to let them know we're here?" Gumpson said.

"It can't be helped," Lasse said. "Be quiet."

Lasse held the tool steady. The light didn't pulse or flicker like a flame, just kept a steady glow. After what seemed like forever, Lasse consulted something on the stick and began to move it up. A huge section of the rock face began to move with it, shifting into the air as lightly as if it was a feather. Only the grinding sound of rock moving on rock marred the ghostly vision of the block of bones lifting out of their once-eternal tomb.

"I tell you, I saw Luther Gumpson on this mountain!"

The shout came from below, so faint that it was very nearly drowned out by the moving rock block.

"He's up here! Everyone get up here and we can catch him!"

Lasse stood stunned with surprise. The rock-entombed beast hovered in the air, a dozen feet above the slab from which it was now parted.

"You've got to let me go!" Gumpson hissed at the immobile Lasse.

Lasse just looked at him. He didn't move the dinosaur or do anything but blink at Gumpson in confusion.

"Jesus, buddy, they're going to kill me!"

He could hear the sounds of shouting as what must have been dozens of men began to scale the hillside. The hill was not that tall. Even in the darkness, the men would get to them soon.

"There's a light!" Gumpson heard one of them shout. "He must be up there!"

Lasse turned to face the sound, and then took a couple of steps back, moving him closer to Gumpson. This situation was clearly a surprise to him; he didn't know what to do, so he wasn't doing much of anything. Gumpson did know what to do. He calculated the distance and tensed his leg muscles. Without a noise, without so much as a loud breath, he baby-stepped up to Lasse and whacked him as hard as he could on the back of the neck with his joined fists.

The alien dropped to his knees, utterly unprepared for an attack from the rear. He dropped the Multi-Purpose Tool, which clattered somewhere on the rocks in front of him. Gumpson did have a bit of luck, after all, because the tool apparently landed on the right control. Its green light went out, and his legs were free. The dinosaur was free, too. The rock containing it crashed back into its mineral cradle. Lasse rubbed the back of his head and issued forth a whistled alien word that sounded a lot like a curse, or maybe a sigh, or maybe both.

Gumpson didn't stay long enough for his foe to stand up. He hightailed it further up the ridge, away from the ascending shouts. If anyone had brains enough to come up the back way, he was a dead man, but if these yahoos were anything like most of the people he had met out here, he was in the clear. He didn't have his gun, which was a major problem, but he figured it was a good idea not to try to wrestle Lasse for it. He reminded himself that under that human exterior was a strong reptile. Gumpson had even shot him, and that hadn't slowed him down much. Getting his pistol back was not worth the trouble of getting clawed to death, or whatever it was that reptiles did to kill their prey.

When he had gained the top of the ridge, he looked back down to where he had been. Lasse had not moved, as far as he could tell. He hadn't even stood up, but was still just hunched there, on his knees. For a member of an advanced civilization, he looked rather pitiful. Gumpson felt a momentary pang of what he assumed to be conscience, but then he reminded himself that he could have been out of here long ago if it weren't for that lizard man. Sure, Lasse had rescued him from the spaceship, but he had just turned around and put him in another kind of bondage. At least the spaceship guys had still let him use his gun.

The decision about what to do for the alien was made for him when a group of men appeared on the ridge and surrounded Lasse. He could hear the excited hubbub of their voices.

TWENTY-THREE

"What's the matter, Digger? You look like you've seen a ghost."

Phelps sat with the other men at the dinner table. Barnum Brown dressed well in the field, but he was not as much of a stickler for good food as Edward Drinker Cope had been. He had skimped on the cook, and the food showed it. But the men were hungry, and ate without complaint.

Phelps was miserable, but he couldn't show it. It was getting late, and soon would be getting dark, and then the big blonde-headed aliens would come. This was not the sort of thing he could talk up around the camp. Having worked so hard to convince Brown that he was off the sauce and didn't believe in such things, it wouldn't do to start talking about them now, especially if it meant convincing the entire camp to walk away from the very bones Brown desired.

"You okay, Digger?"

He nodded to the college students that addressed him. They did not address him with the proper courtesy, he felt, which probably meant they had heard stories about him from some of the other men on Brown's crew. That could not be helped. If he suffered from a poor reputation, he really had no one but himself to blame.

"I'm fine," he muttered back, and the students turned their attention back to their food, though it hardly deserved it.

He wanted to shout that he had met his own self, thirty years younger, but that, too, would be greeted about as warmly as if he produced a large whiskey bottle and downed it on the spot. Sometimes the straight and narrow life constricted one's ability to express oneself. These college students would not even understand the significance. What did they care if he had a younger self? They were young, they would live forever. Look at that one, Harryhausen, tucking into his food. Eating food this bad was dangerous in itself, but Harryhausen was transferring it from plate to mouth as if he couldn't consume it rapidly enough.

Phelps didn't realize he was staring at Harryhausen so fixedly until he felt the pressure of another rump beside him.

"He bothering you?" he heard a voice ask.

It was one of the other men. He wasn't one of the roughnecks whose speciality was the steady hauling of rock. He was dark as an Indian, but with the look of a man who wore suits and ties naturally. This was one of the scientists, Phelps could tell. He just had that sort of scientific air about him. He looked to be fairly tall, as far as Phelps could judge seeing him sitting down, and was thin without being skinny.

"My name is S.L. Burgess," the man said, extending a hand for a shake. He had a firm grip. "The S.L. stands for Sitting Lizard. Sitting Lizard Burgess."

Phelps gave him a closer look. Well, that explained the dark-as-an-Indian part. He *was* an Indian. He was as dark as himself.

"Does that name ring a bell?"

It did, sort of. He just couldn't concentrate. This Indian was sitting here chatting away as though they weren't all about to die at alien hands.

"You were out here with Professor Marsh, weren't you? In 1876? Professor Brown said you were."

Phelps nodded. That's where he had heard the name

Sitting Lizard. An Indian bearing that name had come into camp. He had ended up getting shot, as far as Phelps could recall. Phelps could not recall much else about him, except that he spoke very good English for an Indian.

"You must have met my mother, then."

"I don't recall any women out here then," Phelps said, but then he remembered what Barnum Brown had told him. Al Stillson had really been Alice Stillson. And that meant she must have met the Indian Sitting Lizard, too.

S.L. Burgess smiled as Phelp's shake of his head turned into a nod.

"I guess I did meet your mother. I just didn't know she was—well, a she."

"So you must have experienced all the same things she did when she was out here," Burgess said. He was ignoring his own food to question Phelps. "You must have seen what she saw."

Phelps noticed that Barnum Brown, who had been on the far side of the row of dinner tables, had wandered closer. He remembered what Brown had told him about the book or story, or whatever it was, that Burgess's mother had written.

"I suppose you could say that," Phelps said. "It was pretty quiet out here then."

Burgess gave him a stern look, as if to punish him for lying.

"Didn't anything . . . oh, I don't know, *unusual* go on in that time? Did you see anything sort of out of the ordinary?"

"No. I said I didn't."

Brown was clearly hovering now.

"My mother said she saw a lot of strange things."

"Your mother liked to make up tall tales, son. She was prone to exaggeration."

He couldn't remember speaking more than about five words to the young, dirty-faced Al Stillson, but now was a good time for him to spin some tall tales himself. As he spoke the words, he saw Burgess's already dark eyes grow darker.

"Are you calling my mother a liar?"

"No, I'm not."

"It sounds like you are."

The young man rose to his feet and reached for Phelp's collar, and only then noticed Brown standing close by, pretending to stare out at the horizon.

"But I suppose you aren't," Burgess said, recovering in record time.

"I said I wasn't," Phelps responded lamely.

He stood up and walked past the row of rough tables, past all the dining men, and walked to the base of the rocky cliff that rose above them and that held the bones that the men from outer space wanted so badly. It rose above him stark and beautiful, and a trick of the moonlight made it look like there was a green glow where the men had been working today. This was not going well. The men weren't about to leave their food. He would never get the area clear.

"Back there, what you said—did you mean that?"

He hadn't noticed that Burgess had followed him. The young man must have picked up his stealth from his father.

"Mean what?"

"About my mother making up tall tales."

Phelps could barely see Burgess's face in front of him, but he could hear the note of pleading in his voice.

"I really didn't know her to do that," he said, as gently as he could. "I didn't read whatever it was she wrote."

"But you know what was in the story she wrote."

"I've heard."

"You were here. Is it true?"

He was about to find out that it was true, and in the worst way.

"Please, I beg you," Burgess said. His hands were on Phelps' lapel again, but this time they bore the supplicant's touch of a beggar. "Just let me know if it's true. There's safety in numbers, you know. If you say it's true, too, maybe I can believe it."

Something the young man said jarred him. Safety in numbers. That was the answer. Not fewer people on the cliffside tonight; *more* people on the cliffside. But how? Brown wasn't going to order up a crew tonight, everybody was already tired. Then he remembered the men in the wagons, circled around them like dogs ready to strike. All he had to do was give them a scent.

"Look there!" he shouted, so loud that Burgess took a surprised step back. "Watch out! It's Luther Gumpson!"

He shouted as if he wanted even his momma, dead in her grave in Missouri, to hear him.

"I just saw Luther Gumpson heading up that ridge!"

"What are you talking about?" Burgess said. "I don't see anything."

He stood right in front of Phelps, but Phelps just looked past him and kept shouting.

"There he goes! Luther Gumpson!"

He heard some stirring, both from behind him and off to the side. Those men waiting in the wagons could react pretty fast when they were given the chance to put down their whiskey and pick up their pistols and shotguns.

"Where?" he heard another voice say, from off in the night. "Where is he?"

He felt a hand on his shoulder.

"What is all this yelling about, Digger?"

It was Barnum Brown, bearing a lamp, standing in front of his crew. He did not look pleased at the sudden eruption of noise.

"I saw Luther Gumpson, sir. The man from the wanted poster. He was heading up the ridge where your skeleton is."

"He was?"

"Yes, sir."

Brown exhaled slowly.

"How the hell could you see him out here, Digger? It's so damn dark you can't even see it's night out here. If I didn't have this lamp, you couldn't see me."

Several men from the wagons began to appear out of the night, and they were not inclined to ask questions. A few bore lanterns or torches, while others stumbled about as best they could. He saw the silver glints of guns in numerous hands.

"Which way did he go?" one of them shouted.

"Up there!" Phelps said, pointing up the ridge.

"Can you show us?" the man asked.

Phelps felt the weight of a lamp in his hand. He turned to see Brown letting go of it.

"You don't mind?"

"I don't care to have gunslingers camping out next to my Tyrannosaurus rex. By all means, Digger," Brown said. "Lead the way."

TWENTY-FOUR

Lasse wasn't hurt so much as disgusted with himself. What was bringing all those people running up here? The light? It couldn't be that bright. Had they somehow gotten wind that he was keeping Gumpson here? They couldn't have. They shouldn't have known anything at all, but here they came all the same. Then Gumpson hit him on the back of the head and he dropped the bones of the dinosaur. It was doubtful that anyone could tell that the bones had been lifted and then dropped back into place, but the action was still an affront to Mother Naga, and she had certainly suffered enough of those at his hands lately.

"Hey, mister!" said a man who suddenly appeared around the bend, trudging up the narrow trail that wound up and down the cliff face. "Did you see Luther Gumpson come through here?"

It occurred to him that he should shut up and send the men away so he could get back to work. If they thought Gumpson was up here they would be around all night and he would never get anything done. Anger flooded his mind, and instead he abandoned rationality and decided that Gumpson should die. Gumpson did not care about his own kind, murdering them with impunity, so Lasse should not care about him. It would be worth abandoning a night of work to see him dead, after he had taken off the way he had. Lasse would just get this skeleton by himself, and he would recover Bjorn's bones by himself. He could do it all alone. When the other men straggled up behind their leader, he spoke.

"Yes, I saw him," he said.

The lead man—a ragged old human who appeared to have been greatly taxed by the climb up the hill—appeared surprised at the news, even though he had been the main one shouting about it.

"He went up the ridge," Lasse said. "He's not armed. You can kill him if you hurry."

"Really?" the man said.

"Yes," Lasse replied.

The lights from their torches and lanterns bothered him. He wished they would go away.

"How do you know he's not armed?" asked another man, who was waving his own pistol around to show it was not a problem he shared.

"We wrestled," Lasse said. "I took his pistol."

He rooted around inside his vest and produced the pistol, which glowed dully in the crude light sources the men carried. The men appeared to be impressed.

"*You* took Luther Gumpson's pistol away from him?" one of the men asked.

"Yes. I just showed you."

"You did it?"

"I said I did. Shall I take your pistol, too?"

The man took a step back into the shadows, shaking his head. Lasse finally stood up, and the men gave him a wide circle. He couldn't see how many there were, but there were obviously enough to ruin his work for tonight. He had to give up.

"Don't you want to come with us?" one of the men asked.

"No, thank you," Lasse said. "But you better go, or he'll get away."

That was all he needed to say. The men started heading further up the ridge, their lights flickering and blinking like fireflies. He walked past them, heading the other way, his thoughts a useless jumble as he made his way to the road. He had murdered Bjorn. He had failed to spirit away the messenger of Mother Naga. He had let the human Luther Gumpson escape from him. The wound on his torso allowed some night air to press against his real Nes body, reminding him that he would soon lose his disguise. He was alone, and far away, and in danger.

He was vaguely cognizant of human forms passing him on their way up the slope, but he ignored them. He walked for what seemed like Earth hours but must have only been minutes. After a while, he realized that he was heading toward a sound. It was low and hypnotic, and almost before he realized it he had stumbled into its source: it was one human talking to a group of another humans under the stretched awnings of a tent. The speaking human's voice had been the source of the sound he followed. It was low and sinuous, curling about the night, not rushed, but with an element of urgency.

"Welcome, brother," the man said.

Lasse had not realized that he had walked into the light cast by a roaring fire and by several lanterns hung from the tent poles.

"You're about the only one heading the right way," the man said, motioning Lasse to a chair near the stage. Lasse craned his neck and realized that several men from the tent were indeed on their feet and heading out, retrieving pistols from holsters and waistbands as they went. There were more leaving than there were staying, and Lasse was the only new entrant. The man smiled at him.

"Greetings again, brother. I am the right Reverend Winthrow Parnassus. We are here to talk about the Lord."

Lasse nodded miserably. That was certainly not a name the Swedes would have picked out, but it seemed to fit him. The right reverend was a squat little man, and the glow from the fire made him seem orange, as if he was a plump bit of meat being cooked.

"How many of you are feeling guilty tonight?" Parnassus said. "How many of you have sins weighing heavily on your hearts?"

Lasse found himself nodding before his conscious mind had even picked out what Parnassus was saying. He lifted up his head and decided to pay better attention.

"Sometimes we are forced to do things we don't want to do, and that we know are wrong, and then we feel bad," Parnassus said. "We feel guilty. We know we have done wrong and we want to be forgiven."

The two men sitting next to Lasse grabbed their hats and stood up, forcing him to cant his knees to the side to let them pass. He kept his eyes leveled on the little orange man.

"Sometimes we do things that we know to be wrong, but we do them anyway. Sometimes we intentionally do things to hurt others. And then we want to be forgiven."

Forgive me, Mother Naga, Lasse thought to himself, but let the thought whip away into the winds of his mind and shifted his attention back to Parnassus. More people stood up to go, but Lasse didn't even move to let them pass, forcing them to shove and twist and grunt their way out of the tent.

"Sometimes we do things to harm ourselves, and then we want forgiveness. But I tell you, there *is* a way to be forgiven. It *does* work. It is a way that will free you of your burdens and save you from damnation. Don't we all want that? Don't we all want that, brother?"

Lasse nodded, and with a twitch suddenly noticed that Parnassus had sat down beside him. He looked around the tent. Everyone else was gone. It was he and the rotund human, who upon closer inspection was not orange at all, only a pale white that did a good job of reflecting the firelight. Not unlike the crude human suits once worn by the Nes who had visited this planet thirty years ago, Lasse thought.

"You must be troubled," Parnassus said, resting an arm

lightly on Lasse's shoulder. "I know my sermons aren't that good."

"I . . . am," Lasse said. "Yes, I am."

"Can you tell me what the problem is?"

Parnassus seemed to sense Lasse's discomfort at the presence of his arm, and slowly moved it away. The man almost seemed to know what he was thinking.

"I killed someone," Lasse said. "Mother Naga, I am so sorry."

"You killed Mother Naga?" Parnassus asked, gently.

"No. I killed my partner. I killed my friend."

Parnassus did not seem scared or even particularly surprised by the admission. Perhaps it was the sort of thing he heard every day. The priests of the Nes were used to dealing with the most unfortunate and most misbehaving members of society, and it was undoubtedly no different on Earth. In fact, it could only be worse on such a primitive place.

"Why did you kill your friend?"

He looked at Parnassus for the first time since the man had sat down beside him. Prominent in his rounded face were his eyes, big and almond-shaped. The whites of his eyes were laced with red, as if he was weary of looking at the blood and pain of the world.

"I didn't want to. We were on a mission here. We were in disguise. He was discovered and I had to kill him before I was discovered. It would have destroyed everything we worked for if I had been discovered. But he was my friend. I did not want to kill him."

His human body worked too well. Nes scientists had labored for centuries to create a false body that mimicked the functions of a real body, but only recently had gotten it right. When he was placed into his flesh body, he inherited all the strange mannerisms and reflexes of his monkey-bred vehicle. He felt sorrow inside his Nes self, and he felt tears flowing from the eyes of his false Earth body.

"I can see you didn't," Parnassus said. "But you still feel guilty, don't you?"

"I am not supposed to feel guilt. Guilt is something Mother Naga does not permit. There is no guilt, there is just doing right and doing wrong."

"But you still feel guilty, don't you?"

"I do."

Damned human body. It was tearing up his emotions. His judgment was being clouded by the wrapping of monkey flesh around him. There was nothing he could do about that, not until the body died and he was forced to crawl out of it. In the meantime, the emotions it forced him to feel were real. Mother Naga had never seemed so distant.

"You want forgiveness, don't you, friend?"

There was something frightening in Parnassus' friendliness, but Lasse found himself nodding.

"Mother Naga does not permit forgiveness," he said through lips stained with tears. "There is only moving on and doing what is right."

Parnassus nodded and looked into the fire, as if he saw Mother Naga there.

"I don't know who Mother Naga is, but I know someone who does forgive," he said. "I can tell you about him if you want."

"All right," Lasse said.

"His name is Jesus Christ."

He paused, as if waiting for a response.

"You *have* heard of Jesus, haven't you, son?"

Lasse shook his head. Parnassus' big eyes opened even wider in surprise, as if he had not expected to discover so fallow a field in which to sow his seed.

"Really? You never heard of Jesus?"

Lasse shook his head again.

"May I ask where are you from, son?"

"Sweden."

"Ohhh. And there you worship—"

"Mother Naga."

"Right. I must admit I have not run across many people from Sweden. Or any people from Sweden. I'm from Tennessee, myself. We don't get many Mother Naga worshipers there."

"Tell me more about this man named Jesus."

Parnassus blinked several times, and then started speaking again.

"He is the son of God. He came to Earth long ago, in the form of a man. He taught us that we should love one another and that we should obey God. He said all men are the same in the eyes of the Lord, more or less. He said we are born to sin, that no one lives without fault. But—listen, my friend—he said if you sin, you can get forgiveness, if you are sorry and if you follow him."

So their God became a man, put on a man's skin. It was absurd, but the thought made Lasse feel slightly better.

"What happened to him? This Jesus Christ?"

Parnassus shifted in his seat.

"Some people didn't like what he said and so they killed him. They nailed him to a cross made of wood and he died."

Lasse turned to the man in disbelief. Parnassus gave a little shrug, as if unable to muster a defense for his fellow man.

"But don't worry," Parnassus put in hastily. "He rose again on the third day after his death and went back to Heaven to be with God. By the act of dying, he absorbed our sins. We can be forgiven if we follow him."

"So you killed him, but he forgives you."

"Well, technically the Romans killed him, or maybe the Jews, but yes. That's right. And if he can forgive us of that, he can forgive us of anything. Don't you see?"

Lasse did not follow all of what the reverend was saying. He did like hearing that someone could kill someone else and be forgiven for it. If this Jesus could do it, maybe

Bjorn could. He knew better than to ask that of Mother Naga.

"Tell me about this Mother Naga of yours," Parnassus said. "I don't mean to talk down anybody's religion"—he whispered conspiratorially to Lasse—"except some of this stuff the Indians say is pretty silly. It doesn't sound to me like Mother Naga is very comforting to you in this time of crisis."

"Her role is not to be comforting. We are to rebuild her. She expects that from us."

"I must admit I have never heard of Mother Naga," Parnassus said. "I sort of fancied myself to be familiar with most religions of the world, but I haven't heard of . . . her. I guess it would be a her."

"The gender role is just how Mother Naga translates to your language."

"Oh."

Parnassus had made him feel better by telling him about Jesus, so maybe he could return the favor.

"I can show you Mother Naga," he said, quietly. He had shown Luther Gumpson. If a man who would murder his own kind could appreciate Mother Naga, how much more would a religious man get from the experience?

"Yes, I will," Lasse said, talking himself into it.

"How will you do that?" Parnassus asked.

"Hold still. Trust me."

Parnassus held his head still as Lasse reached his hands toward his head.

"Trust me."

He put his palms against the side of Parnassus' head, hesitated for two Earth seconds, and then concentrated on Mother Naga and sent the images. Parnassus stiffened slightly, and his left heel straightened out, digging a furrow in the dust. After a long moment, before Lasse was even done, Parnassus' eyes flew open and he shoved Lasse's hands away.

"Stop it!" he shouted.

Parnassus leaped to his feet, faster than Lasse would have thought possible.

"My God, what was that thing?"

"Mother Naga," Lasse said, surprised at the reaction, although he supposed he shouldn't have been.

"Jesus!" Parnassus exclaimed.

Before Lasse could stop him, Parnassus stumbled from the tent, holding his hands to his head as if to shut off the images. Lasse would have liked to have heard more about this Jesus, but now he could not. He slowly rose to his feet and walked to the small platform at the head of the tent, where Parnassus had been standing when Lasse first entered. The fire felt good when he passed it. It got so cold here. He had learned that the real Sweden was also very cold, and had resolved never to actually go there.

He reached the platform. There was a bucket there, for no apparent purpose. Perhaps Parnassus had planned to fetch water at some point. He did seem to getting hot while he talked. Behind the platform was a heavy support pole helping hold the tent up. On it was a shape made of two perpendicular sticks of wood. A tiny figure of a man was suspended on them, his arms stretched so far it seemed they would burst from his shoulders. He remembered what Parnassus had told him. This must be that man, Jesus. This was Jesus dying. This was Jesus dying to forgive sins.

It was a gruesome statue, but he removed it from the pole and examined it closely. The woodworking was well done, if you liked that sort of thing. The Nes did not pay much attention to such representations. Still, just looking at it gave him some comfort. This man was not a real man, either. This man was wearing a monkey skin, just as he was. This man was suffering, just as he was. Without quite understanding what he was doing, he tucked Jesus and the cross under his arm and stalked out of the tent.

TWENTY-FIVE

"What is going on around here? I thought your crowd was supposed to be the quiet bunch."

Barnum Brown turned to see Pete Turnstall standing next to him. At least he thought it was Turnstall. He had given his lantern to the excited Digger Phelps, and subsequently couldn't see all that well, but the face of the man standing next to him did appear to be that of the round-cheeked photographer.

"Well, here's our picture taker. What are you doing here?" Brown asked.

Turnstall shrugged.

"I thought I would see if you wanted me to come around tomorrow and take some pictures. What's going on?"

"Oh, one of my men spotted that gunslinger up on the hill, or at least that's what he said. He went tearing off after him, followed by about half the population of Montana, including my men."

Turnstall sighed.

"They *would* catch him at night, when I can't get any pictures. I don't suppose they'd let me do some very long exposures."

"They are not a very patient bunch, as you remember from the last time you took someone's picture. Anyway, you're assuming they're going to catch him, and I'm not so sure. They couldn't catch him on flat land in the

179

daytime, so I doubt they'll collar him at night on the side of the hill."

Turnstall nodded at that, and the two men stood for a moment without speaking.

"Well, hello," Brown said suddenly. "Mr. Turnstall, isn't it? What brings you around tonight?"

Turnstall had crept up on him out of nowhere, but instead of returning his smile, he gave Brown an odd look.

"What do you mean?" Turnstall asked. "We just finished talking about that."

Turnstall must have been in his wagon too late, smelling all the chemicals. Either that, or he was beginning to take unwise portions of that other bottled chemical that was so popular around these parts.

"I don't recall that," Brown said.

"Well, it is dark," Turnstall said. "Maybe you were talking to me and didn't realize it was me."

"That must be it," Brown said, although he certainly didn't think so. He would not argue with a man in an altered state of consciousness.

"So, anyway, would you like me to come by tomorrow?"

"Yes, that would be nice. I think you can get some good shots of the skeleton still in the rock. We've exposed quite a bit of it, but now we're going to start dynamiting some of the bigger bits of rock away. It would probably be a good idea to get some pictures before that."

"That will be fine. What time do you get started? I'll need some good light. Maybe you can get started and I'll shoot while you're having lunch. Will that be all right?"

It was Turnstall's voice. He seemed to have zoomed up out of the night, right up to his face, asking questions. Brown blinked in surprise.

"Will what be all right?"

"What do you mean?"

What was wrong with him? He must have been cooped up in his wagon too long, smelling his chemicals. Or maybe he was partaking of that other bottled chemical, the one that seemed to be so popular out in these parts.

"I mean, hello, Mr. Turnstall, what do you mean running up here like that and asking me questions?"

The chubby-cheeked photographer seemed annoyed. "I didn't come running up here. We've been standing here talking."

"I think I would remember that," Brown said.

"Well, apparently you don't."

This was getting tiresome. Brown wanted to start early tomorrow, since he had missed today entirely, and now his crew was running around the mountain after a fugitive bank robber and he was stuck talking to a mad photographer.

"Damn it, man, what are these games you are playing?" Turnstall asked, a bit louder than Brown thought was absolutely necessary. "Everybody out here is insane. I should go back to taking pictures of mountains and rivers. At least they don't act crazy."

"Well, maybe you should."

"I will. But I will be here tomorrow. I'm going to take pictures of your damn dinosaur whether you like it or not."

With that, Turnstall stalked off into the night from whence he had just come. Brown shook his head as he looked in the direction Turnstall walked. He couldn't see him, could only hear the crunching of his footsteps and the occasional curse as Turnstall stumbled in the dark. He was obviously crazy, wandering around with no light. Brown had looked forward to getting some good field shots of his Tyrannosaurus, but now he wasn't so sure he wanted Turnstall to be the one to shoot them.

Art Kan watched the parade of lights on the hillside with sustained fury. Two small lenses hovered before his Earth eyes, converting the scene to almost normal daytime vision. There were large numbers of humans on the slope, running excitedly back and forth, all of them passing directly by the very skeleton he wanted. They appeared to pay little attention to it, leading him to believe they were after something else. This man Luther Gumpson who had once been in his custody, he supposed. Whenever there was a chase on out here, he seemed to be the focal point of it.

"How many men did Fredrik say were up there?"

"Thirty, at least," Hern said. "Maybe forty. They're moving around a lot, and more are coming all the time. So what shall we do?"

Kan exhaled noisily, and then remembered they were supposed to be quiet. The other crew members were dressed in Earth garb, but he and Hern were in their regulation silver work suits, so they were trying to stay out of sight. They had taken refuge behind a wagon that seemed to be empty, most likely because its occupant was even now traipsing about on the hillside, ruining his plans for the night.

"Earth Reclamation Unit 17 has gone up to monitor the situation, correct?"

"Yes."

"Good. Signal to him that we're going back for the rest of the night."

"What shall we do?" Hern asked again.

"Let's go back to the ship. I need to think of another avenue of approach. I think it's time for us to operate in the daylight. We have wasted too much time here."

"In the daylight?" Hern asked, surprised. "That is against the rules."

"Well, the rules were written by Swedes who don't bother to actually come here and see the working conditions. No wonder Alf Swenson had such a hell of a time, working with nothing but mechanical assistants. My new rule is that we will operate in the daytime. We will show the ship if we have to. They won't know what it is, anyway. We will kill anyone who gets in our way. Those are my new rules."

"Fine."

"In the meantime, is your memory device working?"

From where they were standing, they could see the man named Barnum Brown, although they couldn't hear him. He had been talking with another man, and then the man walked away angrily, and later tripped and fell. These creatures did not seem particularly well adapted to their own planet.

"I think it is," Hern said. "I've been activating it."

"Activate it again. Hard."

"Why, if I may ask?"

Kan gave Hern a ghastly grin. With his night-vision lenses dangling in front of his eyes, he looked otherworldly enough for two planets.

"Just out of spite."

Barnum Brown looked around. He had been standing near the dining tables, trying to eavesdrop on the discussion going on between S.L. Burgess and Digger Phelps. He had been hoping to discover whether Phelps was going to sing a different song about what he saw here in Montana thirty years ago. Now suddenly he was outside. Phelps was gone, as was Burgess, as was everybody else, for that matter. What was happening to him? Was he too tired? Was he sick? Was he just not paying attention?

"Where the hell did everyone go?" he asked himself, before he noticed all the lights moving on the hillside.

TWENTY-SIX

Earth Reclamation Unit 17's heart was beating faster than it should have been, given that the hill was not really all that steep and the climb not particularly arduous. He looked hurriedly through the swarm of light-bearing men who were walking—in some cases, staggering—along the narrow trails that crisscrossed the hillside. What had happened to his older self? Where was Digger Phelps?

Eric found him standing next to the partially exposed dinosaur skeleton, waving his arms around and directing the other men willy-nilly. He would send one further up the trail and another further down the trail, which resulted in a great deal of coming and going without any real results being accomplished. Earth Reclamation Unit 17 was proud of him; it was good work.

"Hello!" he said when he found Phelps. He wasn't sure what to call him. "Digger" sounded a little too informal, "Mr. Phelps" a little too formal, "Hey, you," too distant. He wasn't sure he should even be having these thoughts about a person who was essentially himself. Maybe the concerns over protocol were lingering vestiges of his human mind. Maybe he was turning back into his old self.

"I did what you said, sort of," Phelps said, panting from his exertions. "Only I did it backwards. Instead of getting everyone off the hill, I got them *on* the hill."

"I can see that," Eric said, standing aside as two men

184

of questionable sobriety stumbled past. "I wanted to tell you that it worked. I've just received notice that they have given up the plan for the night. They are going back to the ship."

He put a hand on the shoulder of his old self.

"You did good work."

Phelps' mottled face appeared to be blushing, although it was hard to tell by lamplight. It could just be the shadows constantly playing over his face from the passing lights.

"Thanks," he said. "That means a lot, coming from myself."

Eric sat down beside him, leaning his back against the rocks that held the bones of the dinosaur. The back of his head touched one of the creature's claws, or what looked like a claw; Eric was not trained in bone identification. Kan would be infuriated if he learned of that, but Eric decided he would risk it. He wasn't going to tell on himself.

"Take a load off," Phelps said happily as he did so.

Eric smiled, but then let it fade from his face.

"This is enough to get you through tonight," he said sternly. "Something else will happen tomorrow night. You need to be aware at all times. I don't know what he'll do next, but I'll try to get word to you."

"How will you do that?"

"I don't know. Just know that you must be on the lookout for anything that's even a little bit strange. Get ready to move."

"And do what?"

"I don't know that, either. You'll think of something. You did great tonight."

Phelps relaxed a bit, but he still looked worried. Eric started to tell him not to worry too much, but then he decided that would not be good advice. If anything, he should worry more.

"I can't stay long," Eric said. "Give me another memory before I go."

If he were one of the Swedes, it would be easy. He could simply touch the side of Phelps' head and all the memories inside could be his. Maybe not all—that would take a long time—but some of them. More of them. That worked for the Nes, too, which made Eric a little bit jealous. The Swedes had managed to breed that ability in the Nes. It seemed strange, to give such a gift to a race that was to become your worst enemy.

"What memory would you like?" Phelps asked. "There are quite a few I'd like to forget myself, but you probably wouldn't want any of those."

"I think you're right," Eric said. "I want a good one."

"How about your first real love?"

Eric sat up a little straighter, rubbing the back of his head against the dinosaur bone. Those beasts were treacherous even when they were long dead, it seemed.

"I would like that."

Phelps took a deep breath. Eric closed his eyes.

"Remember this: Kansas. A long time ago. You are seventeen years old, and skinny as a rail. You are working as a hired hand on old man Powell's ranch. All day long you see nothing but cows and weeds and an old horse that can barely get out of the barn, let alone carry you all over the place. Then one day you come to town and see a girl in a white dress, with a white hat on. You realize it's Sunday. You are cleaned up, or about as cleaned up as you usually get, and she smiles at you."

Eric could picture her. She had a thin face but sizable lips. He felt a smile beginning to crease his own lips.

"You come back the next week, clean as a whistle. You even scrubbed behind your ears. You talk to her this time. Her name is Sandra."

"Sandra," Eric said, without meaning to. "I remember."

"You see her every week. You go for walks. You lie at night under the Sunday night sky of Kansas. You kiss. You kiss more, you kiss a lot."

Eric remembered what came next. He felt a strange

stirring in the crotch of his trousers as he remembered the night when Sandra seemed to want to get out of her dress, and he certainly wanted to get out of his clothes, even though he had painstakingly washed them. That was a glorious night.

"Just remember that part," Phelps said, almost as a warning, but then other images crossed Eric's mind. He remembered seeing Sandra talking with another boy one day when he came to town unexpectedly. Just talking, maybe, or maybe more than that. He remembered lots of brown liquor flowing down his throat, some of it splashing on his face. He remembered taking a fist to her face the next time he saw her. He didn't see her anymore after that. He searched for her months later and she was gone, as if she had never existed.

Eric felt the stirring in his pants stop, felt the smile fall from his lips.

"I'm sorry," Phelps said. Eric opened his eyes to see his older self watching him. "You remembered too far, didn't you?"

Eric nodded, and Phelps dipped his head in shame.

"Don't," Eric said, putting a hand atop his own fatter, older hands. "I want to know everything, good and bad."

"That's the problem with me, I guess," Phelps said. "Or, rather, the problem with us. It's all mixed in together."

Eric felt sad, and he didn't want to go back to the ship sad.

"One more. Something easy this time, not so complicated."

Phelps leaned his head back and thought for a moment.

"How about the first time you ever rode a horse?"

The memory of that came flooding back with no prompting at all, so quickly that Eric felt his head digging back into the dinosaur claw. He was seven. His father stood by and watched while he nervously trotted the horse about in the packed earth of the front yard. The horse was so big he felt like he was towering above the world.

He was nearly in the clouds. When he felt comfortable he headed the horse into the open field. Sensing it had a weak master, the horse began charging across the ground, going faster and faster. He began to cry with fear, and felt the tears flowing toward his ears from the speed. He heard his father's excited shouts, faint with distance. But he didn't fall off. After a few minutes, he quit crying. The horse ran as fast as it could and he came to enjoy the ride. He even sat up in the saddle a little and issued a feeble whoop. He liked the speed. Eventually the horse tired of running and walked back to the house. He patted it on the neck and dismounted into his father's proud arms.

"I remember," Eric said. "That was a good one. I think I will leave on that one."

He stood up and dusted off his rump.

"Be careful up here, in case you do meet that Gumpson."

"I will," Phelps said, rising himself.

"Save up some memories for me. Next time we meet, I want to talk for a long time."

Phelps extended a hand, and Eric shook hands with himself.

"I look forward to that," Phelps said.

Eric joined a small parade of men who were heading back down the hill. No one paid him any attention at all.

TWENTY-SEVEN

Lasse took tentative steps into the clearing where the ship was grounded. As soon as he had left the preacher's tent, he was walking down the road when he saw a group of tall men coming toward him, heading for the hillside. He had ducked behind a wagon and watched them pass. They wore hats, but he recognized Fredrik, Mikael and Earth Reclamation Unit 17. They didn't appear to see him. It was rare for them to operate so openly, so they had to be undertaking a major operation. He paused by the side of the wagon for a long time, until he was reasonably sure the road was empty.

Later he thought he spotted some silver glints off in the night. They reminded him of the mission suits worn by the Swede crew, including, until recently, himself. He broke into a sweat. A group of drunken men fresh from the hillside were stumbling down the road with him, so he took pains to insinuate himself into the middle of their pack, which had the unfortunate side effect of forcing him to drink a couple of mouthfuls of their rancid whiskey.

Then it occurred to him. It was entirely possible that the whole crew was off the ship. They had all been working off of it when they were collecting bones, so they might be out of it now. If they were out, he could go in. Unless Kan had gone to the trouble to reprogram it, the computer would still recognize him as a member of the crew. He

189

could find Bjorn's bones, take over the ship, get the bones of the messenger of Mother Naga, and leave. Many more trips would be required to get all the bones for Mother Naga, but that would be something for the Nes council to take up. He could convince them that this was the homeworld after all, and they could put all their resources into one gigantic return mission.

He took a roundabout path getting back to the ship, one that kept him on the road part of the time and off the road part of the time. He was equally skittish about encountering either Swedes or humans: the Swedes because they would kill him instantly, the humans because they would kill him slowly with their foul drinks. He was already dying, or at least part of him was. The wound that Luther Gumpson had opened in his side was starting to itch, which reminded him he was wearing a very mortal outer shell.

Finally he gained the relative shelter of the trees that ringed where the spaceship was hidden. He climbed one thick branch and watched for what seemed like forever, but must have been only a few minutes. There was no movement anywhere around the entrance. There would be no way to tell whether the ship was empty or not until he got down there, and then it would be too late. On the other hand, he was dressed roughly the same as the Swedes he had seen on the road. He reached over his shoulder and grabbed the hat that dangled there on a leather cord. He could put on the hat and no one in the ship could tell if it was him or Mikael, or Hern, or Fredrik or anyone returning. He would likely not get a chance like this again. He decided to take it.

He fished around under his shirt for the button that would open the door. It was sewn into the lining of his Earth clothes, and to the untrained eye looked like nothing more than a regular button. For him, it would be either the key to victory or the key to a quick and painful death. He took a breath and pushed it. The transport tube opened like it always did, giving no sign of any danger that might lurk below. He crawled into the space before it was all the way open and pushed the down button. He exhaled. Just as he did, he felt something slam into the space with him. It shoved him into the far wall of the transport tube.

"Who is—" he started to say, and then he heard a familiar voice.

"Hello again," Luther Gumpson said. "Bet you thought you'd gotten rid of me."

Lasse turned to face his former captive. Gumpson smiled and made no further effort at physical violence.

"What are you doing here?" Lasse said. "I thought you would be long gone by now."

"I would have been, only I have some obstacles in my way. For one, I don't have my gun and I didn't manage to catch anybody out here alone tonight so I could take theirs. Two, I don't have a horse. Now, I could probably have stolen one, but a horse doesn't do me much good without a gun. It just adds horse thievery to the list of my positive qualities."

Gumpson carried with him a strong acidic smell. Probably from urinating in his pants the night before. Lasse couldn't very well hold that against him, since it was technically Mother Naga's fault, but it was not a pleasing scent.

"So I guess you got away from the men who were chasing you," Lasse said.

"Looks that way, don't it? I'm kind of surprised I did. I had to come down the far side of the hill, without any light or anything. I thought those men would be all over me but they didn't seem to come down that way. You threw them off the trail, didn't you?"

"Me?" Lasse asked.

He remembered his instructions to Gumpson's pursuers. He had told them where Gumpson went, that he was unarmed. If they didn't pursue him down, it was only because they were bad trackers or they were afraid to climb down the hill in the dark. He felt a tiny, quick flash of shame about lying to Gumpson, but now was probably not the time to confess.

"You. You threw them off the trail, didn't you?"

Lasse nodded.

"Thanks," Gumpson said. "You saved my life. I'm sorry I conked you on the head back there."

"I'll live."

"I guess so, but I shouldn't have done it. Anyway, things have worked out all right now."

"But why are you *here*? Here, in this ship? You remember what they did to you."

"I certainly do. Like I said, I came down the far side of the hill. I couldn't see where I was going. I didn't mean to come this way, but then again I really didn't have much of a plan at all. I found myself in the trees, and then I heard somebody sneaking around. I heard you step on something and make some whistling sound, so I figured it was you. Then I got to thinking. I don't have a gun or a horse, but maybe I can get a spaceship. If you were going to get back in here, I figured it was okay for me to come back, too. They've got it in for you worse than they do for me."

"You want to take the ship?"

"You got a better way to get me to California?"

He didn't, at that. The transport tube opened up and they were inside. The two men hunched in expectation, but the ship seemed silent. Gumpson took a tentative step forward, but Lasse stopped him.

"Let me go first. I want to see if the alarm system is on. I don't know if it will detect you, or not."

He took a couple of steps and waited, but nothing seemed to happen. He signaled Gumpson to follow. They walked down the short hallway that led to the main room. They approached the center of the ship as if it were filled with rattlesnakes, but there was no movement. Everyone was off the ship.

"First things first," Lasse said. "Come with me."

He thought it best not to leave Gumpson alone on the ship. He led him through the main room and into another hallway, one that led to Hern's office. The rooms lit up automatically as they entered, which caused Gumpson to twitch every time.

"They're supposed to do that," Lasse said.

"It's just strange," Gumpson said.

Hern's office was in typically spartan Swede style, with all its instruments and tables recessed into the white walls until they were needed. The middle of the room was given to a small storage board, which looked like a glass wall studded with tiny pictures.

"What are these things?" Gumpson said, squinting close at one of the pictures.

Lasse didn't look at them, but knew from experience that Gumpson was looking at tiny human bodies, seemingly frozen in the glass.

"Replacement bodies," Lasse said. He was looking for something else, something even smaller.

"*Bodies?*" Gumpson said. "They're so small."

Lasse pulled out his Multi-Purpose Tool when he found what he wanted. Gumpson quit staring at the tiny figures and walked over to watch him.

"What is this glass wall?"

"Storage."

Lasse took the tool, made the adjustments and pointed it at a tiny figure. This figure, unlike the others on the wall, was green.

"That's him, isn't it?" Gumpson said.

Lasse nodded. The figure glowed for a second and then disappeared from the wall. Lasse aimed the Multi-Purpose Tool at the floor and the green figure appeared there, tiny and motionless as a doll. Lasse knelt over him. Hern must have removed his human body. This was Bjorn as he remembered him, but now he looked puny and pitiful.

"What are you going to do with him?"

"Get him out of here."

Lasse took a handkerchief out of his pocket and gently wrapped the tiny Bjorn in it. He was limp and spineless as the handkerchief itself, and Lasse took care not to actually touch him, out of respect. He paused for a second with the wrapped Bjorn in his hand, and then stuck him in his pocket.

"Let's go," he said, his voice thick.

He was almost out the door when he remembered something, nearly bumping into Gumpson as he went back for it.

"What are you getting now?" Gumpson asked.

"Nothing. Come on."

Gumpson meekly followed him back to the main room. He stood and stared up at its rounded dome ceiling, amazed at its height, and then walked over to a control board that jutted from the far wall, just underneath three monitor screens. Distracted with his own thoughts of Bjorn, Lasse didn't notice what he was doing. Before Lasse could stop him, Gumpson pushed a couple of buttons.

"Don't do that!" Lasse hissed.

"Sorry. What do these buttons do? There's nothing written on them at all."

"The Swedes don't need them. They know what everything does. It's wired into the memories of their physical bodies. Do you have instructions written on your gun?"

"I never looked," Gumpson said defensively. "Speaking of my gun, can I have it back?"

Lasse cursed himself for having mentioned it.

"Look, if I wanted to kill you, I could have done it already," Gumpson said. "I have a knife. That works just as well."

Lasse handed over the gun. Luther took it back gladly, like a child receiving candy. He scrutinized it closely and then stuck it in his empty holster.

"It doesn't have instructions on it," he said. "Just says where it was made."

"There you go," Lasse said.

Two of the monitors were blank. The one on the left showed a view outside the transport tube. Shadowy trees waved in the wind.

"What is that?" Gumpson asked.

"It's a view of outside."

"But it's dark outside. How can we see anything?"

Lasse was constantly being reminded how primitive these people were. Something as simple as night-vision cameras were apparently quite beyond them.

"It's set so that it can adjust for the darkness and show us how the scene would look if it were light outside."

Gumpson appeared to be impressed.

"It's also recording, which means it recorded our entrance. I need to fix that. That's the first thing Art Kan will check when they get back. We need to make it seem like we haven't been here at all."

While Gumpson stared, Lasse punched the buttons to rewind the recording. He took a segment from before they got to the transport tube and spliced it several times to cover the time they took in getting into the tube. The resulting record was a little notchy, but it would have to do. Anyone staring closely at it could easily see the forgery, but Lasse was betting they would give it a cursory look, see that all was well, and move on.

"Are we safe, then?"

"No, not really. The transport tube also has a record of its use, but I don't know how to access that. We'll just have to hope they don't look at that when they get back."

"Right. So can you fly this thing?"

Lasse looked at him.

"You think I would come back here if I couldn't?"

Gumpson shrugged.

"It's hard to tell with you people from other planets. If you can fly it, then do it. Let's go."

Lasse was just reaching for the controls when they heard a sound from the transport tube. The ship, Lasse knew, didn't make random sounds. It was the crew, coming back. They were trapped. Gumpson whipped out his pistol, but Lasse grabbed his arm.

"That won't help. Come here."

He dragged Gumpson over to a blue panel on the floor and shoved him onto it. Gumpson disappeared. Lasse followed him, stepping onto the panel. When he opened his eyes again, they were obviously in the hold, below the main deck. It was a cavernous room with virtually nothing in it but more storage walls. To Gumpson, it looked like they had stumbled into a glass plate factory. Gumpson walked to the closest storage wall and saw more tiny figures. These were all bones, nothing but bones.

"There are a lot of dead animals here," Gumpson said, and Lasse nodded. "You don't want any of them?"

Lasse stared at all of the bones with a sinking heart. So many bones, and he had come so close to getting them.

"Maybe later."

Gumpson cocked an ear to the ceiling, but there was no sound.

"You won't be able to hear them unless they come down here," Lasse said.

"So how will we know when they leave?"

That was a good question, one he was not prepared to answer. Instead, he motioned for Gumpson to follow him. They skirted the storage area on the only small path the room offered, and walked to the far side. It wouldn't protect them, but at least they'd have some warning if the Swedes were after them. On the far side, a small platform jutted out from the wall and ran about a dozen feet along its base, three Earth feet above the ground. Gumpson threw himself on one end of it with a grateful sigh. Lasse stretched out on the other end, being careful not to mash Bjorn, who slumbered the final sleep in his pocket.

"So now we wait, huh?" Gumpson asked.

"Now we wait. If they come down here, we can try to overpower them. If we go up there, they'll kill us."

There was a long silence, and then a question occurred to Lasse.

"Luther Gumpson, are you a follower of the deity named Jesus Christ?"

Gumpson laughed, and then remembered he should be quiet.

"I rob banks for a living."

"Oh. So?"

"Jesus Christ argued against robbing banks. Well, not directly, but I'm pretty sure he would be against it," Gumpson said.

"So you are not a follower of his."

"You could say that."

He waited a little while and mulled that over and then asked, "But wouldn't he forgive you?"

The only answer he got back was the sound of Luther Gumpson snoring.

TWENTY-EIGHT

Art Kan stomped into the main control room, hitting his head on the top of the doorframe as he did so. This always jarred his vision momentarily but he did not mind that. There was an odd acidic smell in the transport tube and in the hallway, but it seemed to lessen in the main control room so he did not worry about it. He had already assumed the ship would get smelly if they stayed on Earth too long.

He and the crew members had walked around the area for a while, observing what was going on without being seen. The ruckus on the hillside had interfered with his plans; he was not prepared to grapple with so many humans, especially ones who had succumbed to the influence of the cheap intoxicants they swilled in sizable quantities. They succeeded only in delaying his mission, not destroying it. Still, it was a bother. This planet was not supposed to take this long. It was not considered a hardship duty to come here, so consequently he had not been given a very large crew to get the job done. He didn't want to come back like Alf Swenson had, complaining about interference from the locals. He wanted to get what he was after and get out.

"Hern! Fredrik!"

The two crew members stood before him, their human spines held straight.

"Yes, sir."

"I think I have a plan. We just need to get those people away from that skeleton long enough to get it. Its location on a hillside will complicate matters somewhat, but I think that should not be a huge problem. I have decided that we should not show the ship, not yet."

"So how are we going to get rid of them?"

He really liked this part. Kan was pleased with himself for having thought of it.

"I think we should activate one of the simulations."

"A simulation?"

"Actually, two simulations might work better."

"Simulations of what, sir?" Hern asked, a worried look on his face.

This was the best part.

"Why, the very thing they are after, Hern. They want what they call a Tyrannosaurus rex. We'll give them a Tyrannosaurus rex. In fact, we'll give them two."

Hern and Fredrik gaped at each other.

"I'm really not sure we have enough power for that, sir. We may have to move the ship closer, or take one of the power generators out into the field."

"Let's do that," Kan said. "I don't want to move the ship until I have to."

"But moving the generator means we'll have to shut down power to a lot of the ship's systems. Our weapons, for instance."

Kan thought for a moment. The ship was buried, and the only real enemies on the planet, the Nes, were no threat. One was dead and safely in storage, the other was probably dead, too, shot by Luther Gumpson.

"It is a risk we will have to take. Get that generator mobile and ready, and select our finest simulations. I want them at full power. I want them able to kill."

Three Earth hours later, Kan walked from his quarters back into the main control room. He could barely get in. There, stretching before him, were two magnificent specimens of what the humans called Tyrannosaurus rex. They were each twenty feet long, and the tops of their heads nearly scraped the domed roof of the ship. They would have to duck their heads to get out as it was. At times like these, Art Kan was proud to be a Swede. Their technology was wonderful. Their simulations were the best, almost as real as the creatures they represented.

"How is it going, Hern?"

Hern was kneeling over a cube the size of a small boulder, looking worriedly at its controls.

"Are you sure one of these won't be sufficient?"

Kan, feeling expansive, clapped him on the shoulder.

"Hern, if one is good, two must be better. Is there a problem?"

"It's just the power requirements. Running two of these in any sort of realistic fashion takes a great deal of calculating machine work, especially in an environment where they have never been tested before."

"This is where they came from," Kan said. "It's more realistic than anywhere they have been tested."

"I realize that, but the landscape has changed. It's not as tropical, the inland sea is gone. There's no telling what impact the changed environment will have. These creatures are going to step out there expecting to smell salt air and walk on squishy ground, and they're not going to get either one. They may fall off a cliff."

"No they won't," Kan said. "You'll make sure of that."

"The energy required will be enormous," Hern said, a trace of irritation in his voice at the new responsibility Kan had just placed on him. "As it is, we're not going to be able to operate them for long. They better scare everyone off quickly."

Kan laughed.

"I don't think we'll have any problem with that. Where do you need the generator placed?"

"On a high place overlooking where you want the rexes to be. I need to cover as much ground as possible with the energy wave. Otherwise they may flicker on and off, and that would take away some of the realism."

"But they would still be scary."

"Oh, yes."

"And they will be deadly, yes?"

"Yes. If we can maintain a full-power beam at them, they will be able to run and eat and make as much noise as the real things did."

Kan looked up at the magnificent creature that stood before him. It was a sign of his ancestors' decadence, yes, but what a sign. Its head could nearly swallow him whole. Its legs looked capable of stomping the spaceship itself into dust, although he knew they couldn't. The only things that gave away the beast's artificial origin were its arms. His ancestors knew what they were doing, though, even with those. They were no fools.

"I think it's ready," Hern said.

"Good. Take Fredrik and Mikael and whoever else is free and go. Is Earth Reclamation Unit 17 back yet?"

"I don't think so."

"He is taking his time. I think he is enjoying this visit a little too much. By the way, Hern, when you got the generator ready, did you alter the settings for my private quarters?"

"No. Why?"

"It's awfully hot in there all of a sudden. I had to leave the door open. Can you check and see what's wrong before you leave?"

Hern walked over to the command console and punched the monitoring buttons.

"That's odd. It looks like someone altered it specifically, sir."

"Who in their right mind would do that?" Kan asked. Two crew members had already turned out to be lizards, now someone was trying to sweat him out of his human body.

"I certainly don't know, sir."

Hern punched more buttons, filling one of the monitors with a schematic of the inside of the ship.

"There's more. Apparently someone came down on the transport tube before we got back. He is identified as an intruder."

"What does that mean?"

"It means he isn't one of the crew."

"That is a useful distinction to make. Where is this person?"

"It looks like he went across this room, into my office, then down into the hold, sir."

"Any way to tell what this intruder is doing down there?"

"No. There is not much to do down there, at any rate."

"We'll leave our guest there for the moment. Run a complete diagnostic, now. I want to know everything that's happened here in the last day."

"Yes, sir."

The diagnostic was done almost immediately. The ship was powerful, for a cargo ship, and Kan was glad he had requested it. Because this mission was to a backwater, the powers that be were originally planning to stick him with little more than an underpowered garbage scow, where a diagnostic scan would have taken the rest of the night.

"What is the result?"

"Two things. Someone tampered with the outside camera to mask his entry—my guess, it's our visitor, who is even now in the hold. But there's more. Apparently the other outside camera picked something up that we didn't notice before. When Earth Reclamation Unit 17 took that human away, he did more than just guide him to the road."

"What do you mean?"

"Look at this."

He punched a button, and an image of Earth Reclamation Unit 17 talking with the raggedy-looking human appeared on the monitor.

They were once physical beings—like us—but over time have redeveloped themselves into beings of pure energy, sort of like clouds of gas. They are trying to position themselves among the other races in the universe as being one of the more advanced races, but they're having trouble. They are not well-liked. Their colonization has been pretty clumsy, and they are generally resented for the experiments they performed on virtually everything they came across. There is sort of a governing body of the more advanced civilizations—you'd call it a council or something—and they are appealing to it to be allowed to join the top people, the elite, the . . .

Cream of the crop?

Yes. Good phrase. To help their case, they are trying to downplay the experiments they performed. They are sweeping the universe now, going to their old haunts, trying to get rid of the evidence, you might say.

"That's enough," Kan said, and Hern stopped the images.

"Our Earth Reclamation Unit seems to have a rather bad attitude about his creators," Kan said.

"What shall we do about him?"

"I knew we shouldn't have brought him along," Kan said. "I told them, I told them. I said you should never bring an Earth Reclamation Unit back to Earth unless they have really been put through the wringer. I knew this was a mistake."

He smacked a fist into his palm, but then his mood brightened. Who cared what the reclamation unit told some doddering old human? It's not like the human could do anything about it. He himself, Art Kan, could walk out among the people, or even fly over them in the ship, and tell them all about it, and there was not a single thing they could *do* about it.

"We will deal with him when he returns," Kan said. "In the meantime, we should deal with our unannounced visitor. This creature is in the hold, you say?"

"Yes."

"I think you should seal off the hold and cut the oxygen until he is unconscious. No camera down there, you say?"

"No."

So this wasn't a top-of-the-line freighter after all. Then again, Swedes weren't used to having indigenous creatures invading the hold. That's usually where they tried to escape from.

"It would be nice to know what we are up against, but whatever it is, it needs oxygen if it's been walking around here. Seal it and cut off the oxygen. Let's see how long it takes our visitor to go to sleep."

"That could kill him, sir," Hern said.

Kan gave him an angry look. Hern was something of a scold. Don't hit your head on the ceiling, sir. It could kill him, sir.

"I simply felt an obligation to point that out."

"Obligation noted. Now do it. Mikael! Par! Get ready to go down into the hold and fetch up an unwelcome guest!"

TWENTY-NINE

Lasse felt his eyes growing heavy. He was tired, or at least his outer shell was, but inside his mind was racing. He shouldn't be getting sleepy. Groggily, he leaned up on his elbows. Art Kan knew they were here. He might as well give up. Lasse stood up and began stumbling to the blue transport patch, ready to throw himself into the waiting arms of his captors.

Then he realized why he was getting sleepy. They must be cutting off the oxygen. He wouldn't have to go up to the next level; they would obligingly come to him. Then they would obligingly kill him. He tottered over to the already sleeping Luther Gumpson and shook him violently.

"Wha—" Gumpson said, and then without further ado he produced his pistol and aimed it right at Lasse's chest.

"Stop!" Lasse said. "It's me! You've already shot me!"

Gumpson stared at Lasse through bleary eyes and then put the pistol away almost as fast as he had brought it out. He was pretty quick with that thing.

"What's going on? Where are we?"

"We're in the hold of the ship, remember?"

Gumpson blinked a couple of times and then was fully awake.

"Yes. What's going on?"

"I believe that the crew is coming down here. They know we're here. At least, they know you're here."

"What do you mean by that?"

205

Lasse's head began to hurt; it was getting hard to talk. He didn't have much time.

"I mean that the ship has a method of detecting when intruders are on board. It registers their presence, but it ignores the regular crew."

"I'm getting a headache," Gumpson said.

Lasse positioned his face directly in front of Gumpson's.

"Yes. There's something wrong with the air. They are pumping all the oxygen out of here. They're going to knock us out."

"But they think I'm alone down here. Is that what you were saying?"

"Yes."

"And call me crazy, but you would like for them to think that."

Lasse looked down at the floor, and then back at Gumpson.

"Yes. They don't really perceive you as a threat. They definitely perceive me as one. They'll kill me if they catch me, just as soon as they catch me. You know that."

Gumpson nodded.

"What do you want me to do?"

"Nothing. Just let them find you, they will anyway. But don't tell them I'm here. I'm going to hide."

He stared into Gumpson's eyes.

"Promise me."

"You didn't tell that mob on the cliff which way I was headed. I saw them running all over the place. You must have directed them to go every which way *but* the way I went. I owe you one. Go, hide, before it's too late."

Lasse was suddenly grateful that the mob was so disorganized. He wanted to confess the truth to Gumpson, but now didn't seem like the proper time.

"Thank you. Just close your eyes, don't look at where I'm going. That way you won't be tempted to look there to check on me when they come. The less you know, the better."

"That has always been my motto," Gumpson said.

His breathing was becoming rapid and shallow, and he squinted his forehead and closed his eyes against the pain caused by the lack of oxygen. Lasse dropped something into his front shirt pocket, and then took the chance to walk quickly to the other side of the storage walls. He was nearly gasping by the time he reached a storage bin that was dug into the wall on the other side. Its latch was faulty and had not been fixed, and consequently it was the only wall bin not filled with equipment. He had memorized its location for just such an emergency.

Lasse had barely installed himself in the space before he heard footsteps coming from the blue transport pad, heading for the far wall where Gumpson no doubt slumped, barely conscious.

"Hey, boys," he heard Gumpson slur.

"Get his gun," he heard a voice say. It sounded like Mikael. "He's good with that thing."

Lasse felt his grasp on consciousness fading. He hoped they turned the oxygen back on soon, or he would die here, curled up in a ball in the hold of an enemy ship, his equally dead brother-in-arms a tiny swaddled jewel in his pocket. Just before he blacked out, he said a prayer for his own safekeeping. As the darkness came to claim him, he realized that he hadn't addressed it to Mother Naga, but to a man whose face he had never seen.

THIRTY

Earth Reclamation Unit 17 was lost in his thoughts as he activated the transport tube and rode back down into the ship. He remembered riding his horse, but couldn't quite remember what happened to the horse, and that bothered him. He remembered his first love, and tried to keep his mind focused on the good times, not the bad ending. The bad ending bothered him. He thought about his memories of sunrises and sunsets. For years, after he was created, he had wondered what it would be like to be really alive, to be a full human being. Now he realized that he knew. To be alive was to be bothered by memories and to think back on sunrises and sunsets.

He walked down the hall and into the central control room, expecting to wander back to his chambers and shed his Earth clothes for his silver suit. Instead, he walked in the control room to find the entire crew assembled around the legs of two gigantic dinosaurs.

"Wow," he said, unable to help himself. "Those are huge."

He knew lots about the creature that Earth residents called the Tyrannosaurus rex, but had never seen the Swede simulations. They were magnificent. They took up all the space in the control room, filling it with their towering yellow and brown hides. Their heads seemed to hover far above the floor, and he could see their six-inch teeth jutting from their massive jaws. So engrossed was he in staring at the simulated beasts that he nearly tripped over the metal control cube clumped near their feet.

"Watch out," Hern said.

He and Fredrik were hunched over the box, poking at it and tinkering with its rows of buttons and knobs.

"Don't touch anything," Hern said, a little more harshly than Earth Reclamation Unit 17 thought was necessary.

"They're fantastic," Unit 17 said to Mikael and Par, who were standing atop two scaffolds that stood only as high as the creatures' haunches. They were examining the legs and backs of the beasts—all they could reach—verifying the quality of the simulations. He expected Mikael to give him a look of agreement, but instead he got only a cold glance from above. Everyone on the ship seemed to be cranky. The night's botched operation must have upset them more than he would have thought. Then it occurred to him that Art Kan wouldn't have gone to the trouble to conjure them if they weren't going to be used. He couldn't imagine what use they could be. Suddenly the magnificent monsters gave him a chill.

"What . . . what are you going to do with them?" he asked no one in particular.

"Don't trouble yourself with that question," Art Kan said.

Of the crew, only Kan ignored the beasts. He stood before one of the red chambers, staring at something there. Earth Reclamation Unit 17 walked up and saw the placid face of a grizzled man staring back at him.

"Luther Gumpson," he said. "How did you recapture him?"

"I didn't," Kan said. "He came back in here himself."

"He did?"

"He did. He apparently has killed Lasse, which is suitable to me, and stole his access button."

"But why did he come back?"

"Some might ask the same question of you, Earth

Reclamation Unit 17. That is what we will find out. Hern? Are you done over there?"

Hern straightened up from the metal box that controlled the simulations.

"Yes, I think so."

"Good. Please free up Mr. Gumpson's face so he can answer a few questions."

Eric stewed over Kan's comment while Hern pushed two buttons next to the red chamber. What did Kan mean, someone might ask the same of him? He had to come back, but Gumpson didn't. Gumpson's face didn't move once Hern had released it from the immobilizing beams. He didn't appear afraid, Eric thought. He looked annoyed.

"Welcome back, Mr. Gumpson," Art Kan said.

"Thank you. Your hospitality just made me want to return."

"No doubt it did. If we need to, Mr. Gumpson, we can open up your skull and insert devices that will force you to tell the truth to any question we may ask. It will not take long, but I would rather not have to do it. Why did you come back?"

"I was planning to steal this ship and get away."

Kan stared at Hern for a second, and then both started to laugh.

"You thought you could fly this ship? You seem to have a high estimation of your own intelligence," Kan said between basso chortles.

"You seem to do all right," Gumpson said, which wiped the smile right off Kan's face. "I figured it couldn't be all that hard."

"What happened to the man who helped you escape from here?" Kan asked angrily.

"I shot him," Gumpson replied flatly.

Eric was still amazed at how callous this man could be about shooting other creatures or his own kind. He said it like he was talking about squashing a fly.

"And stole his access button to get back inside the ship."

Gumpson nodded.

"It is hard to put anything over on you advanced civilizations," Gumpson said, which prompted a growl from Kan.

"Spare me your primitive outbursts," Kan said. "Tell me; did Lasse die slowly? Did he appear to be in pain?"

"Nobody I shoot dies slow," Gumpson said. "Slow deaths are what happens when somebody can't aim good. I can aim."

Kan appeared somewhat mollified by the answers Gumpson gave.

"I am grateful to you for killing him, although I am sorry it was not a slow process. To repay you, I will arrange for your own demise to be correspondingly swift. I would have liked to have kept you around, but you apparently are more trouble than I anticipated. It is regrettable."

"You're telling me."

Eric tried to formulate some reason for not killing Gumpson. As cold-blooded as the man appeared to be, he thought Kan shouldn't be allowed to just kill anyone he pleased. While he was trying to think up a compelling reason, Kan turned to face him.

"We have some other unfinished business," Kan said. "Earth Reclamation Unit 17, you know I argued against bringing you along on this trip. I now see my arguments were justified."

"What do you mean?" Eric said, jolted from his thoughts.

"You apparently are not aware of where all our surface cameras are located. You had a discussion with an Earth resident while sitting on a rock that was just to the left of one."

Eric felt his face growing hot. Beads of sweat formed on his forehead. The Swede Earth bodies would only sweat under extreme circumstances, because they found the secretion of fluids distasteful; Eric didn't have that luxury. His body was an almost exact copy, and he was feeling the heat right now.

"I can explain that."

"I wish you would."

Having said that, he wasn't sure how to proceed. He could say the man was his original, but that could lead Hern to want to drag Digger Phelps inside the ship to perform side-by-side tests. On the other hand, without that link it just made him appear to be a traitor.

"I—I just got carried away," Eric said. "It was the first time I had really talked to an Earth resident for very long. I forgot what I was saying."

Digger would thank him, if he ever got the chance, but Eric wasn't sure he would get the chance.

"How charming," Kan said. "That was totally against your orders and your better judgment. You may be a replica of a resident of this planet, Earth Reclamation Unit 17, but you belong to us, body and soul."

"Yes, sir."

"I believe you will not object to being put out of commission until we are safely off this planet. Will you?"

"No, sir."

"Good. I'm glad all of this business is settled. It will be morning soon. Hern, are you ready to go?"

"Yes, sir."

"Good. The replicas look fine. Get that power supply where you need it and get ready to bring our replicas to life. We will have a morning surprise for the humans that they will never forget."

Eric felt sweat break out on his forehead again, only this time it felt cold.

THIRTY-ONE

He couldn't tell what color the big dinosaurs were. Everything looked orange with those damn red lights shining in his eyes. The hulking leader of the otherworldly band was talking to the crew members who had departed, taking with them the large cube that they had been fiddling with. The cube, as far as he could tell, was orange, too. They had shrunk it down with one of their little gizmos before they left.

Luther Gumpson's eyes returned to the dinosaurs. He wasn't sure what they were called, but they looked like the living, if not breathing, reincarnations of the skeleton that Lasse had been so insistent on digging from the hillside. He had never thought much about dinosaurs before. They were supposed to have lived a long time ago, and he did not have time in his life to worry about creatures that were long dead. The only problem now was that they didn't seem dead at all. They were towering right in front of him, their bodies nearly horizontal to the ground. The stripes on their sides, combined with the red light he was forced to view them through, made them look like outsized tigers on the prowl. They didn't seem to be breathing, and they weren't moving at all, but they looked real, all right. They had massive tails that loomed above the spaceship's floor like the limbs of a mighty live oak tree. Their legs looked like trees, too, come to think of it, their three-toed feet forming the roots. Their heads were equally massive, like steamer trunks stuffed with butcher knives.

The only things that seemed out of place on their ponderous bodies were their front arms. Compared to the rest of the beasts, they were absolutely puny. They had muscles—he could see the bulges even from his distant perspective—but they ended only in two tiny claws, not the massive sabers he would have expected. The claws were hooked but it didn't look like they could hold much. As far as he could tell, the little arms couldn't even reach the cavernous mouths above. The dinosaurs were formidable, no doubt about that, but it was the head you had to worry about, not the claws.

The spaceman named Art Kan stood before a picture on the wall. It seemed to show an image of what was happening outside. There was no question, these fellows had some fancy equipment. He had never even heard of anything that could do that. Then again, he was currently imprisoned in a ship that could fly through space, so he supposed he shouldn't be too surprised by much of anything. The picture on the wall glowed orange, so it must be morning, or maybe it was just orange from the lights shining in his eyes. He had passed some of the strangest nights he could remember in the last few days.

"Are you ready?" Kan asked, to no one that Gumpson could see.

"Yes," a voice from nowhere came back. "We are set up on the closest ridge to the ship. It should be sufficient."

The voice sounded like that of the one they called Hern. So Kan and Hern could speak to each other, even thought Hern was far away, and neither one had to shout or even raise his voice. Gumpson was simply not surprised.

"Can you tell if anyone is present on the ridge where the dinosaur skeleton is located?"

"They aren't on the ridge. They seem to be still in camp."

"Even better. Make sure to put the dinosaurs between them and the ridge. I don't want them running that way."

So Hern could see far away, too. Gumpson remained unsurprised. If Hern next announced that he was going to flap his arms and fly around and check things out, he wouldn't do so much as raise an eyebrow.

"It sounds like now would be a good time," Kan said.

"It's your call," Hern said back.

"Fine. Give me two Earth minutes to open the door."

Gumpson blinked. Open the door! They were going to put those beasts outside! There was a rumble and suddenly the whole front of the ship seemed to disappear. It must not be down very deep, because in short order there was a gaping hole to the left of where Kan was standing. Daylight poured in, shining on the motionless predators who already looked like they were lunging toward it. There was a ramp that led up and out, ending on the surface, about forty feet over Kan's head. Gumpson saw that the ship was indeed barely buried. It seemed to be wearing only a light covering of dirt over its outer shell. Now that he could see the edge of it, it seemed a lot bigger than he would have guessed. Couldn't fly through space in a canoe, he supposed.

"It's almost ready," Kan said.

Gumpson suddenly had a plan. He wished it had come to his head sooner, but that couldn't be helped. Fortunately, Hern had left his head unfrozen, although it was still hard to move. He looked to his left, to see the brown-headed man standing there. He was the one that Kan had called Earth Something Unit 17. The guy was in trouble, obviously. He might help.

"Buddy," Gumpson said. "Hey, buddy. Unit 17."

The brown-headed man turned to look at him. Kan and the remaining blonde-headed spaceman were standing on the other side of the dinosaurs, near the pictures on the wall, and didn't seem to hear him.

"Push those buttons," Gumpson said, cutting his eyes rapidly to the left.

The man stared at him.

"Let me out of here. Now. We can escape."

The man didn't seem to know whether to frown or to smile.

"Push those buttons!" Gumpson said, as loud as he dared. "They're going to kill you and me anyway! Let's get out of here!"

He seemed to be considering it, but there wasn't much time. Another minute and the critters would be gone and the door would be shut. The brown-haired man seemed to understand that. He looked over at Kan and the other blonde-haired man to make sure they weren't paying attention, and then with agonizing slowness he reached over to the wall next to Gumpson's head.

"Now!" Kan said.

"Now!" Gumpson said, feeling his limbs falling back under his control.

He lunged out of the hole in the wall and shoved the brown-haired man violently along as he ran for the dinosaurs. The creatures stood blinking in the sunlight, twitching their tails, seemingly uncertain of what to do next.

"What are we doing?" the brown-haired man shouted as he ran alongside Gumpson.

"You can ride a horse, can't ya?" Gumpson shouted back.

"Yes!"

"Then ride that one! He can't reach you with those little claws. Get behind his head and hold on!"

The man flung himself up the scaffolding before the monster could turn its neck to see him. It was still blinking at the sunlight, although it had opened its mouth and its tail was whipping through the air. Gumpson had left himself the harder job; he had to run behind the first dinosaur to get to the scaffolding that led up the side of the second one. This also took him close to Kan and the other blonde-haired alien, who had just seemed to notice that the two resident non-aliens were attempting to fly the coop. The one whose name he didn't know had produced the silver thing that Lasse had called a Multi-Purpose Tool. It was well named, Gumpson decided. That was their answer to everything. As he ran, he felt around his waist, but his familiar gun belt was not present. These weren't even his clothes, he realized. They must have cleaned him up and dressed him in the clothes they used to impersonate good old human beings.

Gumpson glanced left. The brown-haired man had made it up the scaffolding and was climbing up the monster's back. The other dinosaur had turned its face away from the open spaceship door and was staring at this moving figure on its neighbor's back. Time to take its mind off possible lunch. Gumpson put on a burst of speed and snatched the Multi-Purpose Tool out of the blonde-haired man's hand. He had been trying to watch the dinosaurs and the escapees at the same time, and had hesitated just a second too long.

"Give that back!" the man shouted.

Gumpson hit a button at random and saw a green flash, but nothing seemed to happen. Maybe it didn't work on them. He jammed the thing in his belt and kept running, hunching over to avoid the tails swishing above him. If they suddenly decided to slam one into the floor, he was going to be a very flat man. Gumpson tried to climb the scaffolding, but the blonde-haired man was right behind him and had a grip on his ankles. The dinosaurs were getting restless now. They turned their heads, they shifted their weight from foot to foot. The one he was climbing on ignored the brown-haired man to concentrate on the creatures clambering onto its own back. With a deafening roar, it shifted all its weight to its left leg, sending its haunch crashing into its neighbor's leg. The beasts made contact right where the blonde-haired man was hanging; with a screech, he let go of Gumpson's ankles.

Gumpson could have sworn he heard the crunching of bones, but he didn't look back to see how the man was doing. He scrambled up the monster's back. He needed to get in place before this prehistoric horsie got moving. His boots slipped on the monster's scales, but he found enough handholds to allow him to move with surprising speed. The monster was hunched over, for one thing, which made it easier, and the scaly skin was studded with irregular bumps that were just big enough to grip with a fist. He got to the beast's neck just before it started moving, with steps that caused the whole ship to vibrate. If he dug his rump into the shoulder bones, he found he could stay on. He had been right about the claws he glimpsed flailing below—they couldn't reach him. The massive head of the dinosaur rose before him on its curved neck, which made it hard to see ahead, but that wasn't his department any more. He was just along for the ride.

"Get off of there!" he heard Kan shout from behind.

A sudden green beam flashed through the air, but just then the dinosaur shifted to the right. The beam struck the beast on the left side of its neck, causing it to bellow in either pain or confusion. With another shattering roar, it stepped out onto the ramp, its companion at its side. Gumpson felt the air rushing at him as the monsters crashed up the ramp and into a Montana quite different from the one they once knew.

"Hang on!" he shouted to the brown-haired man. "It's going to be a bumpy ride!"

Barnum Brown sipped at his second tin mug of hot coffee. It was brackish and thick, but it was hot, and it would do the trick. He adjusted his shirt at a point where it wasn't quite tucked all the way into his belt. He tied his pick to his belt. He wet his fingers and ran them along his eyebrows. He heard some shouting, and looked up to see something he had not expected—live dinosaurs, running right at the camp.

Brown dropped his coffee and ran past the tables and the fire to get a better look.

"Look at that!" the kid named Harryhausen shouted. There were lots of coffee mugs and breakfasts on the ground. "Those are dinosaurs!"

They did indeed look like the creatures Brown devoted his life to digging out of the ground. They were huge. They were yellow and brown, which Brown didn't quite expect. They had huge heads and huge legs and whipping tails. They looked like he might expect Tyrannosaurus rex to look.

"They're heading right for us!" S.L. Burgess shouted.

"Run for the ridge!" Brown shouted, but even as he did so he saw it was too late.

With a roar, the beasts were upon them. The tethered horses whinnied and stomped the ground in terror, and most managed through brute force to free themselves. The dinosaurs ignored the fleeing horses and ran between the camp and the base of the hill, effectively cutting off that means of escape for Brown's men. There wasn't much else for them to do but run west across the flatlands, ducking behind rock outcroppings or hiding beneath the wagons.

"Go!" Brown shouted. "Everybody run!"

The crew wasted little time in obeying his advice, but Brown himself stood close to the fire, jumping back and forth from one leg to the other. One part of him wanted to run. Another part—the part that was so far winning out—wanted to have a look at these creatures. They were moving fast, and were stomping back and forth between the two smaller ridges that paralleled the main hillside, so he lost sight of them for seconds at a time. What he did see delighted him. They were colored more brightly than he would have imagined. He had always had it in his head that the dinosaurs would be dull-colored, like rhinos or hippopotami or elephants. These creatures looked more like reptilian peacocks, their sides glowing like flowers under the bright Montana sky.

They didn't walk like he had expected, either. He would have assumed they would drag their tails along the ground, using them to balance their massive heads. These did seem to use their tails for balance, but they did so by holding them in the air, not dragging them. This allowed them to walk very fast, which was not a surprise. He would have expected that from such a gigantic predator. Even compared to his imagination, these creatures could get up some speed. They had crossed the flatlands faster than he could ever have imagined.

It was when one of the brown-and-yellow dragons began heading directly toward him that Brown realized he was standing in the open, practically begging to be made lunch. There wasn't time to cut to the left and head up the hill, so he sprinted for the nearest black wagon and dove inside, headfirst. He hoisted himself up on his forearms. The wagon had only one resident, a man whose face was losing a battle with his beard. Brown couldn't see much of him, but the volcanic snores emanating from somewhere in the man's bushy jaw indicated that it would take more than marauding dinosaurs to wake him up.

As he sat up, Brown realized he had seen something else outside that he hadn't expected to see this morning, aside from the dinosaurs themselves. He realized that the dinosaurs had men riding on their backs. He felt the ground shaking outside as the beast that had been pursuing him stomped by. Against his better judgment, Brown stuck his head out of the wagon. The creature was now after S.L. Burgess, who was sprinting for a rock outcropping. It didn't look like he was going to make it.

"What is going on?" Brown asked himself.

He began frantically whipping covers off his unwitting host, which didn't even affect the rhythm of his snores.

At last he saw what he was after—the man's gun, tucked in his holster. Brown grabbed the man's pistol by its butt and began to pull it from the holster. That woke him up.

"Hey!" the man shouted, clamping Brown's wrist in a firm grip.

Brown did not fancy himself a violent man. He prided himself on his calm demeanor. Whatever frustrations he built up usually couldn't survive a day of pounding picks. At this moment, it seemed that a little violence, judiciously applied, might come in handy. He kicked the man in the head, returning him to a deep sleep, and grabbed the pistol.

By the time he jumped from the wagon, he saw that Burgess was only one quick lunge away from experiencing a death that no other human being had ever faced.

"Dinosaur!" Brown shouted.

He held the gun overhead and fired off a couple of quick shots. He could have fired straight at the beast, but it was moving so fast he doubted he could have hit it despite its size. He fired two more shots. It seemed to work. The dinosaur slowed and turned to see the source of such a sharp sound. Burgess, seeing his chance, put on a burst of speed and disappeared behind the pile of rocks. Brown sighed in relief. The other beast was out of sight, as were his crew, but at least this one had been stopped from eating his top man. The downside was that it was now headed straight for him again. The dinosaur spun quickly around, so fast that the man on its back lost his grip and fell off its back. The Tyrannosaur batted the falling man with its tail, but otherwise ignored him and made a beeline for Brown.

Now that he had come face to face with a real, live, stomping dinosaur, should he shoot it? Did he only like his dinosaurs dead? Brown realized his dilemma was unjustified. When he frantically checked the pistol, he saw the cheap man inside the wagon had only loaded it with four bullets, and he had already shot them all.

❖   ❖   ❖

Earth Reclamation Unit 17 couldn't say how long he had been on the dinosaur's back. It seemed like forever. Everything went by in a rush. He had barely managed to process the fact that Art Kan was going to incarcerate him when suddenly he found himself setting Luther Gumpson free, and then, most interesting of all, riding on the back of one of the most advanced predators that had existed on any planet. He knew it was fake, a beam-projected replica devised by a calculating machine aboard the ship, but when it was roaring and crashing around beneath him, he believed. He knew that Hern was off somewhere overseeing this rampage, but he also knew that the fact he and Gumpson were on the beasts' backs wouldn't change anything. If they happened to find themselves getting crunched between those massive jaws, that was unfortunate. Actually, given the disposition of Kan aboard the ship, it would probably even be desirable.

Fear had seized his heart when the creatures approached the camp, but the humans there reacted as if they faced such challenges every day. They ran, they ran fast, and they ran in different directions. It was enough to confuse the beasts, especially since Hern seemed to be steering them to keep the camp residents away from the hillside. That slowed them down and enabled most everyone to escape. Escape, that is, until the dinosaur he was riding very nearly took a bite out of one of the fleeing scientists. Eric had looked for Digger Phelps, but hadn't been able to pick him out. The person his dinosaur seemed intent on eating was obviously not Digger. He moved too fast, for one thing.

Just when the beast was preparing to bite off the fleeing man's head, a loud noise sounded behind them. The dinosaur stopped and then whirled around, dislodging Eric's hands from its scaly back. The loud noise had come from the man named Barnum Brown, who was a good distance away, holding a pistol. Eric scrambled to stay on board, but when the creature lunged forward, he felt himself slipping back. Just as he lost contact with the monster's hide, its tail caught him hard in the side of the head. He didn't see anything else after that.

The world seemed to be blue when he again opened his eyes. He blinked a couple of times, and realized he was looking at a pair of battered blue trousers. A groan escaped his lips, and he heard Digger's voice.

"Don't get up," Phelps said. "You took a nasty fall."

Eric ran an exploratory hand over his face. His fingers came back bloody, but they discovered no apparent loose teeth or missing parts.

"What happened?" he asked slowly.

"Oh, you missed all the fun," Digger said with a laugh that jiggled his knees and caused sharp bolts of pain to shoot through Eric's skull.

"Is Barnum Brown all right?"

"He's all right."

"Where are the dinosaurs?"

"They're gone. Just rest."

Eric felt a persistent pain behind his left eye. He switched on his camera and tried to zoom in on a small cloud that lounged on the horizon. Nothing happened. He attempted just to take a single image of the small cloud. Nothing happened. The cloud looked very faintly like the ship that he had traveled to this planet in, but he could not take an image of it. His equipment, it seemed, was ruined. He was just a human being, that and nothing more.

"Do you feel all right?" Phelps asked.

"More or less," Eric said, then he corrected himself. "Less, actually."

They sat that way in silence for a long time, Phelps stroking Eric's hair.

"The leader of the Swedes heard me talking to you," Eric said at last. "I don't think I'll be welcomed back on the ship."

"You're welcome here," Phelps said. "You belong with us. You're one of us."

Eric finally gathered the strength to sit up. Over Phelps' protests, he sat up to see how the world looked from that vantage point.

"Welcome home," Phelps said when Eric was finally upright.

"Thanks," Eric said with a weak smile.

He actually didn't feel that bad, even with the shattered hardware in his head. He tried to operate the camera again, but found that it would not work at all. He could turn it on, but nothing happened, so it might as well not be on. With a sigh, he switched it off.

"What were they going to do to you?" Phelps asked.

"I don't know. I don't think I want to know."

Kan may have been merciful once, but he certainly wouldn't be now. Eric had betrayed him twice, and that was not the sort of thing Art Kan took lightly.

"Look at your new home," Phelps said, indicating with a sweep of his arm the flatlands of Montana. They were hunched under a rocky overhang, facing away from the hillside and the camp. There was nothing in front of them except for a few scattered wagons. The sun was high overhead and merciless, efficiently draining away the day's color. Right now, his new home didn't look like much.

"Can I ask you something?" Phelps said.

"Of course."

"When I was put into that little red room and copied to make you—why? I mean, why me? I'm not exactly the best specimen he could have run across."

Eric looked at Phelps. He thought about lying, but decided to be honest. If he couldn't be honest with himself, what was the universe coming to?

"The Swede who was here before was a scientist. Swedes are always interested in perfecting the bodies they use for exploration. Swenson must have detected the flaw in your body. When he discovered it, he decided to put you in the red chamber and make a copy of you for further study."

"The flaw in my body? What flaw would that be?"

"Apparently there is something wrong with your liver. It was in its early stages then. I wonder what its condition is now."

Phelps looked ashen.

"How is your health, Digger? Really, how is it?"

Phelps met his eyes.

"Not so good. My stomach bothers me. Sometimes I can't keep food down. Sometimes I—bleed. But you . . . is your liver bad?"

Eric shook his head.

"Part of the reason Alf Swenson made a copy of you was to see how to fix the problems. When they made me, my liver was bad. Then he fixed it."

"So you're in perfect health."

Eric felt his forehead with his left hand. There was a cut across it, but Phelps had clumsily cleaned it.

"Well, not at the moment."

Phelps gave a quick laugh, but his face couldn't hold a smile.

"But you're me, thirty years ago. Except you're in even better shape than I was back then."

Eric nodded.

"Even if I die, you are my life. You are me."

He couldn't go back. He knew that. What Phelps said was true. He was home again. Phelps extended his arms. Dark pools of sweat were suspended below them. The skin under his jaw was loose and shaking, and dotted with an uneven covering of stubble. His eyes were bloodshot, his teeth chipped and yellow. Eric leaned in and gave himself a hug.

THIRTY-TWO

William the Conqueror was getting used to hearing lots of shouting, which was usually followed by lots of looking for Luther Gumpson, which was usually followed by a lot of sitting around and griping. This early in the morning, he was willing to ignore a good bit of carrying-on, especially when he was still having such a nice rest. He wasn't one to rise with first light; he liked for the sun to warm him up a while first.

Then it occurred to him. These were not shouts of excitement. These were shouts of fear. High-pitched shouts of fear followed by rumbling roars of rage. With a start, William Kinney whipped his head from under his blanket and sat up. His friends were gone. He looked behind him to see dozens of running men. When he swiveled to the left, he saw what was inspiring them to run so lustily. It was a dragon. Two dragons, actually, two huge streaking monsters crashing across the ground, kicking up enough dust for a wagon train. He must have read all the wrong books as a child, because he remembered reading that dragons didn't really exist, but here was abundant proof to the contrary.

To make things worse, he noticed that a man was riding on the back of one of the dragons. The man had a face that seemed very familiar. It was a face he had studied, it was a face he had seen in his dreams. It was a face that was worth money, and it was up there riding on the

226

back of a dragon. From what he had heard, that was typical Luther Gumpson style. No subtlety at all.

The other dragon, the one that didn't have a human rider, made a run for a man who was standing out in the open by himself. Kinney didn't really want to see a man get eaten alive so early in the morning, but he found himself unable to look away from the gruesome spectacle. Luther Gumpson's monster, too, was headed for the man, so it looked like a fight over lunch was about to be under way. Then there was some kind of green flash and the riderless monster veered away and bellowed in what sounded like pain. Not only was Luther Gumpson riding one beast, he seemed able to control the other. This was intolerable to William Kinney. This gave Gumpson too much advantage.

Cursing his fearful pals, Kinney climbed to the top of a nearby rock pile to watch Gumpson in action. The bank robber wasn't really controlling the creature, he saw. It was more of a case of just being able to hang on. The monster knew he was there, and apparently was quite willing to get rid of him, but couldn't reach him. It had only two tiny claws on its little front limbs, and they just weren't long enough to yank Gumpson off its back, no matter how much the beast flailed them in the air. Kinney initially thought this was a shame, but then he realized that it left the door open to an enterprising young man like himself.

Before he really thought about what he was doing, Kinney climbed to the very top of the rock formation. It was a steep one, and it put him a good twenty-five feet in the air. When he saw the riderless monster come running under the rocks, he leaped. He slammed his tailbone hard against the giant lizard's spine, but otherwise it was a good fit. It was almost like riding a horse, albeit an awfully bony horse. This creature, too, flailed its little arms, but it couldn't reach him.

Once he realized what he had done, he felt exhilarated.

The wind whipped his hair around his head, stinging his eyes. The beast kicked up a ferocious dust cloud, but it was beneath and behind him. Whatever this thing was, it could really run. William the Conqueror let out a war whoop.

He saw something looming off to the right, coming up fast. He saw the shadow of a man, at about his height. It was the other monster, and that was the bank-robbing Luther Gumpson riding it. Kinney made sure his grip was firm on the critter's scaly back, and then he slowly eased his pistol out of its holster. The way this thing was bucking, he'd have to be careful or he'd drop his gun on the ground.

Kinney waited until the two beasts were running alongside, fifty feet apart. Gradually their strides brought them closer together. Gumpson was looking straight ahead, trying to figure out where his steed was heading. Kinney waited until they seemed to be loping along like two hounds running together, and then he took careful aim. Despite the dragon's crashing stride, he kept his hand dead level.

He had managed to steer the dinosaur away from Barnum Brown, but beyond that he didn't have much of a plan. He was trying to learn how to operate the thing called a Multi-Purpose Tool and ride a meat-eating dinosaur at the same time, and so far he wasn't managing to do either one very well. Then things got more complicated. Luther Gumpson looked to his left, and saw some punk atop the other dinosaur, aiming a pistol at him.

He jammed his boot heel into the right side of the monster's neck. It let out a monstrous roar, but it turned its head in the direction he wanted to go, and where its head turned, its body followed. It wasn't like it was trained, he thought. When it turned its head to the side he pushed on, it was probably just trying to reach around and bite his leg off. Either way, it allowed him to steer the beast, and it got him further away from the pistol.

Gumpson leaned back an inch or two and stared at the Multi-Purpose Tool in his hand. It had several smallish buttons on it, but nothing that was remotely helpful. He knew which way to point it—you aimed the wider end at whatever you wanted to shoot the green beams at—but beyond that he wasn't sure about anything. The Swedes could get all fancy with it, but its operation was eluding him.

He didn't have much time. The clown on the other dinosaur had also managed to figure out how to steer his steed, and was once again trying to get Gumpson in his sights. The real threat depended on how good a shot this guy was. If he was a bad shot, or even an average shot, then Gumpson was safe. The way these creatures thundered along, the average guy would need a cannon to unseat him. This guy might be different. There was something about his gaze that was unnerving, even from fifty feet away. He didn't move his head when he looked at Gumpson. He looked like some kind of hawk who was staring at a mouse. The way he held his pistol was even worse. There the guy was, riding on the back of a creature that had no right to be alive, a creature that would kill him and devour him if it got half a chance, and he was entirely fixated on shooting Gumpson. Gumpson had to admire the man's dedication, but he wished it could be focused on someone else.

He didn't exactly hear the first bullet wing by his head; it was more like he felt it. If the other dinosaur hadn't stumbled momentarily, it would have taken his head off. Gumpson cursed and pointed the Multi-Purpose Tool at his tormentor and pressed the first button his thumb touched. A beam of green light shot from the silver stick. It looked like it hit the man, but apparently it didn't. Nothing happened. The man rode on alongside, looking more deadly than ever.

❖　　❖　　❖

William Kinney had never seen a green light before. Luther Gumpson didn't seem to be shooting at him— he was aiming some kind of green light at him, but it was a light like nothing Kinney had ever seen. Kinney had seen fires and lanterns and electric arc lights and even the new light bulbs, but none of them had ever been green. He had seen *fireworks* that were green. Maybe that's what Gumpson was shooting at him. He hoped so. Gumpson couldn't kill him with fireworks.

Kinney was getting ready to aim again when he noticed that he had lost his gun. He looked at his fingers, but it simply wasn't there. He hadn't dropped it. William the Conqueror had never, ever dropped his gun, no matter what happened. Someone could shoot his arm off and he wouldn't let go. Kinney held on tightly to the dragon beneath him and looked at his palm. He hadn't dropped the gun after all. It was still there, only it was about the size of an ant. When he pulled his hand closer to look at it, the wind carried it away like it weighed nothing.

Of course, he had another, but it took some doing to get that into his hand. First he had to let go of his grip on the dragon's neck, and then get another grip with his right hand. He then slid his left hand down to his other holster and dug out the gun. This feat was managed in what Kinney imagined was record time. He had his other pistol out and aimed at Gumpson when suddenly everything went green and he found himself floating in the air.

"Wait!" he wanted to shout, but he couldn't mouth the words.

His dragon was running away, and he didn't like it. Then something worse happened. His dragon noticed that it didn't have a rider on its back anymore, so it returned to investigate. It noticed something floating in the air. That something happened to be made of meat, and was floating right about at mouth level. The beast stared at him for a few seconds, apparently making sure it understood the nature of the situation. Then it charged, mouth agape. The floating William Kinney wanted to scream, but he could only wait to be devoured.

Luther Gumpson decided that his backside had experienced quite enough time on the dinosaur. He had hoped to entice it to carry him far away, but it didn't seem to want to leave the area. He could control it with his boots only so far, and that level of control was not enough to turn the creature into a usable escape vehicle. All it was doing was allowing everybody who was chasing him to know exactly where he was. They were under the dust cloud, but he was above it, on parade. After he had somehow managed to freeze his shooting antagonist in a floating bubble of green, Gumpson decided his own joyride should end.

He waited until his mount ran by a patch of trees, and then flung himself to one of the scrubby pines. Getting a grip on the puny limbs was harder than he had expected, and he succeeded only in slowing his fall slightly while managing to rub a good deal of skin off his palms. That burning sensation helped lessen the pain of impact, but on the whole it was not a very pleasant escape from the beast's back. At least it was well timed. As the monster rushed away, he heard excited gunshots coming from the direction where it was headed. Apparently the man who had ridden the other dinosaur wasn't the only one who recognized him. The other members of the crowd, having first managed to keep from being eaten, had noticed that he was the man they were seeking. They started shooting at his dinosaur a little too late, but that wasn't his problem.

Gumpson tucked his hands under his arms, but that made them hurt worse. He stood up and grabbed the Multi-Purpose Tool and stepped from the trees, preparing to defend himself against any other gunslingers who wanted to try their luck. A sudden crashing sound made him duck back, and he narrowly missed getting shoved under the dirt by the passing feet of one of the dinosaurs. He couldn't tell which one it was, but it appeared to be hungry. Gumpson followed its dusty trail, although at his own much slower rate. Through squinting eyes, he saw that it was stomping directly toward his tormentor, the one he had left hovering in the air. It served the bastard right to get eaten by his own mount, but a midair meal wasn't something Gumpson had the stomach to watch.

Perhaps he should just put the poor swine out of his misery. What was it Lasse had told him about the Multi-Purpose Tool? If he reversed it somehow, it would crush the man into a tiny little figure. That wouldn't stop the dinosaur from eating him, but at least the sight wouldn't be as gory. Whoever this guy was, his luck had run out. Gumpson pushed two buttons on the Multi-Purpose Tool, aimed it as best he could through the dust and hoped for the best.

Just before his thumb found the trigger button, the problem was solved. The dinosaur stopped moving, and then it disappeared into thin air. With its passing, the earth stopped shaking under its feet. At the same moment, the green cloud that was suspending the man in the air disappeared, dropping him a good twenty feet to the ground. Gumpson lost sight of him in the dust at first, and then walked to where he fell. The man lay on his back, stunned. Gumpson walked over to him, as did Barnum Brown. As they approached, the man seemed to regain some of his senses. He shook his head, sending his own small cloud of dust flying from his dirty yellow hair, and then scrambled across the ground for his pistol.

Gumpson kept his thumb on the Multi-Purpose Tool, although he wasn't sure why. He hadn't released that man from the green cloud. He hadn't pushed the trigger button at all. Maybe the green cloud would only stay a short time, or maybe the Swedes were up to something.

Maybe when they finished playing with their dinosaurs they decided to take all their toys and leave, including the green cloud. While he was pondering this, he walked up to the man. Gumpson was musing about creatures from outer space and their unusual ways, but he was neglecting his own survival. Before he noticed it, he was standing right over the fallen man, who was pointing a very well-polished Remington pistol right at his face.

There it was, the face from a wanted poster staring right at him. Money in the bank. Unarmed and defenseless, looking down at him with the glazed expression of a deer. Easy as pie. Only William Kinney found that he couldn't pull the trigger.

"Damn you," he said to Luther Gumpson.

Gumpson gave him a quizzical deer-stare in return.

"I cain't shoot you now," Kinney said through gritted teeth. "You saved my life. You did something and got rid of that critter."

Another man appeared over him. It was that bald fellow who said he was a scientist. He had a pistol in his hand, but he was only pointing it at the ground. The man had said he was looking for dinosaurs. Is that what those monsters were? Weren't dinosaurs some kind of lizards?

"If you're so grateful and all, and you're not going to shoot me, you could put your Remington down," Gumpson said.

"Well," Kinney said. "I think you saved my life, but I ain't sure. It could of been a trick."

He kept his pistol pointed at Gumpson's face. His sense of gratitude was beginning to fade.

"I'm going to show you something," Gumpson said. "Don't shoot. It's not a gun."

He held up something in his hand. It was a silvery cylinder, with little dark spots on it. Gumpson's thumb hovered over one of the dark spots.

"If I put more pressure on this, you will die a very

painful death," Gumpson said. "Shoot me, and I'll die quick. I'll barely know what hit me. But my thumb will twitch and you'll die a death worse than you could ever imagine."

Kinney didn't blink; he could imagine some pretty terrible deaths. Gumpson had to be bluffing. That was probably just some stick he had picked up off the ground. Then again, there had been all that business with two dragons running around, and the green light Gumpson had been shooting at him, and the fact that most sticks on the ground weren't highly polished silver. Just minutes ago, he had been hovering off the ground in a green cloud. Before that, his pistol had been reduced to something smaller than a toy. Maybe that was what Gumpson would do to him. Kinney did not like the thought of it. He was short enough as he was.

"All right," he said, and lowered his pistol arm to the ground.

Gumpson closed his eyes in a long blink of relief.

"You have no idea what's been happening here," he told Kinney. "You should just clear out."

"What *is* happening here?" the scientist asked.

"It's a long story," Gumpson said. "But if I were you, I'd get up on that hill and check on your dinosaur skeleton."

The scientist's eyes flew open wide.

"Don't anyone shoot anyone else," Brown said, and he was gone.

"You know, if I don't shoot you, someone else will," Kinney said, and the look on Gumpson's face showed the bank robber knew it was true.

Already there were shouts that the dinosaurs had disappeared, which meant that Gumpson had to be on foot. The clouds of dust whipped up by the monsters were enough to shroud him for only a few minutes more, if even that long.

"What do you suggest?" Gumpson asked.

"I came here to shoot you, so let me shoot you," Kinney said. "I'm a good shot. If I don't want you dead, you won't die. You drop to the ground and bleed, and I'll say I killed you. Everyone will believe me if you play it good enough. Then they'll go away."

Gumpson did not appear convinced.

"And you'll do this out of the goodness of your heart."

"I will expect to be paid. It would only be right for you to pay me the reward out of your bank robbery money, plus maybe a little extra for letting you live."

"I didn't make a nickel on that last job. I had to leave it behind to get away. The bank just wanted people to think that so they'd come after me. Which they did."

This was not welcome news.

"What are you saying?"

"Buddy, there *is* no bank robbery money. You shoot me in the right shoulder and there won't be any more, either."

He had to be lying. He wouldn't have stuck around here this long if he didn't have the money stashed somewhere. It had to be so much he could hardly drag it around. Kinney didn't have long to think. He could hear approaching bootsteps, steps that were somewhat tentative, just in case the monsters were still around, ready to pounce. In another few seconds, one or more men with guns in their hands would come upon them, and they would shoot Luther Gumpson in the back without a second thought. He would lose the reward money and he would lose a chance at Gumpson's money. Kinney really should just shoot him, but he had not done a good enough job of burying his Protestant, churchgoing roots. This man had saved his life. He couldn't kill him. Then he saw that Gumpson had also heard the approaching men. It looked like his grip on the silver cylinder had loosened just a bit. Gumpson started to move away.

"Just play along with me," Kinney said, and he shot Gumpson.

He clinched his eyes, waiting for the horrible, painful death Gumpson had foretold, but it didn't seem to arrive. Kinney looked up. Gumpson was sprawled on the ground next to him, writhing in agony and clutching his right shoulder.

"I tried to shoot you in the left shoulder but you moved, damn you," Kinney whispered. "But at least you're still alive. They don't have to know that."

Then he shouted, "I got him! I killed the bastard!"

Gumpson took the cue. He slipped the silver cylinder under his vest, and then he lay as still as death.

THIRTY-THREE

S.L. Burgess scrambled his way up the hill. The rampaging dinosaurs had disappeared, but he was still so stunned by their appearance that he could barely see the rocks in front of him. He'd known the west was wild, but he hadn't known it was that wild. Thoughts and imaginary scenarios stomped through his mind almost as loudly as the dinosaurs had stomped across the ground. Were those hunched-over creatures Tyrannosaurus rexes? The size and the shapes of their heads matched the bones in the hillside, but they didn't walk the way he would have expected. He would have expected their tails to be heavy, but these were held high in the air.

What were they doing here in the first place? Were they holdovers from another age? That was impossible. They would have been found by now, if creatures that huge could have survived that long. Burgess felt a twinge of shame for not knowing more of his Lakota heritage. He figured that some Sioux myths could probably be twisted to describe the beasts he had seen stomping through the campsite, but he never thought they had referred to dinosaurs. No, he had been right in the first place. Their presence out here for so long *was* impossible. If nothing else, the farmers and cowboys who had pushed their way into the west would have said something about beasts that would no doubt have demolished their herds.

He pushed the thoughts from his mind as he topped

the rise that led to the dinosaur skeleton he had first discovered. There could be no doubt; those creatures should not have been here, but he would wonder about that later. First, he needed to see why such a crowd was gathered around the hillside. He could see the backs of the crew, and of Barnum Brown, as they all stood, hands on hips or arms crossed, staring at the rock wall as if it were a new work of art being displayed in a gallery. Burgess's eyes traveled to where the rock wall itself should have been, but to his amazement he saw nothing.

It wasn't *quite* nothing. He saw the wall of the ridge rise above the trail that had been stomped out by the boots of the team, but where the skeleton should be there was instead only the blue Montana sky and a few white puffy clouds in the distance. Burgess pushed his way past Harryhausen and Brown himself to verify that the skeleton was, indeed, gone. It was, and the looks of shock on the faces of the Barnum team members showed its loss. The gap in the hillside bore some scuff marks and cracks, but compared to most paleontological work it was as clean as if it had been cut with a diamond-edged saw. Whoever had done this, they had not done it with dynamite.

"I can't believe it," he heard Brown say, almost to himself. "It's gone. I can't believe it."

What had taken the team days to even halfway uncover had taken someone else only minutes to remove. The skeleton had been there the night before, Burgess was sure of that. He had seen it with his own eyes. Now it was gone, and the rocks that had held it were as smooth and clean as a dinner table, albeit a poorly treated dinner table.

"What happened?" he asked, although he knew it was a question that none of those assembled could answer.

"Somebody beat us to our dinosaur," Brown observed drily.

Burgess took no offense at his tone. He wasn't being

sarcastic. He was as stunned as anyone, or even more so. Brown and the others began discussing the ramifications of what had happened, but the blood started pounding in Burgess's ears and he no longer heard them. He turned and stared back the way he had come, and thought hard.

His mother had said there were creatures out here back when she was here, and they were after dinosaur bones. They could dig them up fast, faster than either the great scientist Cope or the great scientist Marsh. They could perform what seemed like miracles. She had even seen a dinosaur herself, and now he had seen not one but two, running around as if they were still frisky as colts after a couple of million years. A question welled up inside him, but he was afraid to ask it.

Then he saw Digger Phelps heading up the hillside toward him. Phelps had been around back then. Phelps knew his mother. He had already said she made up tall tales, but even her wildest stories hadn't involved two Tyrannosaurs running around with men on their backs, shooting at each other. If she wanted to have made up something wild, surely she would have made up something like that.

"Digger!" he said as Phelps just got to the flat part of the ridge. "Did you see all that going on down there?"

Phelps gave him an accusing look.

"What part do you think I missed, Mr. Burgess? The screaming? The shouting? The shooting? Maybe the two big dinosaurs running around? I saw it all."

Phelps was not much of a pleasure to be around at any time, Burgess had noted, but he seemed especially cranky today. Nevertheless, he had to try again. He grabbed Phelps' arm.

"Wait, just a second, before you go over there."

"What happened?"

"That dinosaur skeleton is missing. Digger, can I ask you something?"

Phelps looked over his shoulder.

"It's missing? Is anyone dead?"

Burgess shook the old man until he quit looking away and met his eyes.

"Why would anyone be dead? You know more than you let on, Digger. What are you holding back?"

Phelps tried to give him an icy stare, but he looked guilty. Phelps looked sort of guilty all the time, but he looked especially guilty right now.

"Nothing. Please let me go. I want to see what's happened."

"You already know what's happened, don't you, old man?"

Burgess moved his face in close. His brown skin sometimes frightened people, he knew, especially white people who had spent some time out west. He had been told that he was capable of making a very fierce face that recalled the visages of great Indian warriors of the past. He didn't get much call for that talent in scientific circles, but maybe it would come in handy now.

"I don't know anything," Phelps said.

Phelps was a tough old bird, but Burgess was losing patience.

"Just tell me this, and I'll let you go."

"No—"

"Did my mother make up tall tales? Or did she tell the truth?"

Phelps looked anywhere but at his eyes, and let out a little moan. The others were probably staring at them now, but Burgess didn't care. He had a right to know. Anger made him strong. He picked Phelps off the ground by his collar, making his eyes bug out and exposing his pasty belly.

"Was my mother a liar? Or did she tell the truth?"

"Damn you," Phelps said through clenched teeth. "She lied about being a boy."

"That's not what I'm talking about."

"She told the truth. Every word. That what you want to hear?"

"Is it the truth?"

The fight was going out of him. Burgess clenched his fists harder and the air started going out of him, too.

"It's the truth. Your mother is not a liar."

Burgess set him back on the ground. Phelps took a long breath and attempted to restore some dignity by straightening his clothes. It didn't help much.

"That's all I needed to know," Burgess said, and Phelps walked slowly past him.

"Don't tell Barnum I told you that," Phelps said. "Please."

"I won't."

"Really, don't."

"I said I won't."

Burgess walked behind Phelps as he made his way over to the crew, who were still engrossed in the mystery of the missing skeleton.

"What was that all about?" he heard Brown ask Phelps, but he didn't wait to hear the answer.

He walked to the other side of the ridge, where he could look past the Widow onto the flatland below. So his mother had been right all along. Everything she had written was true. That was the only explanation that made sense, crazy though it was. He had gotten into fights on her behalf before, but somehow he still felt he owed her an apology. He would tell her just as soon as he got home.

Suddenly he heard a familiar voice. Someone had just climbed up the ridge, following in Digger's footsteps.

"Hello, Mr. Brown," said the voice. "Why the long face? Did somebody take one of your dinosaurs?"

It couldn't be.

"Hello, Mrs. Paul."

It was. His mother was here.

"Well?"

"Yes, Mrs. Paul, we seem to be missing a dinosaur."

Burgess walked closer to the group. That was his

mother, all right, holding up a smoothly folded piece of
paper.

"Hello, son," she called out upon seeing him. "Long
trip, I'll tell you about it later."

He beamed at her, but she turned her attention back
to Barnum Brown. She unfolded the paper, revealing it
to be a map. He had seen that map before, but he had
never believed it until now.

"What have you got, Mrs. Paul? We're kind of busy."

Brown's chilly responses did nothing to lessen his
mother's smile.

"This is a map, Mr. Brown. I believe I know who has
your bones. And I may know a way to figure out where
they're going next."

THIRTY-FOUR

The tent that had served as a mess hall was converted to a scientific command post where Barnum Brown could listen to the insanity in all its glory. His men hauled one of the heavy work tables into the center of the tent, and Brown took a few moments to put some of his equipment on it, including a pick and a copy of one of his monographs. They served no purpose, but he wanted them there to remind him that no matter what he might hear from this odd crowd, his first commitment was to cold, hard science.

Brown's crew looked at him, eyes wide with expectation. They had seen a miracle, and they wanted an explanation, one that he was not capable of giving. He had no idea why dinosaurs had suddenly taken a notion to go waltzing around in modern-day Montana. They *had* been dinosaurs, no doubt about that. He could not explain them away as freak monitor lizards or Gila monsters. If he had been forced to confess it, he was in fact a little bit annoyed that he had not been allowed a better look at the creatures. It had been hard to concentrate on the one that was headed his way, ready to eat him. The ability to clinically analyze the cranial structure of such a beast was severely limited in such circumstances. That crisis had passed, but then it had been hard to see through the dust, and then he had to contend with a vision of a man floating in midair. All in all, the dinosaurs had created too much

243

excitement for his taste, and he was at a loss to come up with any useful theories.

When things seemed out of sorts, perhaps it was time to turn the explaining over to the crazy people. For that, he had Mrs. Paul. He had to hand it to her; her strange manuscript had foreseen not only the appearance of dinosaurs, but also the floating green cloud and any number of other things. She might be crazy, but she seemed to be on to something. Mrs. Paul had a brief reunion with her son, who appeared surprised—but pleased—with her presence. She had kept up with the Montana news as best she could from a distance, and when she heard tales of shootings and mass gatherings, she began heading west. The closer she got, the more her suspicions were confirmed. She seemed pleased to have arrived just in time to have her kooky stories validated.

"Now, if you will, Mrs. Paul, your explanation," Brown said. "I warn everyone here that it will be a strange one, but since Mrs. Paul has journeyed all this way to tell it, I propose that we hear her out."

There was a general rumbling among the crew. The college students especially looked pleased. They had certainly gotten more than they had bargained for by coming on this trip.

"Thank you," she said. She seemed a little embarrassed to be speaking in front of so attentive a crowd, but she lost her nervousness once she splayed her map out on the table.

"I don't suppose any of you read an article about happenings in Montana that was recently published in the *Wild West Weekly*, did you?"

The group of scientists and laborers shook their heads in unison, except for S.L. Burgess, who nodded slightly.

"You read it, didn't you, Mr. Brown?" she asked him.

Brown felt his face flush as he nodded. Lord, this was embarrassing. He might as well be H.G. Wells up here, nodding about some alien invasion from Mars.

"Now then. It would certainly save some time if everyone had read it, but that can't be helped. I have some copies available for sale later if anyone is interested."

"Please, let's get on with this, Mrs. Paul," Brown said, struggling to maintain some vestige of respectability.

She continued.

"What we are dealing with is one, or possibly two, races that live beyond our planet."

That got their attention.

"The members of one of the races appear to be tall, blonde individuals. They look Swedish, and claim to be from there, but they are from much further away. The other race is made up of lizards that walk like men. They are capable of disguising themselves as humans, and may claim to be from Iceland."

Brown detected some snickering amidst the crew, and he did not blame them. Mrs. Paul ignored the response and continued speaking as if she were addressing a Sunday tea party.

"They have been here before, thirty-one years ago, but they did not get what they were after so they are back. Actually, they could have been here many times since then, for all we know. In fact, they could be disguised as any one of you."

No one in the crew was tall with blonde hair, but that didn't stop them from looking askance at one another. One of the men gave the college student Harryhausen an exploratory poke.

"What they are seeking is dinosaur bones. I think I understand their motives, but I am not sure. It's best to just leave that issue alone, and concentrate on the fact that they are pursuing the very dinosaur bones that you yourselves are digging up."

The snickering stopped. Perhaps the men were thinking back to the missing skeleton on the ridge above them. They knew how hard it had been to even uncover the outlines of the dinosaur, and they also knew that someone had stolen literally tons of rock from right under their noses, all in a matter of minutes that very morning. Brown's science had no explanation for that.

"This map—" she said, thumping a finger on it for emphasis "—this map was stolen from one of these otherworldly creatures thirty years ago. I know because I stole it myself. It shows where dinosaur bones are located."

Despite himself, Brown peered at the map. If that were true, the map would be well worth having.

"I have studied this map and I believe that we are here," Mrs. Paul said, tapping their location with a forefinger. "What we need to do is determine where they have gone next, and go there."

"And do what?" Harryhausen asked.

That was a good question. What did one say to a race of people capable of spiriting away tons of rock in a matter of minutes, not to mention unleashing dinosaurs? Excuse us, you have our bones, could we have them back?

Mrs. Paul was not helpful on this point.

"Gentlemen, I must say I can't help you on that. I think I've done enough by telling you what's going on," she said. "How you deal with it is your problem."

There was silence for a long moment. Brown stared at the map over Mrs. Paul's shoulder, and members of the crew walked up to peruse it along with him. It had numerous markings, which he took to indicate dinosaur locations. There were several sites around their current location.

"Look at all that," one of the crew members said. "They could be anywhere. How will we find them?"

"We can try to figure out which is the most likely spot," Mrs. Paul said.

"But what will we do with them if we find them?" Harryhausen asked again.

"I'm still now sure how we could find them in the first place," Burgess said, and there were several murmurs of assent.

Brown heard someone clear his throat at the back of the crowd. It was Digger Phelps.

"I might be able to help with that," Phelps said.

All eyes turned to Digger, who was standing with someone Brown didn't recognize.

"You need to hear from this man," Phelps said, pushing his guest forward.

Brown heard Mrs. Paul suck in a gasp.

"Digger, what's—" she said, but she didn't say anything else.

The man just stood there, looking uncertainly at the crowd. He was fairly young, apparently in his late thirties or early forties. He was fairly tall and more than fairly thin, and had light brown hair and a pleasant face. He looked quite a bit like Phelps, Brown thought. He could almost be his son. Perhaps Digger had some sort of confession to make.

"Folks, I would like you to meet myself," Phelps said.

That wasn't what Brown was expecting to hear, but Mrs. Paul sucked in another surprised lungful of air.

"I'll say this fast. What this lady here says is true. While those space people were here last time, they took me as a hostage. They put me in some kind of little hole in the wall with red lights in it and they made a copy of me. This is him. He is me, thirty years ago. Only he goes by the name of Eric now."

"Hello," Eric said.

Well, the Tooth Fairy and Santa Claus should be showing up any time now, Brown thought. So Digger had sat there and lied to him to his face. When this was over, he would have to remind himself to fire Digger.

"Mrs. Paul, you are the only one here who knew Digger Phelps thirty years ago. Does that look like him?" Brown asked.

She didn't speak. She only nodded quickly.

"So what *are* you?" Harryhausen asked the younger Phelps.

The man—what had Phelps said his new name was?
Eric?—turned to face the crowd.

"I—I am a person, just like you. I am an exact replica
of Digger Phelps, just like he said."

"Where did you come from?"

"I came on the spacecraft along with the Swe—the
people that this lady has been telling you about. What
she says is true. They are trying to collect as many dinosaur
skeletons as possible, particularly those that reflect the
biological experiments that they used to perform on this
planet."

Good Lord, Brown thought. Everyone in Montana must
be completely out of their heads.

"Then what are you doing here, if I may ask?" Brown
said.

Eric looked sheepish.

"Well, we had a little falling out. They didn't really
want to bring me here in the first place. See, when they
created me, they tried to wipe out most of my memories.
But I met Digger here—I met myself, I should say—
and they started coming back. The memories."

"And they kicked you off the spaceship?" Burgess asked.

"Yes. Actually, I escaped. I escaped with that man that
everyone is looking for, the criminal. What happened
to him?"

Nobody seemed to know.

"So you're not going back on the ship?" Brown asked
Eric.

"No, sir. They would shut me down if I did. I am
technically a human being, so I guess I will live here. If
that's all right."

The crew seemed to be feeling benevolent, or maybe
they were just getting confused. Everyone nodded.

"Mr. Eric, since you are here, why don't you take a
few minutes and tell us more about these people from
another planet," Brown said.

Now he was sounding less like H.G. Wells and more

like his namesake, P.T. Barnum. Come see the creatures from another planet, folks! Step right up!

The man went into a rather lengthy explanation that Brown found interesting, if more than a little implausible.

"So that's it," Eric said when his story was finished.

"Well," said someone in the crowd.

"That is a very fine story, young man," Brown said, projecting a voice of authority. "You say you are a regular human being, but you have some sort of mechanical equipment inside you."

"Yes, sir," Eric said. "It's a type of camera, operated by my eye."

The camera wielded by that Turnstall fellow was as tall as a man, including its tripod, but here this fellow purported to have one hidden away inside of him.

"I don't suppose you could prove that? Not that I don't trust you or don't believe your story, but it seems it would go a long way to establishing the factual nature of these rather unusual tales we are hearing today."

The man Eric thought for a moment. Brown assumed he was trying to think of a way to wiggle out of the challenge, but finally he nodded.

"I think some of the equipment is broken, after I fell off the dinosaur. But there may be a way to show you."

How a man broke the tiny camera embedded in his eye by falling off the back of a Tyrannosaurus rex in modern-day Montana. A scientific monograph by Barnum Brown. Brown almost chuckled to himself. That was one paper that would more than likely not get written.

"Is there any way to get us in a dark place?" Eric asked.

The Montana afternoon sunlight streamed under the sides of the tent, reflecting off Mrs. Paul's map. The tent cover itself was thick enough, and maybe they could loosen some supports to hang it lower.

"How about my wagon?" Phelps chimed in. "Most of us could get in there and seal off the ends."

That was a better idea, Brown had to admit, and fifteen

minutes later he found himself squeezing into the front end of Phelps' wagon. It was one of the only ones that wasn't moving. During the ruckus, apparently the young man with the straw hair had shot the bank robber Luther Gumpson. Brown had felt a twinge of regret upon hearing the news, which came as the crew was piling into Phelps' wagon. Brown had been the last one to see Gumpson alive, and was conceivably in a position to have saved him, but Brown had instead rushed off to inspect his skeleton. He was not going to go out of his mind with guilt, as the man was a criminal and had brought his troubles down on himself, but he knew that he could have done more.

"Stop pushing," he heard someone say as he climbed in.

The wagon was not built to handle anything like that sort of load, but somehow the entire crew and Mrs. Paul managed to squeeze themselves into its confines. When properly sealed, the wagon was indeed dark. It was also hot and, when filled with people who had very recently been running for their lives, did not smell so good.

"Let's hurry this up, shall we?" Brown said.

"Yes, please," said a voice he couldn't identify.

"Who's in front of me?" Eric asked.

He was situated in the middle, so everyone could see whatever demonstration it was he had in mind.

"No one. Just the wagon cover," Digger Phelps said.

"Just make sure no one is directly in front of me, unless that person doesn't mind losing their vision," Eric said. "I'm not sure I'll be able to moderate the intensity of the light."

No one had any idea what he was talking about, but Brown heard a good bit of scooting around going on in the dark, and he was suddenly squeezed hard on both sides as people cleared room.

"Watch out, now," Eric said.

There was another moment of clothes rustling, and

then a bright cone of light appeared from out of nowhere. It flared so bright for a second that Brown had to blink and turn away, and even then the afterimage floated in the darkness under his eyelids. When he looked again, the light had dimmed to little more than a glow. He had some trouble seeing around the original light's afterimage, but what he did see was astonishing. The cone of light was coming from the man's left eye, just as he had promised.

"There is a camera inside here, but like I said, it's broken," Eric said. "This is all I can do now."

Everyone sat still, watching the light. It was like he had one of those new electric bulbs stuffed inside his head, in addition to the camera. Whoever those space people were, they knew how to make things small.

"How bright does that light get?" Brown asked. "Don't show, just tell."

"Much brighter than it was when I first turned it on," Eric said. "It was built to be very powerful, so it could record things in most any sort of light."

After a minute more, Eric switched the light off, and returned everyone to darkness.

"I'm sorry, but I'm not sure how much longer the power supply will last."

They clambered out of the wagon. A group of men in a passing wagon waved as they went by.

"Better luck next time!" they shouted, and Brown waved back.

He had seen these men before, and they seemed to recognize him.

"When are you going to use your dynamite?" one of them shouted.

"I don't know," Brown shouted back. "Not anytime soon."

"This trip was a complete waste o' time, then," the man called back, and then they were too far away for more shouting.

They walked back to the meeting tent. Brown noticed that Phelps put his arm around Eric as they walked. His younger self was a little taller than Phelps, but maybe that was because the years and the abuse had combined to pull Digger a little closer to the ground.

"So we are up against advanced space people," Brown said when they were all reassembled. "We know what they are after, obviously, and we have a map that may let us figure out where they are going next."

Eric cleared his throat.

"Actually, I do know where they're going next," he said. "It's not all that far, and they won't be there all that long. In fact, they won't be on this planet much longer."

Brown nodded.

"Well, that helps. So we are up against advanced people from outer space, and we know where they are. They have the ability to unleash live dinosaurs against us whenever they wish."

"That is true," Eric said.

"So what do we do now?" Digger asked. "Do we just let them go?"

All eyes were on Brown. He stood there and thought for a minute. On the one hand, they were up against a rival with unimaginable technology. On the other hand . . . and here the memory of Mrs. Paul's strange story bit hard into his mind. Othniel Marsh and Edward Cope came up against these same creatures, and managed to beat them. They recovered bones, and Cope even managed to get a complete Monoclonius skeleton out of the deal. Was he any less a rugged paleontologist than those two? Was he going to let people from outer space run off with his bones?

"In my opinion, the fossilized bones of creatures that lived on this planet belong on this planet," Brown said slowly, emphasizing the words. "I don't care who else came here and what they were doing, the bones should stay."

He thought of his dear dead wife, just for one second, and then pushed that pain away.

"The past is always with us," he said, trying to keep his voice level. "The past is the future. Those bones are our past, and they will give us knowledge for our future. We must get them back."

He had been talking almost to himself, and was momentarily taken aback when his crew gave out a fairly hearty cheer.

"I see you agree," Brown said, unable to keep a smile from creeping across his close-shaven face. "Now then. Where are they now, Mr. Eric? Can you show us?"

Eric walked to Mrs. Paul's map and studied it before pointing to a location about fifty miles away.

"Tracking the sites wasn't my job, but I believe this is the next stop," Eric said.

Brown was vaguely familiar with the area. It was to the west, and was more mountainous and jagged than where they were now.

"Our guns are useless. We need to figure out what to do," Brown said, as much to himself as to anyone there.

"We have him," Phelps said proudly, pointing to his younger self.

"Yeah," said Burgess. "He can—well, he can shine a light out of his head."

"A lot of good that will do," said Harryhausen. "Are we sure we should take him?" he continued. "I mean, no offense, but he came here with those guys."

Brown looked at Eric.

"That's a good point. No offense, Digger, or Mr. Eric, but how do we really know that you are no longer affiliated with our visitors?"

Eric just smiled weakly, but Phelps started to bluster.

"What you are saying is you don't trust either version of me!"

"That's not it, Digger, it's just that—"

"I saw him on the back of the dinosaur," said one of

the crew, a man named Wiggins. "He rode one for a little bit and then fell off and it hit him in the head with its tail."

"See!" Phelps nearly shouted.

"I promise you," Eric said, "I am no longer with them. I will do whatever you say to prove that to you, but I think I could be of service. I know how the ship operates. I can help."

Brown gave him a long look, but the younger version of Digger matched it with his own steady gaze. Phelps was right, he supposed. Brown didn't want to seem like he didn't trust Digger no matter how old or young he was—even though, after being lied to, he didn't—and it wasn't like they couldn't use all the help they could get.

Well, he could shine a light out of his head, as Harryhausen had pointed out. Shine a light out of his head. Brown felt the stirrings of an idea beginning to form.

"Say," he said, "has anyone seen that photographer around?"

THIRTY-FIVE

The ship shifted imperceptibly, and Lasse could tell they were moving. It didn't rumble or shake—Swede ships were far too sophisticated for that—but it did tilt a few degrees to one side as it slid out from under its thin covering of dirt and rocks. Lasse found himself momentarily envious of the Swedes. The Nes had little money left for space travel, and their ships were relics of bygone years. The last decent ship they had was the one Thornton Grieg had used to come to Earth three decades before, and he had crashed it upon returning. Were the Nes to be caught traveling in space in their current ships, they would be ticketed for unsafe transport. The Swedes, meanwhile, had money to burn, but they didn't spend it on fancy ships. Their ships were only a notch more spaceworthy than any of the antiques the Nes had on hand, and they didn't seem to care. They were after quantity, not quality, so they could send out more ships to more worlds to try to recover evidence of their past meddling.

He had been down in the hold a long time. Unless there was a major operation under way, the Swedes didn't come down here. They could simply drop the shrunken bones through a passage in the floor, without ever setting foot below, which was fine with him. He had passed out for a while when the oxygen went low, but he later woke with a headache, not sure whether he should be grateful

255

to still be alive. According to the timekeeping unit he had hidden in his clothes, it should be daylight, but he wasn't sure. It wasn't like the Swedes to fly around in daytime, but Art Kan was probably frustrated and behind schedule enough to attempt it.

Lasse didn't know where they were going. He didn't think they were through. Maybe the interference they had encountered had convinced them to return home. This planet was not that important to them. The inspectors might not even come here. It was a sacred place to the Nes, now that they realized that it was their birthplace, but it meant virtually nothing to the Swedes. Art Kan had groused repeatedly about the backwater mission.

Lasse huddled at the edge of the hold. He was afraid to walk around too much, afraid the sensors had been set to try to pick him up. He had given his crew access button to Luther Gumpson, who was probably now dead. That meant he didn't have one, but he wasn't sure if he would show up now as being an intruder, or if that only worked when you entered the ship. Probably the latter was correct; otherwise they would have killed him by now.

He idly stared at his fingers, wondering anew at the tiny whorls and swirls on the tips of his Earthman fingers. This skin was so sensitive. He could feel his clothes touching it, could almost feel the air bumping against his face. This skin would soon die, and he would be back to himself, but he wasn't sure what that meant anymore.

The ship was leaving the people who knew who he was. There were only two, granted, and one was a criminal, but at least they knew what he was doing. Now he would go to a place where there was no one to help. It was he, alone against the Swedes. He could possibly leave the ship again, but then what would he do? His outer skin would die, and he would be revealed. The Earth people would kill him as surely and as swiftly as the Swedes.

Then again, he could theoretically complete his mission.

He began to smile as the thought took hold. His brain must not have been operating properly after the oxygen depletion. Of course! All he had to do was wait until the crew left the ship again, climb out of the hold, and fly off. He would have a hold full of bones for Mother Naga. He would be a hero.

His stomach growled, reminding him that although his outer body was dying, it still had needs. Actually, his inner body had needs, too. The downside of wrapping himself in borrowed skin was that he had to eat nearly twice as much to sustain everything, and it had been a while since he had been able to get free food at Barnum Brown's camp. He probably barely had the strength to climb out of the hold, much less overpower anyone.

A sinking fear seized him, making him break out in a sweat. What if they really *were* done here? He would never have the strength to wait for them to get into their sleep chambers, where he could overpower them. They would sleep smugly for ten Earth years, only to awaken to his dead body in the hold. They would laugh at him. The very thought made his head hurt.

Lasse stretched out atop the wall storage bins, completely unsure of what to do. He tried to concentrate on Mother Naga for strength, but all that came to mind was the dead and twisted Bjorn. He adjusted his body to make sure he wasn't crushing his friend any further. He felt a strange feeling stealing over him. Life seemed pointless, all of a sudden. Even if he had the energy to move around, he suddenly just didn't see the point. Perhaps his human outer skin was creating these feelings. He understood that the inhabitants of this planet were prone to various mental illnesses, caused by having an unsuitably large brain housed in a primitive, ape-derived body. That would be enough to unseat anyone. Nes were made of sturdier, reptile-based stuff, but just now he was feeling more like an ape than a reptile.

Lasse saw something gleaming on the other side of

the hold, at just about eye level. It was the same color as the wall, and only betrayed its presence by reflecting light differently. He squinted and saw that it was a monitor. He hadn't known that was down here, but then again he hadn't had much time to dwell over the ship's particulars. He knew it was a standard cargo ship, although one of the nicer ones, but he didn't know much more than that. Lasse sat up and stared across at the blank monitor. It would be tapped into the ship's central calculating machine. Lasse could perhaps gain access to a great deal of ship information by using it. He had never been able to use the calculating machine monitors upstairs for such a purpose, because Swedes were always walking around behind him. Here, there was no one. Lasse sighed. The monitor was so far away, and he was so very tired and hungry. He took a deep breath and let out a long exhale. He could rest when he was dead.

With a groan, Lasse hauled himself to his feet and walked slowly to the monitor. His presence had apparently not been detected, or he would be dead by now, but he still thought it best to be careful. No point in knocking around down here and giving himself away by sound. He slowly sat on the cargo bins and faced the monitor. A hand brushed against the wall produced the button board that controlled the monitor's link to the calculating machine.

It occurred to him that he might give away his presence by activating the monitor, but he didn't think so. He had been tapped into the calculating machine upstairs without being able to tell who else was using it, and where they were. At any rate, it was worth the risk. Here, he could poke into whatever he wanted without having some nosey Swede peering over his shoulder.

He tapped the button board and the monitor came to life, showing an exterior view. The monitor was apparently used to keep an eye on the bottom of the hold, which meant that at the moment it was merely aimed at the ground. Trees and rocks were passing rapidly below them, punctuated by the occasional baffled-looking human being staring up at them. It was obviously daylight, and it was just as obvious that Art Kan no longer cared who saw them go by. Kan was running behind schedule, and he was getting sloppy. Lasse tried to cheer himself with that thought, but it didn't help much.

He decided to examine the information about the ship itself. A few more clicks and he learned that it was actually a warship that had been converted to a freighter. Some of the small offices, such as Hern's, were formerly weapons rooms. No wonder they were so small. Lasse examined the ship's history with growing interest. This could be valuable information, although he wasn't immediately sure. His growling stomach competed in a pitched battle with his concentration.

There was something else he could do with the calculating machine. It contained information about a great many things relating to Earth, to be used as a reference by the visiting Swedes. It even contained information about Earth religions. He looked back to his former seat across the hold, and saw the wooden statue of the man named Jesus laid out there. Luther Gumpson had not been very informative about that religion. Lasse knew only that Jesus forgave people and disapproved of bank robbing, but there had to be more to it than that.

He began tapping the button board, and settled back to read and learn. There was a lot of information in the files of the calculating machine, but then again he had some time, and nowhere to go. Mother Naga would not approve, but he had done all he could for her for the time being.

THIRTY-SIX

"Urgh," Luther Gumpson said.

That was the most intelligent thing he had said for the last hour or so. Kinney was not much good with medical work, so he had basically gotten Gumpson drunk and laid him out under a rock for most of the afternoon.

Kinney had secretly moved camp, lest he bump into Peck South and Trevor Hayes, his former friends. He didn't want them to know he had shot Gumpson but hadn't killed him, and had no intention of doing so. They might take matters into their own hands, and that would be a stain on his honor, such as it was. Then again, they probably weren't even around. They had left him to become dragon bait that very morning, and were probably still running somewhere.

Gumpson stumbled against a rock and nearly knocked both of them over. He was heavy, and leaned hard on Kinney. Kinney had waited until the sun was beginning to hide behind the rocks before he dared to move around with Gumpson at his side. Most of the wagons had already departed, but there were a few still around, and he wanted to steer clear of them. He figured the scientist man would have some kind of medicine, but until he got there Gumpson would have to do with knotted rags to stem the blood and 100 proof to stem the pain.

"Hey, mister!" said a voice from nowhere.

Kinney immediately gave Gumpson a shove, sending

him sprawling on the ground. Gumpson grunted but lay still.

"Who's there?" Kinney said, pistol already in hand.

"Don't shoot!" said the voice.

It belonged to a round-faced man who had apparently just stepped from behind a rock mound on Kinney's right side. He looked familiar. Kinney had definitely seen him out here before.

"What do you want?"

"Are you William Kinney? William the Emperor?"

"William the *Conqueror*. He took over France in 1016. That's who I'm named for. Yeah, that's me."

"Hey, you can put down that gun. I ain't armed. Not with a gun, anyway. I'm Pete Turnstall. I'm a photographer."

That's where Kinney had seen him. He had his head stuck in a box, shooting that man that Gumpson had killed.

"You're the photographer, huh? What can I do for you?"

"Well, I heard you kilt Luther Gumpson."

Kinney holstered the pistol and then gestured at Gumpson's motionless body.

"Sure did. That's him there, dead as a post."

"You sure he's dead? It looked like he was walking just a second ago when you came by me."

Kinney made what he hoped was a fearsome face.

"He wasn't walking. I was a-dragging him."

"All right. But why were you dragging him around?"

"Where are you from, mister?"

"Kentucky. Just outside of Louisville."

"Well, see then. This is a tradition out west. When you shoot a man, you give him a last walk around his territory."

Turnstall didn't look like he was convinced.

"But Gumpson's not from here. He's from Missouri or somewheres along there. You ought to take him back there and walk him around."

"I don't have that kind of time, mister. Say, what do you want with me, anyway?"

"I'm doing some photographs of the Wild West. I thought I could get you to pose with your man here for a photo."

This was an interesting proposal. Here was a chance to add to the semi-legend of the Fort McCagle Massacre. Here was a chance to shine up the legend of the Plains City shootout, with nobody being the wiser.

"Well, all right. But don't take so long this time."

"Okay. Give me a minute to set up."

Turnstall apparently had his wagon nearby, because in another moment he returned, staggering under the weight of his camera. While he set it up, Kinney walked over to Gumpson and gave him an exploratory poke. He didn't twitch. The fall appeared to have rendered him unconscious. Kinney had only vowed not to kill Gumpson for saving his life, but hadn't said anything about hurting him a little.

"Here we go," Turnstall said finally. "That was a record-time setup."

Kinney was not impressed, but he allowed Turnstall to pose him standing behind the sprawled Gumpson, pistol in hand.

"Make sure I have a real fierce expression on my face," he instructed Turnstall. "How long will I have to hold it?"

"Not very long. It's a real bright day, and that helps. You ready?"

Just when he was reaching for the lens cap, Gumpson did a half-roll and let out a loud moan.

"God," he said, his voice barely audible.

Turnstall slowly pulled his head from under his camera's black cloth.

"You sure he's dead?"

"Yes," Kinney hissed. "That was just gas."

"Damn," Gumpson said, quite audibly this time. "I hurt all over. Give me another drink, you bastard."

Turnstall abandoned the camera altogether and stomped over to Gumpson, who has attempting to sit up. Before Kinney could stop him, he stuck his face right in front of Gumpson's, and then wrinkled his nose.

"He's not dead. He's dead drunk. So he *was* walking a while ago. What are you trying to pull here?"

With a groan, Gumpson slumped back to the ground. Kinney sighed.

"All right. I was trying to kill this bastard, but then he saved my life so I felt bad about it. I just shot him to make it look like he was dead. I'm taking him to that scientist man to see if he has any medicine or anything for him."

"Barnum Brown?"

"Is that his name?"

"Yes. I know where he is. I need to see him anyway. I'll go with you."

"But wait," Kinney said, unable to keep the worry from his voice. "Aren't you going to take the picture?"

"But he's not dead."

"So? Nobody has to know. You get a good picture, I get a good picture. Will you give me one?"

"I'll sell you one."

"Well, let's see. Go ahead and take a couple while he's not moving around so much."

"It will take me a little time to develop them."

"That's okay. He's not going anywhere. When you're done, we'll take him to get some treatment."

"Remind me never to put my life in your hands," Turnstall said, but he went back to the camera and stuck his head back under the cloth.

Twenty minutes later, he had a couple of nice negatives of Luther Gumpson, splayed motionless beneath the scowling William Kinney. There was another negative where Gumpson's hand was a blur of movement. He had tried to get up again, at an inopportune moment, but Turnstall promised he would destroy that one.

"Very nice," Kinney said when the work was done. "You take nice pictures."

"Thank you."

"Just shoot me!" Gumpson suddenly shouted.

"Shut up," Kinney said. "I already did. Can we load him in your wagon? I'm awfully tired of dragging him around."

"The fumes are pretty powerful in there."

Kinney looped Gumpson's arm over his shoulder and dragged the bank robber to his feet.

"He can take it. Might even do him some good. Let's go."

THIRTY-SEVEN

"Say, Barnum. I know you're busy, but can I have a word?"

The sun was largely gone now, and most of the crew had gone off to pack up their belongings. Brown had decided it didn't make any sense to try to get a late start, so they would head out in the morning.

"Sure, Digger. What's on your mind?"

Phelps took him by the arm and led him off to the far edge of the tent, away from the others.

"I just wanted to tell you something. Thank you for letting Eric go with us. He's telling the truth, you know."

"I know, Digger," Brown said. He didn't quite know, but there was no point in getting into all that again. "I'm sorry you didn't see fit to do the same when I asked you about your time out here thirty years ago."

Phelps looked stricken. His face made a frown so deep it looked almost comedic.

"Oh, I'm sorry, Barnum, but I was just afraid—you see, I didn't know if—I thought that . . ."

Brown held up a hand to stop the stumbling explanation.

"That's fine, Digger, we can go into that later. What did you want to say to me?"

"There's something else I didn't tell you. Do you know why they made a copy of me in the first place?" Of course he didn't, and Digger didn't wait for a response before pressing on. "I have something wrong with my liver. That man from outer space could detect it even then. He wanted to study that, so he made a copy of me."

"I don't understand."

"He was apparently interested in that sort of thing. The man who was here thirty years ago. Eric said when they made him, they cured that problem. Of course, that doesn't help me. I still have it."

From a scientific viewpoint, it made sense. If you were creating replicas of creatures on another planet, you would want to be able to cure as many of their ills as possible. Brown would like to sit down and have a talk with these creatures, if that were possible. Then Phelps' words sunk in.

"What do you mean, Digger? What are you trying to say?"

"I'm going to die, Barnum."

"But—when?"

"I don't know. But I don't really feel so good."

"Digger—you told me you were fine. You told me you were better."

"I know, Barnum. I didn't think I was lying about that, not at the time. Maybe I just feel bad now that I *know* about it. I don't know why I'm telling you now. I just wanted you to know."

He looked at Brown for a long time, and then turned away.

"Are you sure you're all right to go with us, Digger?"

Phelps stopped moving, and looked back.

"I wouldn't miss it for anything."

Now he felt kind of bad about complaining to Digger about his lying. In the scheme of things, maybe that hadn't been so bad after all.

"Digger—I'm sorry."

"Thank you, Barnum," Phelps said.

He seemed to want something more, but Brown wasn't sure what. Brown walked to the edge of the tent and looked out into the night, which had finally arrived, stealing over the vast Montana skies until it had swallowed them up. The source of Phelps' liver ailment was not hard to figure out. So Digger drinks himself half to death, and in exchange he gets a new, younger body that can live on, free of disease. It was unfair. He thought of Marion, and felt tears stinging his eyes, blurring the stars. She wanted to live, and she had died, and there was no second chance for her, no new body flying in from some faraway world. It was unfair. He was sorry for Phelps, but he wouldn't cry for him. Digger had brought his troubles on himself, and didn't deserve another go-round. His wife had deserved that, and much more. The vast, uncaring universe unfurled above him, indifferent to what tiny human beings thought they deserved.

Some ruckus was going on at the other end of the camp, but he didn't feel like sorting it out just yet. He heard excited voices, but felt no compunction to go find out why they were excited. There was too much going on around here these days, not enough of it related to science. He had come out here partly to take his mind off his troubles, and instead they had multiplied like rabbits. They had multiplied like Digger Phelps.

"Mr. Brown? I understand you were looking for me?"

He turned to see Pete Turnstall, the young man with the camera. Turnstall had a habit of sneaking up on him at night.

"Are you all right, sir?" Turnstall asked, his voice full of concern once he saw Brown's watery eyes.

"I'm fine," Brown said. A couple of quick blinks disposed of the tears. "Just got something in my eye."

"The dust is bad out here," Turnstall said, and Brown nodded in agreement.

"I was wondering if you happened to get a photograph of those dinosaurs we saw running around this morning?"

That he could even ask such a question showed the depth of the craziness that was going on.

"Is that what those things were? I wasn't sure."

"Yes, they were dinosaurs."

"I thought those were all dead a long time ago."

"So did everyone else."

"Well. You know, they really didn't stand still very long. There was a lot of dust, too. And I was trying not to get in their way, of course."

"So you didn't take one?"

Turnstall laughed.

"I didn't say that. I'm giving you all the reasons why my picture isn't very good. I did get one. *One*. I had my camera set up for something else when they came along. Thank God for that, or I wouldn't have gotten anything. But one of the dinosaurs stopped for just a couple of seconds, and I happened to have film in the camera. He was headed straight for me, but I don't know if he could tell what I was. I had my head under the cloth, and brother, you can believe I didn't take it out."

Brown laughed at that, and it felt good to laugh.

"So what I ended up with is a head-on shot of this thing coming at me. He's all blurry, because I didn't have time to focus and he refused to stand completely still. The negative is underexposed, also because he wouldn't stand still for long. You can't really see his arms, because he was waving them around so much. And you can't see his legs at all because of the dust."

"But it looks like a dinosaur?"

"Yes. I'm real excited about that. I reckon I'm the only person to have a picture of an actual living dinosaur."

"I think we can safely say that's true. But what will you do with it?"

"I was thinking I could sell it. I can probably sell it and retire."

"You probably can. I don't suppose you'd consider delaying that for a day or two?"

Turnstall looked at him suspiciously.

"Maybe. Why?"

"It's a long story, but I think your photograph could perform a great service for science."

Turnstall ran his fingers over his rounded cheeks.

"Will this service pay well?"

"I think we could work something out. Actually, if things go well, you could have the chance to take more and better pictures of dinosaurs. It should be well worth your time."

He definitely looked interested.

"What is this service?"

"It will take a great deal of explaining. Actually, it will take some explaining and some travel. We're heading out tomorrow, but we're not going far. Any chance I could talk you into coming with us?"

Turnstall shrugged.

"Nothing around here anymore, so I don't see why not."

"Yes, I guess with that bank robber dead, there's not much reason to stick around."

"He isn't dead."

"He isn't?"

"Actually, he's right here in this camp."

"He is?"

"Yep. I helped bring him here myself."

Brown didn't need to feel guilty for leaving him after all.

"Everyone seems to be able to cheat death out here," Brown muttered, half under his breath.

"What does that mean?" Turnstall asked.

"Nothing. So what do you say? Will you come with us?"

Turnstall looked skeptical, but curious.

"So I'll have the chance to take more dinosaur pictures, you say?"

"Maybe. I can't make you a guarantee. You'll have to

work fast, of course. You've seen how they run around."

"I can work fast."

"How about your horse? Is your horse fast? We've got a lot of ground to cover, starting first thing in the morning."

"My horse is fast, but my cart isn't. With all those chemicals clanking around, you can't exactly gallop along."

Brown hadn't thought about that. All he really needed was the one negative, but he couldn't very well just take off with it. Like Turnstall said, it was potentially worth a great deal of money.

"I tell you what," he said. "We really need to travel light, and fast. Leave your wagon and most of your chemicals here. Our cook is staying behind, and we'll have him watch it. Bring only your camera and a few plates, and just enough chemicals for those."

"But I'd rather have all my things if I'm going to have a chance at these pictures."

"You may not have a chance at these pictures if you bring all your things, because the chance may not still be there when you get there. You've got to bring only the barest of essentials. Break your camera down and we'll distribute it amongst the men so it's not so heavy for you to carry. Do the same thing with the chemicals."

Turnstall made a face like Brown had just asked him to saw off an arm and leave it behind.

"I hope this is worth my while, like you said."

"Mr. Turnstall, if you do as I said, I can at the very least guarantee you that you will see things you have never seen before."

That appeared to be the way to a photographer's heart.

"I'll do it."

When he smiled, he looked like a big kid.

"Great. I don't suppose you have that negative of the dinosaur with you?"

"It's in the wagon. Just over there."

"Could I borrow it for a moment?"

"It can't leave my sight."

"Fine. Actually, I'll need your help anyway. Go get it, please, and do you see that tall man standing there? The one with the brown hair? His name is Eric. Could you ask him to join us?"

THIRTY-EIGHT

It was a beautiful day, and they were making very good time. Dusk would be upon them soon, but they still had time to set up camp. Eric could not get over how beautiful this planet was. He had to remind himself that he was home, but every time he did he was glad. Brown, leading the way, rounded a ridge to begin the descent into a small valley shaped like a cup. It was actually a complete tea set; the northern edge of the bowl rose steeply and then ended abruptly, dropping two hundred feet to a flat rock outcropping that resembled nothing so much as a saucer. The illusion ended just beyond the saucer, in the form of a black rock wall that rose nearly vertically. It didn't look like anything that belonged near a cup and saucer.

Suddenly Brown halted, which nearly caused a multiple collision of horses.

"What is it?" asked Alice Paul, who was riding behind her son, having refused Digger Phelps' offer to ride in his wagon in place of the bewildered preacher, Winthrow Parnassus, who was under the impression they were attending some kind of religious meeting.

Brown cantered his horse around to face the crew that followed him. He looked surprised, as if he had just discovered that people had been following him all day.

"What is going on here?" Brown asked, his voice sharp and angry. "Why aren't we digging out that skeleton?"

"Oh, no," said the photographer, the man named Pete Turnstall. "He's doing it again."

"You mean he's done this before?" Eric asked.

"Yes. It's like he suddenly forgets what he's doing."

Eric felt a sinking sensation. He spurred his horse and rode closer to Brown, not that looking at him would help.

"Do I know you?" Brown asked as Eric rode up to him, but Eric ignored him.

"I forgot," Eric said. "You had a memory revoker implanted in your head. They had it set to interrupt your memory every thirty seconds."

"Who are you?" Brown asked.

"Does that mean we're close now?" asked S.L. Burgess, ignoring Brown's angry look.

"Yes, I think so."

He had thought they still had a few miles to go, but maybe Art Kan had stopped at a closer site.

"The device operates within a two-mile radius," he said to Burgess. "They had it turned off, but apparently they turned it back on, as a precaution. It seemed to hit him pretty hard. Maybe the rocks here were blocking the signal, because I'd say we're actually closer than two miles. I'd say we're right on top of them."

There was something else he was overlooking, but he couldn't think what it was, until he heard a shout coming from the wagon driven by his older self. The preacher Winthrow Parnassus was riding in that wagon, along with the straw-headed young man who said his name was William the Conqueror and—Luther Gumpson. Eric's heart began to beat just a little bit harder.

"Luther shot that boy!" Parnassus shouted.

The sounds of a scuffle wafted to the front of the column. Eric turned his horse around and galloped to the back, where he found William the Conqueror on the ground and Phelps and Parnassus wrestling with Luther Gumpson, who seemed rather baffled and wasn't putting up much of a fight.

"Ow, he shot me," William the Conqueror moaned. "He shot me in the back, the yellow dog."

"This is not very helpful!" Phelps said between grunted breaths.

"And killing is a sin!" Parnassus tossed in for good measure.

"He can't help it," Eric said from atop his horse. "The Swedes put some equipment in his head that gives him an uncontrollable urge to kill."

Parnassus and Phelps looked at Gumpson's sweating face and then started to loosen their grip.

"Don't let him up!" Eric said. "The urge comes back every thirty seconds."

They tightened their grip again.

"You're hurting my arm!" Gumpson said. His face was shiny with pain-induced sweat. "If he hadn't shot me in my good arm already, he'd be dead," Gumpson said. "I had to shoot him with my left hand, and I'm not so good with that."

William the Conqueror did not seem mollified by the explanation. He reached for his gun, only to realize that it was the very one Gumpson had shot him with.

"Somebody loan me a gun," he moaned. "Now I can call it self-defense."

"No more shooting," Parnassus said, and Gumpson nodded.

"I didn't want to shoot him. I don't know what came over me."

"I just told you what came over you," Eric said as he dismounted from his borrowed horse. "The problem is, it's going to keep coming over you twice a minute."

He looked at his older self.

"Now would be a good time to pry the gun out of his hand."

"Here, have it," Gumpson said, and began stretching his fingers out. Suddenly he tightened them again and flexed his arm.

"He's doing it again!" Phelps shouted as he pinned the arm to the ground.

Gumpson fired one shot, but it went along the ground and bounced off a rock. William the Conqueror flinched as if he had been shot again.

"Give me that gun!" he said.

"No," Eric said. "No more shooting. I'll take the gun." Gumpson gave it up.

"I didn't mean to," he said.

"I know you didn't. It's not your fault, but we can't just let you try to kill someone every time we turn around. Whether you mean to do it or not, you would thin us out pretty fast."

"Excuse me," the shot young man said. "Can I get some help over here? I'm bleeding."

Eric walked over to him. The rest of Brown's crew had gathered around, but they didn't seem to know much about stopping bleeding. Dead animals were their speciality, and the longer dead, the better. Eric calmed the twitching gunfighter and then slowly pulled away his vest. Despite what he had claimed, Eric couldn't see any bleeding. The vest wasn't even stuck to his side. When he got it clear, Eric saw that there was no bullet hole.

"Hold on," he said, and slowly pulled the shirt away from the skin.

There was a long red welt just under the boy's ribcage, but nothing else. When he dropped the vest flap back, Eric saw a matching streak there. He had assumed it was just dirt.

"He just grazed you," Eric said. "You'll be fine. Just try not to touch it for a while."

"He *missed* me?" William the Conqueror said. "But it hurt like hell."

"I'm sure it did, but you'll be all right. Just try not to touch it."

The boy got to his feet and slowly tucked his shirt back into his pants. Brown's crew turned away as he did so, tactful enough not to see his obvious embarrassment. Even Eric could recognize that.

"What the hell is going on?" he heard Brown shout from what had become the rear of the crew. "Everybody get back to camp! What are we doing out here? We've got a skeleton to collect!"

"So what are we going to do with these two?" Eric's older self asked. "We can't go in against them Swedes like this. We've got our own worst enemy right here with this one."

"I'm sorry," Gumpson said. "Can you get off my arm?"

"You're right," Eric said. "We'll have to leave them back that way, out of the range of the ship."

"But where?" asked S.L. Burgess. "We can't just leave them out in the open."

Phelps offered the use of his wagon, which was covered and would keep the sun off their heads. No one wanted to leave them alone, but no one wanted to stay with them, either.

"I can't stay," Eric said. "I know what Brown had in mind."

Burgess tried to get his mother to stay, but she wouldn't hear anything of it.

"I'm the only person here who has faced these people before," she said, a claim to which Digger Phelps objected. "One of the only people," she corrected. "I'm not staying out here."

"Fine," Eric said. "Why don't we just tie them together, in case something happens and the range gets extended? If Luther tries to kill Mr. Brown, he won't be able to, and in any case Brown will forget he's tried it."

That was the course finally agreed to. Just as the sun was setting, a seething Barnum Brown was tied to Luther Gumpson, who alternately submitted to the ropes passively and tried to bite those who were tying him up.

"Where are you going?" Brown shouted.

A minute later he shouted again.

"Where is everybody?"

THIRTY-NINE

A big —— covered in —— sauce would be nice. Maybe a ——, cooked just to the edge of hardness, with a side dish of ——. Lasse felt his mouth watering at the very thought of it. He was starving, and he couldn't wait for the crew to leave so he could sneak to the food cache and get something to eat. They didn't have any of the Nes food he craved, but he would eat just about anything right now, including the stuff that kept human beings alive. When he was this hungry, no sacrifice was too great.

He watched the monitor as, one by one, the crew left the ship for the night's work. He couldn't tap into the dig plans, but knew from memory that they were atop a particularly rich bone field and they had a lot of work to do. The crew was so shorthanded, what with deaths and defections, that it appeared they were all going outside again. Lasse knew that Art Kan had originally intended not to set foot on the planet, which he considered an inferior world, but circumstances had forced his feet and he had already been out quite a bit more than he wished.

Lasse had been spending his time with the monitor wisely. He had plumbed the depths of the calculating machine that controlled the ship and probably knew more about it than did the rest of the crew. He had a plan in mind, but he knew it would do no good without food.

277

The puniest specimen of Earth creature could come along and knock him over right about now. The delicious Nes food of his childhood swarmed around his mind, so convincingly that once or twice he found his hand floating in midair, grasping for sustenance and flavor that wasn't really there.

Lasse held on to the top of the cargo bench with both hands, to keep himself from lunging after a floating lunch. He had nearly fallen off the last time his hallucinating mind pursued a hovering ——, and he didn't want to succeed the next time. Aside from the danger that the crew might hear the sound of his head hitting the floor, there was also the danger he would knock himself out and just die right there, which was hardly how a hero of the Nes race should make his exit. He held on and watched the blips of light on the monitor, which indicated where the crew were located. The last one exited the ship; it must be dark now. Time to get his food.

Just as he prepared to drag himself up to the top deck, he spotted another blip, this one coming in from the other side of the ship. It followed an erratic course, unlike the others. He stared at the blip. Now who could that be? Then he remembered Earth Reclamation Unit 17. Yes, the ship would recognize him as a crew member; that had to be who it was. Unless things had changed, Earth Reclamation Unit 17 had given in to his human past and had parted ways with the Swedes. He could be a valuable ally. But how to reach him? Surely Lasse could wait just a minute or two, until he had some food. Then again, maybe not. Lasse sighed. He remembered that Earth Reclamation Unit 17 was hooked to a communicator, but it didn't seem to work. He consulted the calculating machine and was reminded that Earth Reclamation Unit 17 also had a camera system implanted in his head. The Swedes were never content to leave well enough alone. They always had to tinker with things.

Lasse would have preferred the voice communication system, but that couldn't be helped. He sat and pondered, staring vacantly at the purposeful blips on one side of the screen and the lone, straggling one on the other.

Code. That was it. Earth Reclamation Unit 17 would have been versed in Swede code. The people of Earth had a similar system, which they called Morse code, but the Swede version was simpler and at the same time had more depth. It was worth a try. He thought about how best to do it. He could have the camera in his eye turn on and off to represent the binary code, but that could damage the mechanism and possibly Unit 17 wouldn't even notice. Perhaps it would be better to turn the light source on and off. Even if the camera was turned off, doing that would momentarily blind Unit 17's left eye. Surely that would get his attention. Lasse coded the message and sent it. He kept the visions of food at bay as best he could, and settled down to wait.

S.L. Burgess was deep into a discussion with Digger Phelps, when they both nearly tripped over the man named Eric. They were walking behind a ridge, just at the edge where the saucer began to swoop up and away from the plate, when suddenly Eric came to a complete halt and groped for a rock to steady himself against. It was almost fully dark, and Burgess and Phelps were so intent on their discussion that they nearly fell right over him.

They were talking about dynamite, and its potential uses against a spaceship from another world. Dynamite was the only sort of weapon they had that could be conceivably useful. Guns alone wouldn't work. Anything that could fly through space could surely take a couple of potshots without trouble. Dynamite would be better, they decided, but they weren't sure for what. Raining rocks and debris down on the ship probably wouldn't do anything, since the ship had already dug itself in under the dirt. Lobbing a stick or two through the open doors would definitely do *some* kind of damage, they decided, but there was the sticky problem of getting the doors open in the first place.

Eric had said this ship was not using what he called an energy field, which, in Burgess's mother's book, had been called a ghost wall. It kept people away from the ship, generally, but it was also an energy drain and the leader of the space people had decided against it, since he wasn't just one space person by himself, but had a crew to work with. So that problem was solved, but that still didn't mean they could get the doors open.

"Eric, what's wrong?" Phelps asked when his younger self stopped moving and began flashing the light from his head.

"My eye," Eric said. "I can't see out of my left eye. Oh wait, now I can't. Now I can again. Now I can't."

"Is your camera thing acting up?"

"Yes, I guess so. No. Wait, that's—I recognize this. Be quiet for just a minute."

They stood in silence. The rest of the crew, which had been following them, stopped too, even though a couple of the stragglers were still above the ridge, out in the open. It was almost too dark to even see them, but they flattened themselves down as close to the ground as they could just in case.

"What is it?" Burgess asked after a minute, when the light flashes had stopped.

"It's code. A man named Lasse is inside the ship."

"They've found us?" Phelps asked fearfully.

"No. It's a long story. He is from that lizard-man race your mother told you about. He is a spy. He's trapped in the bottom of the ship, but he's tapped into the calculating machine that runs it. He will help us."

"How?"

"He wants to know if we have any weapons."

"Dynamite," Phelps and Burgess said in unison.

"Hold on," Eric said.

His light flashed some more, and he was careful to point it at the ground.

"He wants to know the properties and strength of dynamite."

Burgess looked at Phelps.

"Tell him it's pretty strong. It can bring down a rock wall."

"Hold on."

There was more light flashing, and then Eric straightened up.

"He also wants to know if we have any food. He's hungry."

"They came all this way without food?" Burgess asked.

There was a general ransacking of pockets, and eventually a bundle of crackers and some hardtack was produced.

"That will have to do," Eric said, looking at the rather pitiful assemblage.

Everyone had eaten as they traveled, and the food being saved for the morning was back at the wagon.

"How does that work?" Burgess asked. "Your signaling, I mean. How can you send back and forth to him?"

"He can tell when I turn my light on and off. I do that as a code."

"Like Morse code."

"Yes, only better."

Burgess didn't take that as some kind of anti-Earth slight, seeing as how Eric was in the same boat as the rest of the human beings.

"Enough about that. Give me the dynamite. I need to take it to him. He has some use for it in mind."

"There's more than you can carry," Burgess said. "I'm going with you."

There was a general squawking among the crew at that.

His mother didn't want him to go; Phelps wanted to go in his place; some of the crew didn't want anybody to go anywhere.

"I'm going," Burgess said to his mother, his voice as firm as he could make it. "You've seen a spaceship. I haven't. That goes for you, too, Digger. You've seen more of one than anybody here. It's my turn."

He and Eric went back to the horses. Just as they were about to mount up, the college student named Harryhausen appeared.

"I'm going with you. There's too much dynamite for even both of you to carry. I want to see what a spaceship looks like, too."

They argued with him but that quickly became evident as a lost cause, so they gave up and used the light of the rising moon to ride to the wagon. They tried to discourage Harryhausen by forcing him to ride behind Burgess, without a saddle, but he was not deterred. The dynamite had been strapped to the wagon's bottom, under the carriage. Brown hadn't wanted to bring it, but was afraid it would get stolen from the camp. Now it would come in handy.

"We're back," Burgess announced as they dismounted.

He pulled aside the covering. The wagon was empty. No Barnum Brown. No Luther Gumpson. Only loosened ropes.

"Oh, my," Burgess said.

Food—and an Earth explosive called dynamite—was on the way. Lasse did not know exactly what to think about the dynamite, but he awaited the food with great expectation. The blood had rushed to both his heads, his real inner one and his fake outer one, when Earth Reclamation Unit 17 had signaled that it was coming. Everyone was out of the ship, Lasse signaled back. Earth Reclamation Unit 17 still had a crew identification button and could get on board. He could get the food, get down in the hold with Lasse, and then things would really get interesting.

He was so far gone he would consider eating the dynamite. Actually, he wasn't sure what it was. With a burst of energy he hoisted himself up to consult the calculating machine to see what dynamite was, and how it worked. He had barely begun to read when the monitor wiped away the information and showed a blip entering the ship. Someone was back. Earth Reclamation Unit 17 couldn't sneak aboard now. Lasse groaned, loudly, almost to the point of not caring if anyone heard him. Now he wouldn't get either food or dynamite.

"What's a good curse word I can say?" Eric asked Burgess. "Damn?"

"Damn is good. You can find a lot of uses for it. What's happened?"

"Lasse signaled that someone has reentered the ship. They probably have Gumpson and Brown now."

"Well, how are you going to get in there with the dynamite?"

"That's a good question. He said if I could somehow get it under the ship, he could get to it."

"But the ship is underground," Harryhausen pointed out.

"I know. That's the problem."

They sat in silence, mulling their non-existent options.

"How about if there were a way to get the ship to come to the surface?" Harryhausen asked. "You were on that thing. How would you get it to surface?"

Eric tried to think, but couldn't come up with anything.

"How about the dynamite?" Harryhausen asked. "Light it and throw it on top of where the ship is. They might think they are under attack, and will come to the top. Then you throw the dynamite underneath the ship and let that guy have it."

Eric thought about it. Art Kan might come to the

surface and stay there, it's true. Or he could fly away somewhere else and they'd never rescue Lasse or Brown or Gumpson.

"It's better than sitting here doing nothing," Burgess urged, and Eric could not argue with that. "Get the dynamite and saddle up. Let's see what happens."

FORTY

Art Kan stared at the two men who were motionless in the red-light chambers. He had not intended to stay at this location long, and it would be helpful if he and Hern could be outside with the others, collecting the bones. Instead, he was again tormented by these humans.

"Mr. Gumpson, I see that you do not seem to comprehend that the purpose of *escape* is to *get away*. You have exited our ship in some interesting and even stylish ways, but here you are again. And Mr. Brown, I can only assume that you are here once again because of professional envy. Because I have your bones, and I'm not giving them back."

He leaned in and glowered at both men, but got no response. Of course, he couldn't get a response because they were frozen solid. He was tempted to unfreeze them a little, to see if he could tell by their faces if they were afraid, but when he did that they tended to talk and he didn't want to hear anything they might have to say. He had heard quite enough from both of them.

"Hern, what is the situation?"

"I found them, sir. I was examining the far ridge just before we went out when I saw something that looked familiar. I went over and found them in a wagon, tied together. Immobilized. The man who shoots well has been wounded. Our equipment controlling him was shattered, except for the implant that makes him helplessly violent every thirty seconds."

285

"That's the most important one, anyway. How about the other man? Mr. Brown?"

"He is as we saw him last. His memory revoker is still installed and working, and in fact seems to have been used quite a bit. His thoughts must be a jumble. He probably doesn't remember how he got here, or why he is here at all."

Kan made a humming sound and stared at Brown, who stared back at him in frozen passivity. Alf Swenson had come here and run afoul of an Earth scientist. Two, actually, and the end result had been that he collected very few of the bones he traveled all this way to get. Here he was, confronted with the same sort of problem from the same sort of individual. Perhaps on Earth the warrior class instead became scientists as a way to channel their aggressive, stubborn energies. This easy, backwater job was becoming something of a challenge, and Kan couldn't decide if he liked that or not. What was the Earth phrase he had run across—know your enemies?

"Those gadgets of yours, Hern—how do they work? Can you connect me to that memory revoker you have planted in this man's mind?"

Hern looked confused.

"You want to forget something, sir?"

"No. I mean, can you reverse it, so I can read his thoughts?"

Hern frowned.

"That's not a bad idea, but it won't work. I can't get it to call up individual thoughts. It's possible that it can pick up strong feelings, however. It could perhaps detect feelings—and maybe even a few thoughts—that are old and deep and therefore have become quite prevalent in the brain."

Kan was not sure what the difference was, but he didn't press the issue. Hern was better at doing things than he was at explaining them.

"How long will it take?"

"Not long. I already have him hooked to the scanner, so I will just have to hook you into that. I will have to install a connector into your own human brain, sir."

"That's fine. Stick anything in me you want."

"If I may say so, sir, it sounds like you are becoming interested in scientific explanation after all."

"You may not say that, Hern."

"Yes, sir."

Ten Earth minutes later, Kan stood facing Brown. A metal tube snaked from his head, just above the ear, and ran into the wall.

"Ready," Hern said.

"Do it."

Kan closed his eyes. There was nothing at first, but then the feelings started to flow. He felt rage, such that his whole body quaked. It was a helpless rage, directed at him. Kan smiled. So he was getting through to Mr. Brown, after all. There was a lot of fear, too. He would have been disappointed without that. Fear, rage. Kan could feel those things through his own human form, but he could keep them in check.

"Enough, sir?" he heard Hern's distant voice say.

"No."

His own voice sounded thick, like he was on one of these Earth intoxicants. He wanted to know more. Fear and rage did not explain why this man would work so hard to keep the dinosaur bones on his planet. Surely they meant nothing to him, aside from intellectual curiosity, and that was supposedly not something that would lead Earth residents to do much of anything. There had to be more.

Kan thought he detected something much deeper. Swimming through the emotions was a little like flying over the landscape of the Earth. You could see mountaintops and you could see valleys, but there were things that went even deeper than the valleys. Kan waited for the feeling to come up, whatever it was. He tried to think of things to spur it along. He thought of the landscape of Montana. He thought of people.

When the feeling actually hit him he almost buckled at the knees. He held on to the wall to keep from stumbling.

"Sir—" Hern said.

"Cut it off," Kan said hoarsely. "Cut it off."

When he opened his eyes again he found he was sweating. Barnum Brown stood before him, his face suffused in red light, no emotion on his frozen face at all. So that was the cauldron that bubbled below that quiet surface!

"What was it, sir?"

"Unhook me first!"

Hern fiddled with something at his forehead and then removed the connection.

"What was it?"

It was hard to explain. It could not be put into words. So that was what it felt like to live in a body made of meat. It had been so long for the Swedes that they had forgotten. It was a prison. The only connection came through these skins, these awful monkey skins. A life spent in them could be short, and no one knew what happened to you when you died. Even you could not know what happened to you when you died.

"Sir?"

"His wife died, Hern. He misses her."

"Sir?"

What else could he say? Life was uncertain. The past was the only guide. The past. The bones were past.

"I don't know how to explain it to you, Hern. I just know they want these dinosaur bones more than we do."

"Well, they're not getting—" Hern started to say, and then the ship was rocked by a violent blast.

Kan was nearly jerked off his feet.

"What is that?" Hern shouted.

"I don't know. Some kind of weapon."

"What are they doing?"

"I told you, Hern, they want those bones. Get everyone back in here. Punch up that monitor and let's see what's going on."

The screen showed three men on two horses, tossing what looked like flaming sticks at the ship. After each stick was tossed, it would explode.

"Is there any damage to the ship?"

"No, sir."

"Fine. How are our replicas doing?"

"They're ready to go, sir."

"Let them out. Put them at full power. Let them eat some people if they want."

Maybe he had a vague understanding of what was driving these people, but now he didn't care. He had superior technology, and he would use it.

"I can't, sir. I need to get the controller outside, and I can't open the door the way this thing is shaking around."

Kan hated to raise the ship so soon after going to all the trouble of burying it. Maybe he'd just quit burying it at all. The ship could be stable once it was in the air, explosions or no. It was powerful enough to resist whatever it was they were throwing. Its weakness came when it was buried and under attack. Maybe it was time for a change in Swede policy. No more hiding the ships. Let the Earth people see them, and be afraid.

"All right. Wait until everyone is in, and then take us up. Hover just off the ground. Put the controller in the doorway, and show me some dinosaurs, at full power. Let's finish this once and for all."

FORTY-ONE

"I am going to provide you with a once-in-a-lifetime scientific opportunity," the big man said to Barnum Brown.

Brown was frozen in a tiny chamber, red lights beaming into his eyes. This was the sort of place where Digger Phelps said he had been kept thirty-one years ago. Brown wondered if he was now destined to meet a younger version of himself someday. Maybe they would create one with more hair.

"Are you ready, Hern?" the big man shouted.

"Ready," came the reply.

"Now, look at these, Mr. Brown. Take a good long look. These are what you have been seeking."

Standing before them were the two Tyrannosaurus rexes that had previously attacked the camp. Brown would have flinched if he could have moved. The dinosaurs weren't moving either, though, so he mentally relaxed. This spaceman was right. He should take a good look while he could. They were huge, magnificent. He tried to commit every inch of them to memory, for use later in recreating the pose of their skeletons. They had huge, broad tails, legs as big as tree trunks, heads more toothy and fearsome than any shark. Then his eyes came to rest on the front arms of the beasts. They were muscular, but were very, very short; monstrous compared to his own arms but almost tiny in comparison with the rest of the creatures to which they were attached.

"I see you looking at the front claws," the big man said. "Let me explain something to you, to demonstrate why we are interested in these creatures. You see that those front arms are small. Do you know why?"

He didn't. He couldn't even shake his head.

"I'll tell you. Long ago, my forebears visited this planet. They were quite taken by some of the flora and fauna, and set about trying to improve on it. However, after a time they became a bit—decadent is the best word. Somewhat like your own later Roman Empire. My forebears decided they wanted to create a special creature just for them, from the available dinosaurs. They wanted something fierce, something memorable. They took a fairly humble carnivore that was basically a scavenger. They created these."

He swept back an arm to indicate the T. rexes behind him, as if they needed pointing out.

"The creatures were bred to create huge, impressive heads. However, they were essentially beasts of burden. My forebears liked to ride on their backs, just as you do your horses. The arms were reduced to an almost pitiful size, so that the creatures couldn't rake their masters off their backs."

This did not seem very likely to Brown, but he couldn't think of a better explanation. He had never heard of a dinosaur with only two tiny, almost vestigial, claws. He would have assumed they would have three, and on longer arms at that.

"Now you know something that virtually no one else on your planet knows," the big man said. "For all the good it's going to do you."

The ship had been lurching and shuddering, but the big man had ignored that during his talk. Now the ship was firm and steady, and Brown watched as part of the room disappeared, to be replaced with a door that descended into the darkness of the night.

"Through extensive research, we have been able to

replicate these creatures, in a simulated form. They are
not technically real, but they are awfully close. In fact,
they are quite real enough to eat your entire crew. I think
I will prove that to you right now. Hern, let them out."

"Look at that!" Alice Paul shouted when the explosions
started.

The heads of the crew began popping up to peer over
the ridge. There was apparently no need for secrecy, now
that dynamite was being lobbed at the spaceship. At least
that was what they presumed was happening; there was
no way to tell from this distance. If the space people
didn't realize they were here by now, then they had some
serious problems.

"What's happening?" a voice asked.

"I can't see," said another.

"I don't know," Mrs. Paul said. "But why don't we find
out? They probably need some help up there."

Like a ragtag group of Cossacks sweeping across the
plain, Brown's crew began running across the small valley,
pistols or rifles in hand. No one expected those to be of
any real use, but no one opted to leave them holstered,
either, just in case. The ground began rumbling as they
neared the explosions. They could hear the frightened
whinny of horses and the shouts of Eric, Harryhausen
and her own son, out there somewhere in the darkness.
Alice Paul had already lost one man in her life out here,
and she did not want to lose another.

"Sitting Lizard!" she shouted, but heard only chaos in
reply. "Where are you?"

"Mother!" she heard. "Get back! Everyone! Get back!"

She had thought the ground was rumbling from the
dynamite, but it seemed that something more powerful
was at work. An eerie green glow began emanating from
the ground, and then the edge of something huge and
round began to appear. It was the ship, coming up out of
the ground. The light silhouetted the two horses and their

three riders, as they abandoned the attack and got out of the way. Rocks and debris poured off the ship, kicking up a dust cloud that made it seem like the ship was on fire. It was like watching a phoenix rise from the ashes.

Suddenly a horse stopped in front of her. It was Sitting Lizard, sharing the horse with that college student Harryhausen. There didn't seem to be any more room, but her son offered his arm.

"Get up here!" he shouted. "We don't know what they're going to do!"

The ground stopped shaking. She looked back at the ship. It hovered about twenty feet in the air, and the green glow coming from it was stronger now.

"Let's go, Mom. Let's get away from here."

"Wait."

They stood, watching the ship. The kid Harryhausen seemed to be drinking in every inch of it, as if memorizing it for later. After what seemed like eons, but must have been just minutes, a door opened in front of the ship. After a moment the ground began shaking again, but for a very different reason. Two giant monsters appeared in the doorway and pounded their way to the ground. She knew enough about dinosaurs to know what they were and, besides, she had already seen them. They were T. rexes, and they looked hungry.

Earth Reclamation Unit 17 breathed a sigh of relief when the ship surfaced. The dynamite was heavy, and he and the others were forced to carry the sticks under their arms, which made it hard to control the horses, and which also hurt like hell. He dropped a few sticks when he forced the horse to run under the ship. It didn't want to go, and the vigorous spurring that was required made him lose his grip. It couldn't be helped. He waited until most of the dirt and rocks had fallen off the ship, and then galloped to a spot underneath its middle. The ship's silver surface hung just above his head.

Drop it, Lasse signaled in his head. Just drop it and get away. Eric did so, but saw that Burgess was having trouble convincing his horse to proceed. It pawed at the edge of the ship, unwilling to go all the way under.

"Just throw it!" Eric shouted. "Throw it where mine is!"

Burgess and Harryhausen had loosened up their arms throwing the dynamite on top of the ship, and their aim was pretty good, too.

"Now go!"

Lasse said he could get to the dynamite through a portal in the bottom of the ship, using his Multi-Purpose Tool, but he didn't want them around when he tried it lest he snare them, too. Eric took the warning seriously. He didn't want to get back in that ship, no matter what happened. He breathed a sigh of relief when he got out from underneath it, but his relief was remarkably short-lived. The horses weren't the only animals pawing the Earth. The dinosaurs were loose, just as Brown had feared, and that meant he had even more to do.

Earth Reclamation Unit 17 rode his horse to the members of Brown's crew, who had been running toward the ship but were now running away from it, and making good time at that.

"Pete Turnstall!" he shouted. "Where is the photographer?"

He found Turnstall toward the back of the pack, lugging a leather bag that contained his camera and plates.

"Where is my tripod?" Turnstall shouted, but no one was listening. "It's dark! How am I going to get a picture?"

Eric reined the horse up alongside him and stepped down. The horse, freed of its rider, took off into the night. Just as well, for him. A horse made a bigger target for a Tyrannosaurus than did a person.

"Where is that plate you made of the dinosaur?" Eric shouted to Turnstall. "I need it!"

◆   ◆   ◆

Turnstall fished around in the bag and produced the plate. Eric grabbed him by the arm and began running to the far side of the little valley. They needed to get to the lip of the valley, away from the light of the spaceship and close to the black wall that rose in the background.

"Slow down! You're breaking my plates!" Turnstall shouted, but Eric didn't let up.

Nobody seemed to care much about his plates, but he could understand the rush. The longer the dinosaurs were loose, the better the chances that someone from the crew would end up as dinner.

When they got as close to the high point of the ridge as they dared, Eric grabbed Turnstall by the shoulders and positioned him. Turnstall was used to doing this to others for portrait shots, but wasn't used to being on the other side of things. Eric was a little rough, and Turnstall hoped his own camera-side manners were better.

"Hold the plate steady. Steady!" Eric shouted. "Now look away! Don't look at me, whatever you do!"

Turnstall, stunned, did as he was told. He could hear Eric positioning himself close to the image, to Turnstall's right, and from the corner of his eye could see a bright light.

It worked. Brown was a smart man. Rising behind them on the black wall of the cliff was a dinosaur, or at least a reasonable semblance thereof. It was a little blurry, but it was appropriately huge and menacing, twice the size of the actual dinosaurs. You couldn't see the legs, and it wasn't in color, but it was unmistakably a dinosaur. Turnstall craned his neck around to look over his left shoulder and stared up at it in awe. Then he made the mistake of turning his head back and squinting down at his plate. The light almost blinded him, but what he saw filled him with horror.

"You're melting the emulsion!" he cried.

"Turn away!" Eric hissed.

"But you're melting it!"

"Turn away! Don't move it! The dinosaurs haven't seen it yet!"

Or maybe they had. Turnstall faced away from the rock wall, squinting his right eye shut against the light from Eric's head. He heard a bellowing coming from that direction. It was getting louder.

"Pete! What are they doing?" Eric asked.

"Coming this way," Turnstall said. "Right at us."

"Stay steady."

"They're coming right for us!"

"Duck down, slowly."

Moving as one, Eric and Turnstall got as low to the ground as they could, without losing the image. Turnstall could feel the ground shaking underneath his feet, but he saw that the beasts were going to pass just to their right.

"Where are the people?" Eric asked.

"Don't know," Turnstall said. The dinosaurs were close, and his hands were starting to shake from the pounding of the ground. "Can't see."

"Hold steady."

The shaking increased. The dinosaurs towered over them. He could hear their breathing.

"What are we supposed to do when they get here?" Turnstall asked, his voice a tense whisper, his words almost mangled by his panting.

"Just keep them here. Distract them. Maybe move the plate around. Make them think they're facing another dinosaur."

"What if they step on us?"

"Then we move."

Eric felt something brush by him. A claw the size of a man's forearm pushed a furrow in the ground just inches to his right, but he didn't budge.

"That was awfully close," Eric said. "Wish you had told me about it."

"Wasn't looking at that one," Turnstall said.

These creatures were moving awfully fast. They pounded on by, heading for what they must think was a showdown with a big bruiser.

"They're not slowing down," Turnstall said.

Indeed they weren't. Brown had conceived of the idea as a way to keep the beasts occupied to give time for his crew to run for cover, but now it seemed the geography of the area was making for a different solution. The green light from the ship played along the backs of the dinosaurs, and as Eric craned his neck to watch, the shimmering creatures ran up to the edge of the cup and careened right over it, disappearing into darkness where the feet of their imaginary attacker should have been. A prolonged angry howling echoed up the black wall, and then there was silence.

Eric switched off his light. Turnstall swiveled to see where the creatures had been.

"They went right over the wall," he said.

"That they did. They must have gotten too excited and didn't look where they were going."

Turnstall stood up on shaky feet and walked slowly to the lip of the cliff, some twenty yards away. He peered into the darkness, but could see nothing.

"I can't get a picture of anything down there, it's too dark," he said.

He walked back to where Eric was sitting, holding a hand over his eye.

"Are you all right?" he asked Eric.

"I burned through my cornea," Eric said dispassionately. "It wasn't made for such a prolonged exposure to high heat and bright light."

"Does it hurt?"

"A little. I'll be blind in that eye."

"Sorry."

Turnstall turned to face the ship, holding the glass plate up to the green light still pouring from its open door.

"You melted some of the emulsion," he said glumly. "I'm not sure I can print from this."

The illuminated dinosaur had been getting even more unfocused as the beasts approached it, not that the beasts had noticed.

"It saved a lot of lives," Eric said, but Turnstall was not consoled.

He supposed Eric had made a greater sacrifice, giving up his eye, but that didn't make him feel any better.

"That damn Barnum Brown," he muttered.

FORTY-TWO

"Where are my dinosaurs?" Art Kan thundered when the beasts disappeared off the monitor.

"They seem to have fallen into a hole of some kind," said a worried-looking Hern.

He had better be worried. Those dinosaur replicas were his responsibility.

"Get them back!"

Kan knew this was an impossible order, at least right away. The creatures that were recreated within the depths of the calculating machine and were then beamed into the real world required a huge amount of energy, and behaved exactly like the real thing. If they performed some stunt that would kill a real dinosaur, then they died. When they died, the calculating machine would actually let them begin to decay. To restart the simulations, Hern would have to start from scratch, with a dinosaur embryo. It was a time-consuming process, and time was something that was running as short as Kan's temper.

"You know I can't do that, sir," Hern said, as diplomatically as possible. "I'll shut them down."

Kan pounded a fist on his thigh in frustration. These ape-derived bodies tended to encourage apelike behavior.

"Take us up!" he ordered. "We'll go somewhere else."

He turned to Barnum Brown, whose frozen face still stared at the blank monitor where the magnificent dinosaur recreations had been displayed.

"What are you smiling at?" he shouted at Brown, although he knew Brown couldn't do so much as twitch an eyebrow. He knew Brown would laugh if he could, and it infuriated him.

"Take us up!"

Just as the ship began to rise, there was another series of explosions. The ship stayed steady, but they pounded on its exterior like someone was beating on a giant drum.

"What now?" Kan shouted.

"Sir," Fredrik replied. "We have lost the cargo hold."

"You mean the cargo?"

"I mean the cargo *hold*. It has broken away from the ship. See for yourself."

He activated the lowermost camera. The floor of the ship suddenly became translucent, and Kan could see the bottom part of the ship falling away, crashing to Earth, colored green by the light that was now oozing from the ship's broken hull. When it hit, a cloud of dust obscured the whole thing from view.

Kan held his fingertips to the side of his head. The entire crew stopped whatever they had been doing and looked at him. Hern was probably worried that Kan was going to tear his own human head off, and then he would have to fix it.

"Slowly," Kan said. "Somebody tell me, slowly, what just happened."

"Just a guess, sir," Fredrik said. "This ship used to be a war ship, not a cargo ship. The cargo hold was added later, and was attached at only a few points. Some well-placed explosives could blow it right off. And apparently did."

"That's very nice," Kan said. "And to think I was actually proud of this ship. I had good, positive thoughts about it. Who did this?"

"I don't know."

"Lasse *is* dead, isn't he?"

"As far as we know."

Kan let out a disgusted breath.

"I suppose we can't fly through space, now."

"No, we can," Fredrik said. "The original hull is intact. I can check, but it will almost certainly seal itself off."

"So all we lose is all our cargo space."

"Not all, sir. There is some up here. We can still make a good collection."

Kan stared through the floor at the mess below. Human beings were now swarming through the dust of the broken part of the ship. He could go down there and get those bones, but they would fight him every inch of the way.

"Hern? Any chance that we can freeze all of these people down there long enough to recover those bones?"

"Not at the moment, sir. The dinosaurs used up a lot of power. I'll need some time to recharge."

"How much time?"

"One Earth day."

Kan turned and stared back at Brown and at the equally motionless Gumpson. Who knew what kinds of trouble they could stir up if given a whole day?

"I have a better idea. Let's go home."

"Sir?"

Fredrik's stunned voice apparently spoke for the whole crew. They stared at him as if he had announced he was taking up the Earth practice of ballet dancing.

"You heard me. You don't understand what these people are like. They will not give up. If they put up this much of a fight over these bones with us, imagine what they'll do when the inspectors come through. Let them walk around with their big gray heads and big eyes and see how far they get."

"But, sir—" Fredrik started to say.

"That's my decision," Kan said harshly. "I will take the blame. Let's let these gentlemen out and go home. But don't set down right here. Go a little ways off where no one will get to us."

The ship drifted slowly over the landscape, setting down near the wagon where Brown and Gumpson had been discovered in the first place.

Brown and Gumpson appeared a little disoriented when they were first released from the red chambers. They flexed their fingers and shook their legs, making sure everything worked.

"Mr. Brown, you win," Kan said. "These bones are yours."

"Thank you," Brown said, a little uncertainly. "And thanks to you, I know what the dinosaurs looked like. That will be invaluable."

"Don't thank me for that just yet," Kan said. "Mr. Gumpson, you had a fine shooting arm, but not anymore. I shudder to think what your fate will be now, but I leave you to it."

"Thanks, I guess," Gumpson said with a frown.

"I could take you with us and see to that arm," Kan said.

Gumpson's eyes opened wide.

"I think I'll take my chances here."

"As you wish. Now, both of you please go."

Gumpson went first, descending down the ramp with a hesitant air, as if expecting a trick.

"Mr. Brown," Kan said as Brown began to follow him. "Yes?"

Brown had a steely gaze, one befitting a Swede. Give them time, Kan thought, and maybe they'll be like us.

"I'm sorry about your wife."

The words seemed to rock Brown back on his heels in surprise, but he quickly recovered.

"Thank you."

He started down the ramp again, but suddenly turned and took one step back up.

"You know, I would have wanted the bones anyway," Brown said.

"I know that. Now go."

As soon as Brown had left and the door closed, Kan stomped over to Hern.

"Your implant still works?"

"The memory revoker? Yes, it does."

Kan smiled.

"Give him one more blast of it before we go. Make it a really good one. You might say it's something to remember us by."

FORTY-THREE

"You are sure you want to do this now?" Earth Reclamation Unit 17 asked.

"I'm sure," Lasse replied. "I've never been so sure about anything."

With that, he waded into the water of the small creek where Winthrow Parnassus waited, his hands joined together in front of him. When Lasse reached him, Parnassus murmured something to him and then dipped him under the water. When he came back up, Lasse was smiling.

The baptism was witnessed by only Eric, Digger Phelps and Alice Paul. Brown and his crew were back at camp, trying to figure out how to transport their windfall of fossils. Lasse and Eric had painstakingly combed through the wreckage of the Swede ship's cargo hold, enlarging relevant skeletons with their Multi-Purpose Tools. Some of the bones in the hold weren't from Earth, so they left those in miniature form. Brown had been delighted with the pile of bones that rose before him, although he seemed baffled as to their origin.

"Congratulations," Eric said when Lasse waded back ashore.

He was still wary around the Nes. Swede training had painted them as fanatics, and Eric had seen little to change his mind. He couldn't forget the sight of Lasse killing his own partner.

"Thanks," Lasse said.

He couldn't keep a smile off his face.

"So what are you going to do now?"

Lasse ran his hands over his face, pushing away the remnants of water.

"I'm going to travel with Winthrow for a while. Help him preach. Maybe I'll go it alone after a while."

The first thing Lasse had asked for when he was pulled out of the wreckage was food. The second thing was Winthrow Parnassus. Eric didn't ask him about it, but it was clear that at some point when he was trapped in the ship, Lasse had abandoned his plan of going home with the fossils of his distant kin. He had decided on an entirely new course, and Eric couldn't find it in his own heart to blame him.

"What about—your disguise?" Eric asked.

"This body will die," Lasse said matter-of-factly. "It has already started to smell, in case you hadn't noticed. It will hold up for a while, but then I've got this."

He held up a small pouch. Within it was a tiny Swede body. Eric recognized the crewman that had been named Bjorn.

"I stole it from Hern's office. I don't think he noticed. I don't really care to wear these things, but I'm getting used to it. This one is still alive, and it should last me for a long time. Long enough. I can become Bjorn, at least in this way. I feel I should, after what I did."

Eric looked at the ground.

"What about you?" Lasse said. "What are you going to do?"

Eric scratched the patch that had taken the place of his left eye.

"I'm going to stay out here with . . . with myself, I guess you'd say."

He pointed at Phelps, who was talking with Alice Paul and Parnassus.

"I don't know how long he has left. I want to spend as much time with him as I can."

"I don't suppose you'd like to hear me preach a little bit before you go?"

"No thanks."

Lasse laughed.

"All right. Maybe next time."

"Good luck, though."

"Good luck to you."

"Thanks," Eric said. "We'll both need it. We're both far from home."

The sunlight sparkled in the water drops that hung from Lasse's hair.

"No," he said. "We're not."

FORTY-FOUR

It actually felt good to have a suit on again. Barnum
Brown splashed some water on his face, taking care not
to let any run down into his collar, and then headed down
the hall to his office. He was glad to be back in New
York. Pound for pound, there seemed to be more crazy
people in Montana than in New York. Brown was in a
strangely good mood today. His recent memory lapses
seemed to have gone away, and he had a whopping pile
of new bones to go through.

"Your appointment is here," Miss Lord said when he
appeared. "The reporter from the *New York Times*."

Brown was in such a good mood he didn't even mind
speaking to a reporter, and he was pleased to note that
he hadn't forgotten about the appointment. Things had
really been slipping his mind in Montana, but he felt
better and sharper now that he was back home.

"Fine. This shouldn't take too long."

The reporter rose to shake his hand. He was a youngish
man, but already his eyes had bags and his hair carried
more than a bit of gray. He looked pleasant enough but
had a slight air of boredom, as if this interview was not
his dream assignment.

"Welcome back, Dr. Brown," he said.

"Just call me Barnum, thank you."

"As you know, I need to ask you about your recent
trip to Montana. I hear you made some very good finds."

Suddenly, he didn't feel like sitting still. He didn't mind talking to the reporter, but he had too much energy to be motionless.

"I did indeed. Would you like to see one?"

The reporter looked less than delighted at the prospect, but he said, "Of course. I'd be delighted."

Brown led him back down the hall to a collection room where he had already unboxed some of his prizes. Resting on the table was the head of a Tyrannosaurus rex, if such an eating device could ever be said to be resting. The reporter gasped at the sight. The head of such a monster could impress anyone.

"That is amazing," the reporter said, walking around it, too engrossed to even take notes.

"Look at the teeth," Brown said.

"Good Lord. He could eat a whale like I would eat a chocolate-covered cherry."

Brown suddenly had grave doubts about this man's ability to write a good scientific story, but he pressed ahead.

"We don't have all the bones, but altogether this is a fabulous specimen. When we get it assembled, it should stand nearly forty feet long."

"Wow."

"It will rear up most impressively on its hind legs," Brown said. "We don't have the arms, and some other bones here and there are missing, but overall it's a great find."

The reporter was taking notes now.

"Show me how it stood, if you don't mind."

Brown frowned in thought for a moment, and then complied. He hunched over just a bit, held his head high and formed his arms into three-clawed weapons.

"This is sort of what one would look like if it wore a suit," he joked, and was pleased when the reporter laughed. "Of course, it also had a tail."

"It would rest its weight on the tail, I guess," the reporter said.

"We believe so, at least some of the time," Brown replied, shifting out of his carnivore role.

"Now then," the reporter said. "Can I ask you some other things about your trip? I've heard reports that some of your crew reported seeing some pretty amazing things out there."

Brown knew it would get around to this.

"I don't know why they say these things. I've lost some very good scientists over this. I cannot put in a good word for Mr. Burgess. He will not amount to anything useful, I fear."

"He is supposed to be working on some sort of book," the reporter said. "Kind of an H.G. Wells type of thing."

"Well, good luck to him on that," Brown said. "That's the kind of thing he's suited for. I had some problems with several of my crew, which disturbs me. Even the younger ones. That Mr. Harryhausen is just not suited to any kind of life with dinosaurs, I'm afraid. But I'd rather not talk about my crew."

"One last question about that. I understand a photographer is pressing some sort of suit against you."

Brown closed his eyes and shook his head.

"Oh, that. Yes, he has some sort of foggy plate and claims I ruined it, whatever he means by that. Says it was very valuable. I barely remember meeting the lad. I suspect it will be thrown out of court."

The reporter squinted at him over the top of his notebook.

"So you didn't see anything strange while you were in Montana? Anything at all?"

Brown sighed and gave the reporter his best level gaze.

"Well, of course I did."

He motioned to the Tyrannosaurus rex skull, which gleamed a deep brown under the lights.

"I saw this right here. Just look at it! Look at those teeth! If that isn't strange enough for you, I don't know what is."

PRAISE FOR
LOIS MCMASTER BUJOLD

What the critics say:

The Warrior's Apprentice: "Now here's a fun romp through the spaceways—not so much a space opera as space ballet.... it has all the 'right stuff.' A lot of thought and thoughtfulness stand behind the all-too-human characters. Enjoy this one, and look forward to the next."   —Dean Lambe, *SF Reviews*

"The pace is breathless, the characterization thoughtful and emotionally powerful, and the author's narrative technique and command of language compelling. Highly recommended."   —*Booklist*

Brothers in Arms: "... she gives it a geniune depth of character, while reveling in the wild turnings of her tale. ... Bujold is as audacious as her favorite hero, and as brilliantly (if sneakily) successful."   —*Locus*

"Miles Vorkosigan is such a great character that I'll read anything Lois wants to write about him. ... a book to re-read on cold rainy days."   —Robert Coulson, *Comics Buyer's Guide*

Borders of Infinity: "Bujold's series hero Miles Vorkosigan may be a lord by birth and an admiral by rank, but a bone disease that has left him hobbled and in frequent pain has sensitized him to the suffering of outcasts in his very hierarchical era.... Playing off Miles's reserve and cleverness, Bujold draws outrageous and outlandish foils to color her high-minded adventures."   —*Publishers Weekly*

Falling Free: "In *Falling Free* Lois McMaster Bujold has written her fourth straight superb novel.... How to break down a talent like Bujold's into analyzable components? Best not to try. Best to say 'Read, or you will be missing something extraordinary.'"   —Roland Green, *Chicago Sun-Times*

The Vor Game: "The chronicles of Miles Vorkosigan are far too witty to be literary junk food, but they rouse the kind of craving that makes popcorn magically vanish during a double feature."   —Faren Miller, *Locus*

MORE PRAISE FOR
LOIS MCMASTER BUJOLD

What the readers say:

"My copy of *Shards of Honor* is falling apart I've reread it so often.... I'll read whatever you write. You've certainly proved yourself a grand storyteller."
—Liesl Kolbe, Colorado Springs, CO

"I experience the stories of Miles Vorkosigan as almost viscerally uplifting.... But certainly, even the weightiest theme would have less impact than a cinder on snow were it not for a rousing good story, and good storytelling with it. This is the second thing I want to thank you for.... I suppose if you boiled down all I've said to its simplest expression, it would be that I immensely enjoy and admire your work. I submit that, as literature, your work raises the overall level of the science fiction genre, and spiritually, your work cannot avoid positively influencing all who read it."
—Glen Stonebraker, Gaithersburg, MD

" 'The Mountains of Mourning' [in *Borders of Infinity*] was one of the best-crafted, and simply best, works I'd ever read. When I finished it, I immediately turned back to the beginning and read it again, and I can't remember the last time I did that."   —Betsy Bizot, Lisle, IL

"I can only hope that you will continue to write, so that I can continue to read (and of course buy) your books, for they make me laugh and cry and think ... rare indeed."
—Steven Knott, Major, USAF

What Do You Say?

<u>*Send me these books!*</u>

Shards of Honor	72087-2 ◆ $5.99	☐
Barrayar	72083-X ◆ $5.99	☐
Cordelia's Honor (trade)	87749-6 ◆ $15.00	☐
The Warrior's Apprentice	72066-X ◆ $5.99	☐
The Vor Game	72014-7 ◆ $5.99	☐
Young Miles (trade)	87782-8 ◆ $15.00	☐
Cetaganda (hardcover)	87701-1 ◆ $21.00	☐
Cetaganda (paperback)	87744-5 ◆ $5.99	☐
Ethan of Athos	65604-X ◆ $5.99	☐
Borders of Infinity	72093-7 ◆ $5.99	☐
Brothers in Arms	69799-4 ◆ $5.99	☐
Mirror Dance (paperback)	87646-5 ◆ $6.99	☐
Memory (paperback)	87845-X ◆ $6.99	☐
The Spirit Ring (paperback)	72188-7 ◆ $5.99	☐

LOIS MCMASTER BUJOLD
 Only from Baen Books

If not available at your local bookstore, fill out this coupon and send a check or money order for the cover price(s) plus $1.50 s/h to Baen Books, Dept. BA, P.O. Box 1403, Riverdale, NY 10471. Delivery can take up to ten weeks.

NAME: _____

ADDRESS: _____

_____

I have enclosed a check or money order in the amount of $